Wakefield Press

In Search *of* Anna

Valerie Volk is an award-winning Adelaide writer of poetry, verse novels, short stories and longer fiction. A self-confessed voyeur of other people's lives, she is fascinated by the perennial question 'What if ...?' Valerie loves travel, opera and cats – not necessarily in that order. *In Search of Anna* is her ninth book.

By the same author

In Due Season

A Promise of Peaches

Even Grimmer Tales

Passion Play: the Oberammergau Tales

Of Flowers and Forebears

Indochina Days

Bystanders

Of Llamas and Piranhas

In
Search
of Anna

VALERIE VOLK

Wakefield
Press

Wakefield Press
16 Rose Street
Mile End
South Australia 5031
www.wakefieldpress.com.au

First published 2019

Cover designed by Liz Nicholson, designBITE
Edited by Julia Beaven, Wakefield Press
Typeset by Michael Deves, Wakefield Press

ISBN 978 1 74305 611 0

A catalogue record for this
book is available from the
National Library of Australia

Wakefield Press thanks
Coriole Vineyards for
continued support

'We're all ghosts. We all carry, inside us,
people who came before us.'

Liam Callanan, *The Cloud Atlas*

For my grandchildren

James

Alicia

Madelaine

Ellen

Isabella

Poppy

in the hope they will allow those who have gone
before them to live on,
as loving presences, in their minds.

Prologue

Let the dead rest in peace.

It's a fine sentiment. But they don't. Rest, I mean.

My dead hover around me. Almost like a flock of Giselle's Wilis, wraith-like, transformed into the sylph dancers of the night. I've never forgotten that ballet, or the night when my father took me to see it at Melbourne's Princess Theatre. Twelve years old, an eager child. Way up in the gods – there wasn't money for dress circle tickets.

I have never forgotten those dream-like characters who floated across the stage, creatures from another world, fragile, ephemeral, restlessly seeking spirits, doomed to dance forever. It comes as no surprise when I find ghost-like faces from the past drifting in and out of my life. Especially now that I'm getting on in years. Perhaps we become more receptive.

I reach out to them, to see what my past has been. But they laugh lightly as they float away. *Who am I?* they mock me. *I am Anna.*

Which Anna? There were so many. How maddening – that old German custom of using the same name over and over. A nightmare for the historian. Generations of them with the one name, even within a family they're often called the same. *Anna Amelia*, says the first. *Anna Kristina*, smiles her sister. And then, laughing at my confusion, comes the third. *I am, I was, Anna Helena.*

So when an Anna comes to me I have to first look closely to see which one she is. Now that I've got to know them I can see how many Annas I could be searching for.

I stand in the stairwell and look at the gallery of photographs. The old ones go way back, well over a hundred years, in fact almost a hundred and fifty. They've hung there ever since we moved into this house, and they're company when I go up and down the stairs. Not that I do that too often these days. Too hard on my legs. The days of bounding up and down are well and truly over.

Now I just stand at the bottom and study their faces. They look back implacably. There were no smiles in the photos taken in those days. No 'Say cheese' and none of these modern contraptions, like the one my niece uses in her obsession with her own image. I wonder what Anna – what any of the Annas – would have made of her selfie stick. I think my grandfather's phrase, 'Bloomin' nonsense', might have summed it up.

I can see them now, dressed in their best, off to the nearest big town to a photographer's studio with its potted palms and ornate chairs. They were usually cane, with elaborate curved arms and curlicues on the back rests, and most often the men were seated, staring at the photographer. And at us, several centuries later, scrutinising them.

The men sat, all those big burly German farmers, slightly uncomfortable in their Sunday best, legs crossed and heads held high, an odd curl to the lips, almost supercilious, you could say. This was their day, after all, their wedding clothes marking a move into a new status in the community.

No sitting for their brides. They stood, just a little behind. Symbolic? I think so. Those women, gazing out unsmiling, knew that their lives too had altered. Hair drawn tightly back and frizzed on top, in the fashion of the era, an orange blossom wreath holding the filmy white veil cascading to the floor. Wasp-waisted, some of them, though that fashion was just starting to pass, the era of the black wedding gowns not yet over. They look strange to us today. These women, married not in our traditional white, but in the conventional elaborate black gowns that even the shrouding pale veils did not relieve. Was it the granting of sober matron status that they denoted? Or just something more practical for the life to come?

I consider the photographs in their oval frames, trying to identify the Anna I am seeking. Here is one, an interesting face, my grandmother Emma. She fascinates me, and she too is an Anna, Anna Johanne Emma – but always known as Emma. No, she is not the one, though I study her as she stands, one hand resting lightly on Kurt's shoulder, looking at me to see what I make of it all. Is hers a proprietary hand? 'This one is mine, and don't you forget it.' Or is it for support? 'I am your responsibility, and I can depend on you.' Or is she reminding herself that this is now, and this man is her husband, and he's not the one she was expecting to be joined with in holy wedlock. It's not the way it was meant to be.

And what about him, about Kurt? A smaller man than all those other hulking farmers. A different man, not part of this close-knit inbred community. Maybe that was his appeal. Or was it just that she was twenty-eight, and her younger sister wanted to marry, not possible until the older one was safely matched? There were unspoken rules, and if it wasn't the marriage she'd expected nine years earlier, at least he was a newcomer, a touch of glamour about him too.

I shake my head. These two can wait; their time is still to come. They are a part of this story, and they will have their place – but not yet. This Emma Anna is not the woman I am searching for. I move a step higher among these pictured faces, all offering themselves and their lives, all wanting the immortality they are hoping I might give. Not you, I say, and step up, one further.

Finally, I find it, another photograph, tiny, really just a miniature. It's slightly tinted, and she looks not at me, but past me, to someone else. She is the one I really want; that wandering spirit, the woman who gave birth to my grandfather and could not let him go, even when he had separated himself from her, from the land of his birth, and from all that he had known.

His mother, this older Anna, the one who came across the world in pursuit of her missing son, roams restlessly through the blur of these past faces as I reach through the fog of years. For they are me, and I am how they might still live. They call to me, their hands outstretched, begging for life. Take me, each says. Take me, and let me return through your words.

I search among the wraith-like figures, seeking her, seeking Anna. She passes through that ghostly company, and yearns towards me.

Take *me*, she says. Then perhaps I will rest in peace.

Part *One*

CHAPTER 1

Lewin, Silesia 1886

The fire is burning low, and outside a light snow is falling. On the other side of the wall I can hear the soft snuffle of the animals safely housed in their winter quarters in the long low room next to me. Sometimes I think that they are better off, better cared for, than we are. Certainly by Otto, anyway.

He would not miss the birth of their offspring, and his huge workman's hands would be strangely gentle as he cradled a newborn lamb or calf. Much more gentle than his hands ever were with me, or with our children.

I look back on the days of our courtship, and even further to our childhood together, the days before Lewin and the life we now lead. Even then, at the little village school, Otto knew what he wanted and few would dare cross him. Not the other boys in Rauschwitz, our town, the place where we were born and where we went to school. The school was so small that there could have been little satisfaction in being the schoolmaster there. Herr Ladner must have looked back on his days in the teacher training institutions and wondered how he had come to this place. Even without Otto, it would have been a miserable job.

We straggled out each day from the little cottages around,

few of us valuing those hours in the schoolroom, with our slate pencils scratching in their spine-shivering way over the flat slate boards. For me it was easy; I could copy the line of copperplate letters quickly. I would sit, perhaps a little smugly, and watch the others. Amalia, her straggly long plaits always escaping the crown around her head, her pink tongue poking out the corner of her mouth, labouring at the letters. And Jacob, feet scraping on the wooden floor as he toiled.

I would look at Otto, and he would smirk back at me. We were the quickest in this mixed group of village children, and Otto was not going to make the teacher's life an easy one. Even when his insolence and misbehaviour had finally driven poor Herr Ladner to his last resort, the cane, Otto would smile through the performance, as if daring the ineffectual teacher to draw blood from his outstretched hands. And at the end he would laugh, and Herr Ladner would know who had won.

I could not understand why Otto persisted in the school. It might have been compulsory, but if he had not wanted to stay he would have defied parents and village leaders and gone his own way. I doubt his parents would have cared, anyway. The small plot of land his father had use of in the Count's estate was not enough to support them, and his mother spent long hours knitting the worsted stockings that she would take each week to the traders in the market square. Then to hastily buy what was needed before her husband appeared to seize the few coins she had before setting off to the market tavern.

I knew how Otto hated his father and when I looked at the bruises on his mother's arms and blackened eyes I could see why.

'This is not going to be my life, Anna,' he brooded. 'I am going to do something different.'

Another reason I am so often surprised when I watch him today. When he beats our son for some tiny fault, or pushes me to one side when the meal displeases him, I see again that he is the father he did not want to be. Yes, well, we know not what we may become ... That line comes back to me from something I once read.

It was escape we all wanted. Otto sought it through the new railways beginning to criss-cross our land. He was fascinated by the power of these huge metal beasts, and they gave him a reason to continue at the school he hated, where his only pleasure was to torment the mild and helpless master.

'Why do you treat him like that?' I asked one day, when I had seen the effort the poor man was making to suppress humiliated tears.

'Because he's weak!' was the scornful response. 'Anyone as feeble as that should learn to take his punishment.'

'Why stay then?'

'Because one day I am going to drive those trains, and for that I must go to the technical school in Glatz.' Otto knew that to be accepted into the training college in the town he would have to complete the work at our village school.

'Besides, the more Herr Ladner wants to see my back, the more he will try to get me a place at the college.' Otto knew how to manipulate people.

'You will see,' he spoke with confidence, 'that railway line in the north will be brought first to Gorlitz, and then to Glatz.'

It took longer than he had thought, but he was right. Soon after our children were born, the railway line reached us. The Silesian Mountain Railway they called it. And Otto, who had anticipated so well, and worked on so many other lines, now became one of its first drivers.

I did not think, in those early years at the little school, that one day I would be his wife. I would not have wanted it. Perhaps I would have been happier if I had stayed at that school and learned to know my place in the world. Yet who can judge this? Our life becomes what we make it – or, truth to tell, what others make of it.

If the Countess had not looked on my mother with favour, my life might have been very different. But she was a kindly woman, and also, I now think, a lonely one with her husband, the Graf von Striebenow, so often away from home. His palace in Berlin saw him more often than the hunting lodge in the mountains here, south of Glatz. Was it his political life that kept him so long in Berlin? Or did it suit him well to leave his wife and daughter here, many days' journey away?

There were few companions for Christiana, the Countess. For all that she had her painting and embroidery, her music and books (she was a great reader, and rarely to be seen without a book in her hand) and, of course, her daughter, there were no others she could talk to. Perhaps this explains her kindness to the servants, for they at least were company. And my mother seemed her special favourite; they were close in age, and both had daughters.

'Johanna,' she would call. 'Leave your work and walk with me in the garden while I gather flowers.'

So my mother would put aside her mending or polishing, and wander through the grounds, holding the basket for the Countess's flowers. Later those flowers would brighten the rooms of the dark and forbidding lodge, and the two women, so alike and yet so different, would have spent a happy hour. What did they talk of, I wonder now. I suspect the Countess talked, and my mother simply followed and listened. And absorbed. For the Countess was an educated woman, who read widely and thought about issues of the day. While my mother, who knew nothing beyond a few years at the village school, still had a fund of commonsense and a willingness to think.

Later, when I was older, I came to love those gardens, and learned to bury my face in the heavy-scented roses that were her special delight. Imitating her? Yes, for by then she was the model of all I wanted to be. Today I tend the single rose bush I keep alive outside our cottage; breathing its perfume takes me back to those happier times. I stroke the softness of the dark red petals, and remember the softness of the Countess's hands. For I was often with her, and felt her touch.

'You may bring your Anna when you come.' This gracious offer was a relief to my mother, who would otherwise have been forced to leave her new baby with a neighbour for long hours each day while she trudged the two miles to the chateau. It would be well after nightfall before she returned home to prepare my father's meal. He would be back from his small plot of ground where he spent most days, and hard at work with his carving.

The land was too small to provide for us all, already a family of six when I was born. So he continued at his trade of spoon carving, just as my mother spent long weary hours in the evening spinning thread for the linen lengths she would take to the weekly markets. I accompanied her at times, and watched as she sighed, accepting whatever small sum the Breslau traders gave her for her work. A small reward for her weary hours.

At home we watched my father until it was time for us to tumble into the big bed we children shared. My brothers were helping, learning the trade. One day they would be apprenticed to the guild, already partly skilled. I wished that girls might be permitted to learn this work. But no, our place was the home, where we learnt the womanly arts that our minister, Pastor Liebelt, praised so highly.

But even when I was a child this trade was falling away. All those lovely crafted spoons, started as a hobby by herdsmen in the fields and growing to become the export trade that took our spoons into countries far across the seas, were no longer needed. Replaced by earthenware and metal. Practical, and the wood was giving out, it's true, but nothing will take away our simple pride in what we created by the single lamp in our cottage.

We knew that my mother's work at the chateau was a necessity for us. Also for the Countess, as it turned out, because her child, only a little younger than I was, needed a wet nurse when her mother's milk failed. Lydia and I were as close as sisters. In a strange way we were sisters, suckled by the one mother.

The Countess was a second mother to me. She treated me just as she treated her own daughter; we shared our playtimes, our sleep times, our meals as if we were of the same blood. I loved Lydia dearly, more in fact than my own sister Gertrud, and I enjoyed my time at the chateau more than in my father's cramped house.

When did it begin to bother my mother? Was she jealous of the way I loved the Countess and her daughter? Or was it because my father growled one night when I refused the food at our table, and told me I was getting to be too like the fine ladies on the mountainside?

'Ideas above your station!' he roared. 'You eat the food we provide here, and no more airs and graces!'

Even as a small child I could see the differences in our tables. There the fine china, embroidered cloths and delicate food; in our home the rough wood my mother scrubbed with her reddened hands and the stewpot from which she ladled our evening meal. Mine was an observant eye, even then.

But schooldays came, and it probably relieved my mother to see the pattern of our lives changing. I could only be at the chateau when there was no class for me. I laboured at the slate, perfecting my letters, and grappled with the simple number work, which soon was too easy. Only Otto could equal me. We were the same – we both wanted more.

I missed Lydia, who now had a governess as her teacher. But more than that, she had the Countess, who took a major part of her daughter's teaching.

'Why can't Anna come more often?' my friend lamented. 'It's so lonely without her here.'

I suspect her mother felt the same; perhaps she had come to think of me as another daughter. It was a logical suggestion: rather than the inadequate village school, let Anna come each day to share lessons with Lydia ...

I wonder that my parents permitted it, and I will never cease being grateful to them. Those were the days that made me what I am – both my faults, and God knows there are many of these, and also my virtues come from those years and the Countess's training. I know now that she was a remarkable woman, with an eager curious mind and a good grounding in many fields of knowledge. For those she did not know so well, for the work in numbers, and for lessons in geography and the world around us, she had engaged governesses and, later, tutors. She believed in a well-rounded education.

Her passions were literature and history, and these and the classics were fields in which she was more knowledgeable than any of the teachers she hired.

'You are like a little sponge,' she said, smiling at me one day. 'I could wish that Lydia was as willing a pupil as you.'

Dearly as I loved Lydia, I understood what she meant. We were different. My friend's passions were dress and ornament, and her favourite lessons those with the drawing master and the singing teacher who came each week from Breslau, preparing her for the life ahead. She has now gone from here, first to Berlin as her father's hostess, and then as a society lady herself, with a husband from the Emperor's court. We see little of each other. Yet when we do, the old Lydia is still there, warm and affectionate, and still grieving for the shared mother we both lost.

The Countess died so unexpectedly that today I still feel the sense of shock that hit me when they brought the news. She had been returning from Glatz in storms when a thunderclap startled the horses, and they had bolted, overturning the carriage. She was thrown from it, her neck broken. I wept long hours into the night, grieving for the woman who had been so much a part of my earlier days.

The life of the chateau came to an end, though by then I had already been separated from it. The Count had used it rarely, with occasional parties of hunting friends coming to our mountains. I think now that the thoughtful cultivated mind of a wife who preferred books and music to politics and horses had been little inducement for him to spend time with her. And he had, as we later discovered, many consolations in Berlin. With his wife's death Lydia became for a time his hostess, until she made the marriage he approved of.

There had been some talk that I might have accompanied my friend to Berlin, but the Count had no real interest in the suggestion. I suspect I might have been too like his wife in character and interests, whereas Lydia fitted his lifestyle well. Impossible anyway; Otto would never have permitted it.

Lydia. When I think of her a smile always touches my lips. Lydia was like that. She made the world happy, just as she was always happy. A little doll, her mother called her, and it was true. It pleased the Countess to dress her like a princess, in clothes ruffled and lacy, embroidered like a flower garden. I have often seen my mother sigh over the pressing of those dresses, as she lifted the black flat iron from the old stove and tested it for heat with a drop of water from the pewter jug. I do not think she would have wanted to dress me in that way, even if there had been coins to pay for it. They were not clothes for playing. I remember Lydia with her music and her beloved cage birds. Books bored her, and she quickly grew tired and vexatious when the Countess and I lingered over volumes from their library.

What a library it was. Such joy when the Countess and her daughter went to pay calls, and I was left to roam free among the books, even the foreign language ones. Lydia and I were tutored in French and English. Two days of each week we were not permitted to speak, even to each other, in our own language, but one day for French, another for English.

'Mais, maman,' Lydia would pout, 'pourquoi?' Until she discovered that if she was ever to take her place in Berlin society she would need these skills, especially the French that all fashionable ladies would talk. Ah well, now she is part of that world, and I hope that marriage to her father's old friend, the Graf von Nicklenberg, has brought her happiness as well as the town house, country estate and carriages that are part of her trappings.

Today I see her only rarely, when they open the Chateau for a hunting party of guests. The old bonds remain but beneath the smiles and embraces, I see a different Lydia. This one has the look, at times, of a small hunted animal. There are stories among her servants, for they speak more freely to me – after all, am I not really one of them? – about the Graf's ways with maids that make me fear for my once light-hearted friend.

'Does your husband ever hurt you, Anna?' she asked on one of their visits to her old family home.

I looked at her in surprise. She rarely talked of anything except her social life, the card parties, balls and salons they attended for concerts that held little appeal for her. But never of marriage, or what it had meant to her.

Had we still been close and able to speak freely, I might have told her of Otto's drunken rages and the nights I sent the children to sleep in the adjoining stables with the animals, but those days of intimacy were long past.

'Why do you ask such a question, Lydia? Does yours?'

Her eyes slid away from me, and she laughed her tinkling unconvincing laugh. '*Mais non, cherie.*'

Those times together, so seldom, were precious to me, for they took me back to a happier time of life spent in two worlds. As I climbed into the wooden bed I shared with Gertrud and our brothers, I would think of Lydia, in solitary splendour in the four-poster in her room, the silk curtains draped from the carved and gilded tester above her head. So different from our shared horsehair bedding, where each time one of us turned in the night we were all jostled out of position. Oh, the luxury of a bed to oneself.

Yet envy was rare, for the Countess treated me with such kindness, and I knew that dearly as she loved her daughter, what she shared with me was special. When a box of new books arrived from Berlin, we would fall upon them with excitement. She had made a point of collecting complete works of her favourite authors, and Lydia could not understand why her mother and I could be happy for hours reading aloud the great Shakespearian plays, switching from role to role as the stories unfolded.

She introduced me to the great German writers of the classic period – to Goethe, Schiller, Fichte, von Humboldt. And to to Racine and Voltaire, the French tragedians of an earlier age. We read the novels of Fontane and wept over the miseries of Effi Brest. Little did I realise as we agonised for Effi that in a few years I would also be in anguish, over whether or not to confess what I had done.

Too late to think about these things, for I hear the bridle bells jangling on the path outside, and then the heavy tread of Otto as he lurches close to the door. A good wife would open it, to welcome in her man, no matter what his condition. But I have never claimed to be a good wife. After all, I had never wanted to be this man's wife.

CHAPTER 2

Rauschwitz, Silesia 1861

When the hunting party comes back at the end of the day, there is always one face I look for. Dare I hope that before he dismounts, he looks for me too?

The chateau has become once again the centre of neighbourhood life, for this is the hunting season, and the Graf loves his sport. I am not so sure that the Countess enjoys this time so much. The house now rings with life and activity, but these men are not so congenial to her. The Prussian Junkers are heavy and stolid, and their days at the hunt are followed by evenings of drinking and talk of political events. They spend much time re-living the glory days of fifty years ago when Napoleon was finally defeated, and our country became again a powerful participant in world affairs. Much of their talk is outside my understanding and when they bemoan the failure of the German Confederation I have little interest in this.

Or had little interest, until now. It was Lydia who pointed out new arrivals at the chateau as we stood at the windows from her room and gazed down at the coaches, the horses steaming and sweating from their labours and the grooms lifting the travelling chests for servants to carry to the guest rooms.

'See, Anna,' she exclaimed in delight. 'Papa has brought some younger men in this group.' Her blue eyes were alive with excitement, for she had reached sixteen, and the next season she would be going to Berlin, to sample the pleasures of life there. And, we both knew, to find a suitable husband. The Countess sighed when she talked of this, for she did not share her daughter's anticipation of the delights of this life.

'I would prefer, Anna,' she had confided to me, 'if we could just continue our lives here. But what must be, must be. And it is important to my husband that our daughter marries well.'

She shrugged her shoulders wearily, then smiled at me. 'But what of you, *Liebchen*? Your mother tells me there is a young man courting you ...'

I could feel my face redden as the blood rushed to my cheeks. I tried hard to meet her gaze steadily. '*N'importe, madame.*' But she looked disbelieving.

'I find that hard to accept, *ma chère*. There must be many young men in the village who would find your style of beauty much to their taste.'

It is certainly not the blue-eyed golden-haired beauty of Lydia. I am not one who would ever be chosen by artists or the makers of daguerreotypes as a model, though I confess I would love to see just how these pictures are made. This capturing of one's image on paper fascinates me – but not our village pastor, Herr Pastor Liebelt, who thundered against it from the pulpit last Sunday.

'It is a work of the devil,' he roared. 'God made us in his own image; it is a sin to try to copy him and make further images of his creations!' He waved aloft an old copy of the *Leipzig Advertiser* that had come his way, and quoted its words: 'Blasphemy! Would God have allowed a Frenchman to give to the world an invention of the devil?' Pastor Liebelt often found himself interpreting the Almighty's wishes to the rest of us sinners, I had noticed. But then, perhaps such a man of God is granted a special insight into the mind of his maker ...

From what I have heard, these condemnations have not stopped inventors and they now have much better ways of capturing images of people – not just once, but many copies of the same image.

One of the many wonders of our age, indeed. But unlikely that I would be chosen as a model for such reproduction. I stand behind Lydia in her bedroom and view us both in the looking glass and see the contrast. I am much taller – too tall for beauty – and my hair, though lustrous, is dark and straight. Even coiled around my head it does not have the appeal of her fair ringlets. My eyes are dark, and my skin is not the pink and white of apple blossoms, as is hers. We are very different.

So I find it strange when village lads look at me with interest. But only from a distance. Otto has made it quite clear that I am his property, and it would ill behove anyone to forget it while he is away in Glatz. There are many times I feel trapped by the force of his will.

But is this what I want for my life? I am not sure. Soon he will demand it, and I confess that the stirring in my blood when his hand moves from my waist down my wakened body makes me uneasy. But I do not want Otto.

'By sixteen,' my mother tells me, 'I was already wed and had both Willi and Georg. It is time you too are wed. And Otto will give you a secure future. You will not have to work the way I do.'

Yet I think, for all her words about 'her labours', she enjoys being part of life at the Chateau. Even if my father is suspicious of the effect on his youngest daughter, and spends many hours reminding me that I am only a workman's child, perhaps he too, like our mother, has a grudging respect for what I have become.

It has separated me from my family, and even more from the village boys who might have wished a closer knowledge of me, in spite of Otto. When he returns each week from his time at the training college in Glatz, it seems to me that he becomes more demanding, and wants from me liberties I will not give. Yet everyone seems to expect that we will marry. No doubt this is what my mother has told the Countess.

'Quickly, quickly, Anna!' Lydia was all haste now, rearranging her dress more becomingly, and fixing small blue bows in her hair. But I was not forgotten, and had to submit laughingly to her attempts to smarten my plain grey dress with a linen cape and scarf. She surveyed the outcome with a critical eye, pinched my cheeks to make a little colour rise, before she nodded in satisfaction, pointing to the picture in the glass.

In truth, I did look my best. She led the way along the gallery with its mounted deer heads lining our route, down the curved staircase with the gleaming wood that my mother so lovingly polished. Into the large salon, where the evening candles were already being lighted and the gentlemen were gathering for the traditional stirrup cup before dinner – a notion the Count had brought back from the Russian Imperial Court.

So it was that I first saw Kurt. Even now, weeks later, I still catch my breath at the memory of the moment our eyes first met. As he was to tell me often in succeeding days, it was the same for him. A recognition, a spark that flew between us.

'Why,' I asked him later, 'did you look at me and not at Lydia? She is so pretty.'

'True,' he responded. 'She is pretty. She will be a great success at court. But you, my dear one, are beautiful – and I would not wish to see you at court.'

'Besides,' he added laughingly, 'she only had eyes for Gustave. And he for her.'

Did he not think me good enough for court? He would have been right. For all my education and the careful cultivation by the Countess, I was still only a peasant girl. No linen capes and scarves were going to change that. And while they saw me as Lydia's companion, not as a servant, there was a gulf between us.

Kurt was a student, he told me, dragged unwillingly from his university by a father who said he needed to get out of Berlin and live some life away from books. But those same books gave us a life to share that became more and more important as the days passed. The Countess saw us with concern, but did not interfere, or even warn my mother that the hours I spent at the Chateau were no longer with Lydia. Her mind was on her husband and her guests, and she had little time to chaperone two flighty girls.

It was Kurt's mind that I first loved. That thoughtful probing mind that looked at and showed me things I had not understood about our country. Certainly I knew how our society was changing – one only had to look at the misery and need in so many households around us. The closing of mines had brought poverty and the new manufacturers were destroying the home industry we all depended on. It was no wonder that so many of our neighbours were fleeing to the towns in the hope of work in factories that were springing up like mushrooms.

'My father fears my politics,' Kurt admitted to me. 'I see the awful injustice of our lives, and he thinks that I may become a socialist.'

I listened in fascination as he described events and political movements I knew nothing about, such as the Silesian Weavers' Revolt, which I dimly recalled my father, always one for law and authority, exclaiming against. Now I saw it with Kurt's eyes, as a beleaguered craft guild fighting vainly against the industrialisation that was ruining their livelihood. I burned at the injustice of the Prussian Royal Court banning the song that expressed their anger, and felt for the poor singer who had been imprisoned in 1846 for daring to sing the song in public.

'I would have sung it too!' I burst out passionately, and Kurt smiled at my fury.

'Yes, my little one. I could see you there, marching with your pickaxe and smashing the looms in factories just as they did. It is no wonder that Marx called it the first great uprising by the proletariat.'

I looked at him askance. I had heard of this Marx, whose name Kurt spoke with reverence.

'But surely he was a revolutionary? An evil man, against religion?'

His lips twitched. 'Not all revolutionaries are evil. Had I been a little older, I would have joined them in 1848.'

That date meant nothing to me at the time, small child as I was, but the thirteen years that have passed have not erased it from people's minds. In the taverns where the men gather at night, it remains raw and new. They still fight that battle, though not all agree that it should have happened. I have seen it through my father's eyes – that those hotheads, sinfully rebelling against the old ways, were put down was only, he was certain, God's will to keep us safe. But there were those who had listened to the speakers in the towns and argued a different viewpoint. My father came home at night, confused and bewildered, asking how men of sense, men he had known all his life, could possibly have listened to such evil rebellious ideas.

'See!' he would insist. 'See what happened in France when the people are out of control!'

We all shivered. France might have been our old enemy, but the horrors of that revolution struck fear into all neighbouring countries. Tales of the monstrous killing machine, *la guillotine*, were enough to terrify any mischievous boy. Yet even when that bloodstained time was over and order restored, it did not last, and the restored king had to flee from France to London. My father shook his head gloomily.

'No good will come of it when people resist their God-appointed rulers!'

Now I started to see a different view as Kurt showed me his ideas. I listened fascinated as he told me of the professors at the university, and their evenings in the taverns of that seething city. His eyes lit up as he described their passionate discussions and the plans they were making for a new world.

Kurt was charmed by my mind as much as my body. All those years under the Countess's guiding hand, all those hours in her library, had opened different worlds to me, and I could listen and explore with Kurt the ideas that were so important to him. How could I have expected that he, a student at the famous Friedrich-Wilhelms-Universitat, the University of Berlin, would take seriously the ideas of a village girl?

Yet it seemed he did and oh, how much I learned from

him. He told me how he had been influenced by the theory of philosopher Hegel, and I learnt to accept that the evil and revolutionary ideas of Karl Marx and Friedrich Engels might actually have sense behind them. He described Count Otto von Bismarck, who they say is likely to become our next Minister President in Prussia; he too was a force in his student days in Berlin and now, in his forties, his powerful influence lingers with today's youth.

How Kurt's eyes shone when he talked of this man. 'He, my dear one, has a vision for what our Fatherland can be. If anyone can unite our land he will be the one.'

I nodded, and felt the passion of his words, and his wish to be part of this future. He was able to stir me – and not only by his vision.

'Be careful, child,' the Countess warned me. 'He is an attractive young man, and I can see that you are drawn to him.'

'He is like no one I have ever known,' I admitted.

'He finds you very appealing, that I can see. He enjoys your company. But you know that nothing can come of this. I would not like to see you jeopardise your honour. You are very dear to me.'

I blushed, and as the pink rose in my cheeks I found it hard to meet her eyes. For she does not know how my heart races when he looks at me, and how my blood burns when Kurt's hand touches mine. We walk in the pine forests and there, where we stop under the old trees to rest a little, his arm around my shoulders, I can feel the throbbing ache that is unlike any feeling I have had before.

She continued: 'And there is Otto too. I know that your mother believes that you and Otto will wed as soon as he returns from

Glatz. You need to be careful with your reputation, my dearest.'

Yet what did reputation count when Kurt's hands moved quietly, insistently, exploring my body until I forgot who he is, who I am, and the ache to belong to him became impossible to bear? The pine trees looked down on us as we lay together, and I recalled words I had read in her books – 'the world well lost for love'.

The first time it happened, he was aghast when he saw the blood. 'I did not know that I would be your first,' he stammered. 'I had thought that you – '

I stopped him before he could say more. 'I could wish nothing better than that you should be the first one who loved me,' I assured him. 'It was with my full consent.'

And I meant it. I had not known this sort of feeling before, and there was no one I could talk to about it. Certainly not my mother, we had never been close. And the sounds that came from my parents' bed in the dark hours bore no relationship to the swelling feeling when Kurt's body stretched above me.

Not Lydia, for while the four of us would set out to walk together, she and Gustav would happily part to go their own way. She came back a little flushed and laughing merrily, but her gown never looked the product of anxious smoothing down, as mine did. Somewhere in Lydia there was, I knew, a cautiousness I did not have. I would not have talked to her about Kurt. The days of girlish sharing were over.

What happened once continued, even though I knew we had no future. When the hunting season comes to an end, and that is soon, Kurt will disappear from my life, and I will return to being Anna, a village girl. Perhaps in Berlin he will remember a girl he once knew in the Silesian countryside. I hope I will not be a tale he will tell his companions, about a conquest made. I do not think so. He is a honourable man, and I believe he truly cares for me. But not enough to see this as more than a country idyll, a lovely word I learned from the English poets in the Countess's books.

If Lydia was more perceptive and less involved in her own flirtation – for I do not believe it is more than a flirtation – she might have realised how I have changed in these weeks, but Kurt's and my discussions have bored her, and she has had no wish to share our walks. Only her mother has watched warily.

Now he tells me it is time to part, and we walk for one last time through the forest and towards the grotto high on the hillside. Today it is crowded, with country carts and tethered horses. A picnic crowd has come, for this is a favourite destination for holidaymakers from surrounding estates. Kurt has recognised people there. He turns me away hastily, and we make our way back through the trees. It is clear to me: Anna is a passing entertainment, but not someone to parade as a companion.

I know my place.

In a hollow under the pines we lie together for a last time, and as he enters me I do not feel the familiar surge of joy, but a sadness that brings tears to my eyes.

'Oh, little one, don't cry. Let us be happy for this last time. It has been so joyful, so many happy memories.'

So I blink back the tears and concentrate on pleasing him, which I know so well how to do. One day I will remember, and recall the pleasure we have had in each other's bodies as well as each other's minds.

CHAPTER 3

Lewin, Silesia   1864

Three years ago – how quickly those years have passed. Yet there has not been a day I have not thought of Kurt and wondered where he is, how he is, and, more than all else, who he is now loving.

At times I think myself a greater fool than anyone I have known, to have been so easily seduced. But then I remember him, and the tenderness of his passion, and I feel I would not have missed this experience, even though it has spoiled me for anyone else. Spoiled me. Yes, that's a fitting word to use.

Just how much I had been spoiled was not immediately apparent. It was only some weeks after we had parted, after he had returned to his real life – and I back to everyday living – that I realised I had missed my monthly bleeding. And then a second time. And so I knew. As always, my mother took her problem to the Countess, who shook her head gravely.

'I feared this. I was remiss. I spoke to the girl, but I should have also spoken to you, and sent her away. Now we must think what to do for the best.'

'I do not want her publicly shamed,' said my mother. I knew what she meant. The year before I had seen my friend Liesel make her confession before the congregation, and endured the censure of Pastor Liebelt and the condemnation of the members. She had crept from the back of the chapel at the end of communion each Sunday, and been permitted only to kneel and ask for forgiveness. Taking communion was denied her, and when in despair she took her own life she could not be buried in holy ground but in a small unmarked grave outside the churchyard gates, her unborn infant with her, both doomed to hellfire.

I knew this was what my mother feared.

'She must marry quickly,' the Countess decided. 'I think there is a boy who wishes to wed her?'

'But when he knows?' My mother was uncertain.

'I will provide a good dowry to compensate,' the Countess promised. 'Anna is dear to me, and I should have guarded her better.'

How well she understood the world, and the way that gold can sweeten all manner of bitter cups. Otto shut his eyes to the hard truths, and our marriage was a hasty affair.

I have often wondered how the Countess managed the matter, for it had been agreed that she would see him and offer the dowry. How skilfully she must have put it, without explicitly shaming me, to convey to him that this was a needed marriage. And Otto, who had always taken it for granted that one day I would be his, had now found the unpleasant truth blurred by enough money to purchase this small holding and the little thatched house that was part of it.

He must have made calculations. The value of land it would have been impossible for him to purchase weighed against taking on a used girl and a child he had not fathered. The

Countess had judged shrewdly; Otto always had an eye for a bargain.

It is good that my figure is slender, and even better that the swelling of my abdomen did not show until I was many months gone. We were able to have the pretence of a normal wedding, and Otto showed the world the face of a happy bridegroom.

I did not think we would escape the usual noisy festivities, and our charivari was a rowdy affair. Even the most chaste of weddings would bring crowds of young men to rattle saucepans and kettles, play pipes and whistles, and make as much disturbance as possible. I dreaded that it might have been planned for the night before our marriage, a sure sign that people realised I was with child, making this a public condemnation.

I waited in some fear the eve of my wedding, lest the sounds of my humiliation should come. Was it suspected? But no. It was an undisturbed night, and the charivari was, as usual, the night after the ceremony, surely not an ideal way to have your first bedding together with a crowd of drunken louts banging their instruments of noise. It is an unpleasant ritual, but one that it seems we must endure.

Otto saw it differently. For him it was important that our marriage should look as normal as possible, and we did not talk about the coming child. Nor did we discuss the discreet payment of the generous dowry, which Otto had seized upon to buy this small piece of land near the village of Lewin. He did not talk to me about it, and I was given no say in the place where we would live. Here we have built a start to our lives in the small wooden house that is our home.

It is a satisfactory dwelling. Under the thatched roof the loft gives ample storage for the winter fodder, and we have been fortunate with our small crops. While there is only one room for our living and sleeping, there is good space for our animals in the adjoining room, and it has a separate entry. In many of these houses the animals must trek through the family living space to reach their quarters. We are lucky.

Otto has not asked me about the child's father since our wedding. That too I find strange. I know that in his own way he loves me, but now I have become a possession. But instead of buying me, he has been paid to take me. There was little love on our wedding night; or since.

'You are with child?' he questioned me only once before our marriage.

'Yes.' There was no point in denial.

'Is the father someone I know?'

'No.' It was the truth. Otto had had no dealings with the Chateau guests. I sensed his relief that there would be no other father for my babe.

'This will not be discussed elsewhere. The child will be mine.'

It was as my parents had hoped. It would simply seem that the baby had come early. There were many other families in which this had happened. No one would question it.

I lay on our marriage bed and waited for him to come to me. But he had joined the roistering crowd of the charivari. It was, after all, his obligation to provide them with drink, and as the evening passed the noise grew louder under the influence of our strong local beer. The stench of beer and the pain of his lovemaking are all that I recall of my wedding night. This was not the delight of my time with Kurt.

It would have been easier, perhaps, if I had been able to lie there and imagine that Kurt was parting my legs and thrusting himself, urgently, inside me. But that would have seemed a desecration of all that he had meant to me. I heard Otto stumble as he lurched through the doorway of our new home, and I heard the raucous laughter of the men outside as they cheered him on his way. At least they believed that he was on his way to deflower an innocent, even if I was far from that.

Perhaps that is why there was no tenderness in the way he tore my shift from my shoulders and stared drunkenly at my naked body. I was glad that the child did not yet show. This way he could pretend that he was the first to take me. I knew this was important to him. So I closed my eyes and tried to avoid the heavy beer-laden breath as it came closer. But it was not what he wanted.

'Look at me, Anna!' he ordered, then turned to strip his wedding trousers, fumbling clumsily with the fasteners. 'Look at me! See me! I am your husband now.'

The words were slurred, but the anger in them was clear. It was not the wedding night he had anticipated all those years he had been waiting. Always there would be that shadow of the man who had taken what he felt was his right. So I would pay a price. Three years on, I am still paying the price.

Was it a sin? I ask myself that question over and over. I think of those days in the pine forest with Kurt and the joy I felt in loving him. Could this have been wrong? Yes, Pastor Liebelt would have thundered at me from the pulpit if he had known. Sin! Fornication! Only in the marriage bed should you abandon yourself to a man. You will be punished for those acts.

Had I loved Kurt? As time passes, I am no longer sure of that. I loved the ways our minds connected as well as our bodies, and after he had gone I was desolate. The yearning, the wretchedness, they were so agonising that I doubted I could bear it. I had never expected anything more from him, but to lose that sense of being beloved was like a plunge into a well of unhappiness. But now? It is becoming harder to recall his face and I wonder if he ever thinks of me. I wonder how long I will think of him.

Otto knew, his look as my body swelled was dark and brooding. I think he tried to blot out the past by force – it has always been his way to take control. I understand his love of the monstrous engines in the trains that he now drives, because these forces are under his guiding hand. He is their master, and the power they unleash as they thunder through the countryside is Otto's power.

If the child had lived, I would have had a part of Kurt to cherish. Even that has been taken away. All my memories have been clouded, tainted, by the horror of the night the baby was coming. I sensed there was something wrong. I have seen women in childbirth; I have watched animals in labour. I knew what should happen.

But this was different.

Otto had never been a gentle lover, but in those last months before the babe was born his hands, his body, had been more demanding, less careful of my body. My mother had worried over the dark circles beneath my eyes, and I wondered what she would have thought if she had seen the purple bruises on my thighs.

If I remonstrated or tried to resist it only seemed to anger him more. So I learned to endure in silence, and to try only to protect my womb. That too gave offence.

'You think to mock me with your body?' he snarled one night, when I dared to put out a feeble hand to weaken the impact of his battering flesh as he entered me.

'Did you stop him, the other one?'

It was the closest he came to admitting the fury that was driving him.

When my pains began, and I moaned that we needed the neighbour who had offered to help deliver the child, he pointed to the driving snow outside our door.

'You won't get Frau Schmidt in a night like this. I doubt the devil himself would come to you tonight.'

'The devil is here,' I gasped from where I lay, doubled up in agony. 'The devil is in you, Otto – ' but I could not finish my words. My waters had broken, and I lay in a flood of wet warmth.

'Otto, in God's name get Frau Schmidt. I beg you, Otto, help me.' Then the wave of pain seized me again.

As the hours passed, I think he came to understand that this was not a normal birth, but by the time he returned with the stooped figure of our neighbour it was too late. I lay shuddering in the mess of blood and waste, trying to reach to hold the twisted body of the dead child. It was a boy, and the cord that bound us together was still coiled tight around his neck. Frau Schmidt's hands were gentle as she cut the cord and laid the child for a moment on my limp body. Two exhausted bodies. We had both fought for his life, and we had both lost.

I relive it in my nightmares. I relive also the moments when we laid the small body, wrapped only in a swaddling cloth, in the little grave in the children's section of the churchyard. He was not baptised, but in my heart I had brought him to God, and silently named him for his earthly father.

Now those days have passed, and I think back over the blur of the months that followed. I know that I must have eaten, slept, talked to people, but the days came and went.

At least Otto was gentler with me. Perhaps the death of the child had shocked him, as he watched the agony of my labour. Or perhaps it was that now there was no baby for eager faces to peer at, wondering why they saw no trace of Otto in the little face, or at the size of this seemingly early child. Whatever the cause, one source of misery and anger had been taken from him, and a near peace descended on our house.

He comes and goes, as the network of trains bring our land and people closer. Some day, Otto says, the railway will also come through Lewin, because it will bring us closer to Glatz, but for now he is happy to stay there for part of each week. For me too, that is a relief.

Especially now, for this new child has brought me back to life. Perhaps it offers hope, for this time Otto watches my body swell with pleasure. It is his seed, his child, not a bastard foisted on him.

The house that he purchased for us with the money from the Countess is small, but comfortable. It is typical for this area, with its wood and plaster walls and the deep overhanging eaves giving us shelter from the winter winds. It is a haven for me, especially in the times when Otto is away.

After my son died, I found solace working in the plot of ground around our house, and the vegetables I grew were sufficient for our needs. True also of the potatoes, which make the potent schnapps that all our men drink – so often too freely! I have come to like the daily walk. I drive our animals easily to the small field he bought, finding comfort in the slow rhythm of the beasts as they plod contentedly toward the ground where they graze, their long tails swishing idly as they pace. The clear blue of this summer sky is a tent, stretched taut above me.

In his times at home, Otto works hard, and his sowing of the rye crop has been profitable. When he returns from the mill we estimate how much I need for the dark pumpernickel bread he likes, and the rest brings us a small sum of money. It is better than the sugar beet planting he first tried, like our neighbours. It was soon apparent there would be little profit in the new crop.

There are times of peace between us, when he shares with me the excitement of the new world of steam that fascinates him. While it means little to me, I rejoice to see him so absorbed.

I have been existing, as if in a dream, and I watched the changing seasons as summer brought its golden glow over the fields around our township, to be followed by the colours of the autumn woods blazing against the pine forests.

But I do not go to the forest. That part of my life is finished.

CHAPTER 4

Lewin, Silesia 1866

Today I watched Johanna as she tottered across the room to where the crib stands. Although almost two years old, her walk is still unsteady, and it tugs at my heartstrings when I see her sturdy little body.

She is her father's daughter. There could be no doubt about this child. She has his dark and curling hair, and I think when her face has passed babyhood she will have the nose that has been part of his family for generations. Her body is solid, her temperament his. Already she likes to take control, and I foresee a time when she will clash with her father.

Otto dotes upon this child as if there has been no other. She is his first thought each evening when he returns from the fields, and during his times away in Glatz she wanders the house searching for her beloved Vati. His name, *Vati, Daddy*, was the first word she tried to say, and her joy each time he comes back is lovely to behold. At last I feel I have brought happiness into his life.

In character I think she will have something of me. While she is not a dreamer, she loves stories, and the books carefully stored from my times at the Chateau give her great pleasure. I read to her in the evenings, and *story* is one of the clear demands she makes.

Otto is not happy that this is her liking. He is fiercely protective of her, and I think he fears that she may become attached to me. I do not resent her love of him. In a way I feel I owe him this. But at times a wistful sadness fills me, and I wonder if he, the other, might have been more mine than this little one will ever be.

Perhaps the new one? For once again my belly is swollen, and this child is not like Johanna, who kicked fiercely and strongly in my womb almost as soon as I became aware of her. This one is more considerate, and at times I am filled with fear. If I do not feel him move – for I tell myself this is another boy – I panic lest he too should not survive the womb.

This child will be mine, I have decided. Otto can have Johanna, whom we named for my mother, but this one I will call Kurt, even if Otto insists that the first name must be his. In my heart he will be Kurt, and Otto need never know why. I shall ask Lydia to stand as godmother at the baptismal font, and only she will understand what lies behind the choice of name. I will talk to him as Kurt, because Otto will understand that there cannot be two Ottos in our small household. Kurt Werner – a fine name for this babe who moves within me.

I still go to the Chateau, for the Graf has asked me to keep it in order for the times when he comes with his new wife and his hunting parties. I know them all, the maids and the gardeners, so it is little trouble to oversee the house. There are times when I do not feel that I have earned the coins he provides for me.

It is a longer journey than when we lived in Rauschwitz, when I was young and free, but even big with child I am happy to go.

We now have a horse, an old staid beast that pulls the little cart that Otto has made for us, and I can take Johanna with me. Most importantly, I can find books in the library to bring back and to hide myself away, lost in other worlds.

But the languages the Countess taught us so carefully are fading. How could it be otherwise when there is no chance to converse? I try to teach my little daughter some English, and she giggles when we lay out the stones on the path.

'One ... two ... three.' But I tell her it is our secret. I do not think Otto would approve. It is not a game she enjoys, and soon she is off, chasing the hens through the dust of our small yard. She is not a student. That is already clear. It will be different with the new one. With him I will talk in English, very quietly, so that some of the things I have learned can be passed on.

I know that this is important, for the child's early years can form the man he is to become. The Countess impressed this on us, for she had read deeply the works of Friedrich Fröbel and how with this method of educating small children a vast impact could be seen. I had listened in wonder as she told of the new institution he had started and the happy name he had given it ... the *kindergarten* ... and the way these children's gardens had flourished throughout Germany.

I have tried to talk to Otto about this, but he refused to listen. 'Socialist nonsense' was all he said, and bade me get on with serving his dinner.

Fröbel had his enemies, though no one could understand why the Prussian government had forbidden his infant schools for almost ten years. It seems that new thinking must always arouse opposition. But I hear that five years ago they relented and the ban was lifted. As it should have been. Other countries are now establishing these kindergartens and I have read the Chateau's copy of his most famous work, *The Education of Man*. It makes good sense to me. But poor man, I think the ban on his work may have killed him; he died the year after it was imposed, and never saw how his work would grow.

Why is this of such interest to me? My child will have all that this movement can offer. We may not have a kindergarten in Lewin, but I have access to all Fröbel's theories – even to his songbook for mothers and teachers, his *Mother Play and Nursery Songs*. Did I not mention that he believed that women are natural teachers, and were employed in his infant schools? A shocking idea, I admit, but one that gives me confidence to teach my own children.

In another life I might have trained to be one of these women teachers, and perhaps even started a children's garden in Lewin. Dreams, dreams. I had never imagined that my life would turn out like this. Who can see ahead where choices will take us? If I had not walked into the pine forests with Kurt, if I had not lain with him under the dark trees, would I now be planning to educate Otto's child the way I believe Kurt would have wanted our son to be taught?

It will be soon, I think. Frau Schmidt looked at me yesterday and asked if I had things ready for the birthing. I know she remembers that poor dead infant she laid on my breast. This time it will be different. This time Otto can go to the inn and boast he has a son – of this I am sure. But I am also sure that this child will be my son, from the moment that he leaves the safety of my womb. I have wondered if Johanna senses my love for this child. She came to me yesterday while I was reading.

'*Mutti!*' Her small face was wide-eyed, considering.

'Yes, child?'

'*Mutti*. Baby there?' pointing to my swollen middle under the loose smock I was wearing.

I nodded, only half hearing her words. Then I looked up as she spoke again.

Her little face, Otto's face, was considering the matter.

'Baby stay there,' she announced, and I realised she did not view this birth with pleasure. This is not uncommon. A child who has had sole care from two parents is, of course, not going to be enthusiastic about sharing the attention. And the affection. Though I am sure that Johanna's place in Otto's heart is firmly fixed. About my own I was not so certain.

I spoke as lovingly as I could. No child should feel threatened by a newcomer. Even Johanna, a contrary little miss, and often disobedient. Sometimes cheeky, especially when she realised that it amused her father to hear her flout my authority. When I told her to do something I would hear '*Vati* won't make me'.

And she was right. Rarely did he support me. More often he encouraged her with a smile and a wink of his eye as she ran to him for protection. If she was like this at such a tender age, I feared for the future. Did she love me, I wondered. Her feeling for Otto was clear. She would nestle on his knee, and play with his hair, or pat his hand in an almost maternal way. It was comical to watch. Not so with me. When I picked her up to cuddle her, her little body would stiffen.

I tried to talk to my mother about it.

'Your little namesake is so unloving,' I told her one day. 'I fear she will never feel for me the way she feels for her father.'

My mother only looked at me curiously. 'But what do you feel for her?'

I stared at her, quite taken aback.

'Why, I love her, of course.'

'Sometimes I have wondered. When you hold her, it is more as if this is something you must do, but your heart is not in it.'

I was offended, and, yes, hurt by her comment.

'You are quite wrong.'

She did not look convinced. 'Think about what I say. But I know how it hurts to feel that your child does not love you, that she loves someone else more.'

'What do you mean?'

'Remember the Countess. You idolised her, and always wanted to be there, to be with her. I always felt second-best in your eyes. Whatever she said, that was what counted.'

I felt a hot flush burn my cheeks. 'But she was your friend too. She was so kind to us both.'

My mother sighed. 'Do you not understand, my child, that one can admire, even love, someone, and yet be jealous of them? You and she were so close, and she was so good to you, but there were times I almost hated her. You gave her the love that should have been mine.'

What could I say? Her words had cut me to the quick, because I knew that they were true. I had given only little affection to my mother, the woman who had borne me and cared for me – and had encouraged and protected my place at the Chateau when my father would have stopped it. She had been generous.

And I had rarely given anything to her; I had preferred another. So perhaps there was a justice here, that now my own daughter was following in my footsteps.

I looked at my mother where she sat, her aging hands for once idle, no longer working at the stockings that she still made for the little extra money they brought. Work-roughened hands, not the Countess' slender white fingers I had so admired. Even now, I made comparisons. Penitent and regretful, I could only say, 'I am sorry.'

But when the child heard the sound of Otto at the door, and ran eagerly from us, crying, '*Vati, Vati!*' my mother looked at me and smiled. We both knew that the wheel had come full circle.

CHAPTER 5

Lewin, Silesia 1871

Such a year this has been. Even here, in tiny Lewin, we have followed the events with passionate interest. For Otto, his new hero has triumphed, a man of iron who can fulfil all his own wishes for power.

'Even my name,' he exclaimed with a sort of passionate pride. 'Otto von Bismarck!'

Little did I think, in the days Kurt talked to me of the changes that would come to our land, that I would live to see it come about. Now I remember him talking (so often I recall those days with Kurt), telling me of the way he and his companions idolised this man who, they foresaw, would unite our separate kingdoms.

Who would have believed it could be achieved so rapidly? Even my Otto, who so admires the man, shakes his head in wonder.

'Eight years!' he says, marvelling.

Yes, well. Eight years of wars, and no mother can feel pleasure in her country at war. Yet, even I could feel my heart swell with pride when news came of victories. First the war in the far north against Denmark that brought the Duchy of Schleswig to Prussia. Now it is all Prussia, Prussia, Prussia, and we in the southern kingdoms could see that the Prussian Junkers, those powerful landowners who controlled the Parliament, were the ones who had vision for the future.

What a strategist the man is. I blessed the Countess yet again for the reading she had encouraged, for I could follow the events of these tumultuous years – even my Otto at times would listen to what I said. Reluctantly – for I was a woman – and what do women know of the world of politics and warfare?

My world is the world that women have always known, here in the home we have made. When Otto is away in Glatz I can escape into the books I love, and teach the children, though already Hanna goes daily to the little school near St Michael's church. I still walk with her each morning, for in spite of her fierce independence she is but a little girl of seven years. Soon she will walk with the other children from this part, but for now Kurt and I walk with her.

When we have waved farewell to her (and sometimes she will turn to wave again to us) I will often take Kurt into the big white building next door, although it is a Catholic church and we are not of that faith. Yet the Countess was a believer, so sometimes I light a candle and pray for her soul, though my strict Lutheran pastor would be angered by this pagan idolatry if he knew.

The statues intrigue my small son, for he is not used to a church that contains so much to look at.

'Who is this one?' he asks, as he looks at a side altar with its figure of St Anthony. So I tell him stories of the lives of saints and hope that he will not repeat them to our dour and upright Lutheran pastor. Then, while I pray, Kurt wanders fascinated round St Michael's, more decorated and colourful than our plain and unadorned place of worship. He gazes in wonder at the statues and the paintings, for in its 500 years this church has seen passing armies and the trade route that has made this little town important. I look at the famous painting of the Madonna that Richter made and pilgrims come to pray to, and wonder at how much she has known. How many supplicants, how many armies. Some of our youths have joined the army that now fights in other lands.

Five years ago a war with Austria – another master stroke, for here our chancellor, our Iron Duke, began to forge the idea of a separate 'Germany' quite apart from the old Hapsburg Empire. Yes, we'd had a German Confederation, but our separate smaller kingdoms would never have given the power that he and the Prussian king craved. Now we were beginning to see what might be achieved if all our Princedoms united.

But oh, the panic when an assassination attempt on our leader's life was reported. (For by now we saw Bismarck as our leader. Even the Prussian king yielded to his words.) Five shots! And at close range! But his injuries were minor, and there was a sense of justice when the assassin suicided in prison.

The church bells rang out in joy when news came that our leader lived. And last year the final momentous events were set in train. War with France. All the traditional hostilities and distrusts were brought to the fore, and no matter which princedom people lived in, we were happy to join behind Prussia and the Northern Federation in the war that showed the French that they could not insult our Fatherland.

As the war came to an end we rejoiced in the news that the Prussian King, Wilhelm, had been crowned Emperor of a united

Germany. The sweetness of crowning our Emperor in the Hall of Mirrors in the Chateau at Versailles. What a stroke of genius. No wonder when Otto von Bismarck returned to Berlin some months ago, as our first Chancellor of the new Empire, there was an outpouring of adoration for the man who had made our country great.

Otto felt he had been involved – hanging on the great man's coat-tails, perhaps. A pity he did not also follow the Chancellor's religion, for his deep pietism was well-known, and the Lutheran faith that he and his wife espoused was an important part of their lives.

Not ours. Otto had little time for religion and made his feelings clear. So our Sundays, when little Hanna and Kurt and I set off for services in the white church in Lewin, are days that also separate our paths. As I tied the ribbons on my bonnet over my lace cap, in keeping with the old ways, he would laugh and swing our little girl high in the air.

'Stop, Otto! She is too big for such play! She is seven now.'

But Hanna would laugh. 'Higher, *Vati*, higher!'

'Now you,' as he turned to Kurt.

Trapped, the child would look at me, his eyes wide and fearful. But there was nothing I could do, and so he would advance hesitantly towards the huge figure of his father. It was the sort of rough-house play he dreaded, and Otto's face would flush with fury.

'Bah! You have made the boy into a milksop. He's fit only for reading your books and singing hymns in your church. Is he indeed my son?'

As he raised the child high in the air, I could see the panic on the small face, and my heart ached for my son. I could also see the small smile on Hanna's, and I knew that she triumphed in her father's favour.

If Kurt had been more like his father, would things have been easier for him? I doubt it, for I had kept my resolution that this child would be mine. He was dark, yes, as both Otto and I were, but his build was slighter, more like me, and his face was my face.

Hanna's old days of 'Story, *Mutti!*' were truly over. I think her father's scorn had withered away even that slight bond between us, and now she makes it clear that my role in her life is limited to providing for her daily needs. If she has others, she does not let me see them.

With Kurt it was so different. From babyhood on, his face would light up when he saw me, and all his first stumbled words were for me. I cradled and sang to him, and he nestled against me in a way that his sister had never done.

I look at the way this has been captured for all time in the pictures that have just come to us. Such pictures reveal truths that we may otherwise be able to ignore, and then forget.

It has been the talk of the place in these last weeks, an event to make even the most miserly open their purse strings. A travelling photographer came to Lewin with his horse and hooded cart and, like many of our neighbours, we took our children, all of us dressed in our best clothes, to the small studio he had established. There was much discussion of the new methods that were being developed, for the days of the daguerreotype were passing and new methods of paper printing and glass negatives had captured public fancy.

To my surprise Otto wanted this. I think he was anxious to show off his new high-collared shirt which, I had to admit, looked fine with its new fashion wide tie and waistcoat under his coat. He was putting aside the old dress for our region and taking on the new ways. He tells us this is common in Glatz, that few there will wear the traditional clothes our small town still favours, and that Glatz has several of these new photographic studios.

So there we stood, carefully posed by the dapper Frenchman setting up a business for a time in our town. Otto was seated and looking most impressive, while I stood, in my new magenta gown with its broad skirts and long puffed sleeves and many petticoats. Thankfully the days of the crinoline are passing, though it seems that the material is now to be drawn to the back. I have heard talk of a new fashion – a silly word, a *bustle*, for an even sillier idea. Such a travesty of nature to poke out at the back like this, I feel, for who can believe there is beauty in a protruding lump behind the body.

With my hair drawn back and the cluster of curls behind my new bonnet, I felt ready to be captured by the photographer as he crouched beneath the heavy black curtain over his equipment. Even Kurt, who has just this year changed from the loose robe of childhood into the required clothes for a five-year-old, now looks a little boy in his miniature leggings and coat, while Hanna thinks herself a true little lady in her hooped skirt and the matching tartan jacket with its lace ruffles at her wrists. We had never dressed like this before; it is indeed a special event that I know will not happen again. Otto will not countenance such extravagance another time.

Even here the tension in our family is captured for all generations to see. Otto's arm is around his beloved daughter, while I stand behind him, careful not to touch either of them.

My hand rests lightly on Kurt's shoulder, keeping him with a family group that he seems eager to separate from. Ah well, the camera doesn't lie, they say. Perhaps they are right, and maybe Monsieur Delroix, when he posed us, had an intuitive understanding of our family life.

Could he have heard the disputes over my teaching of the boy, or seen the way Hanna simply ignores my requests, my commands? Could he have seen the increasing coldness of our married life? There will be no more children, that is clear. Otto finds his satisfactions elsewhere and makes it clear that our marriage bed is a cold place that gives him no pleasure.

'At least your Count von Bismarck has a happy marriage. And three children, though they are grown now,' I tell him.

'Two of those sons went to war last year,' he replies. 'They were in the cavalry and fought bravely against the French upstarts.'

'I wonder how their mother felt,' I ponder.

'You will scarcely need to worry for that. Your little runt of a son would run from battle. He quakes when I come near.'

'That cannot surprise you. You are too rough – you frighten him.'

'I should beat the fear out of him. He needs to learn to stand up for himself.'

This photograph may be the last time that we stand together as a family. For the divisions that were always there are likely to become deeper and more damaging as the years go on. I sense that will be the future. Perhaps it is a mercy, that we do not see too far ahead.

CHAPTER 6

Lewin, Silesia 1883

I had been right to fear the future, and the changes that would come. That before he was twenty, I would be losing the son who was the one bright spot in my life. The day he went will never leave my mind. My son.

I sit these days at my loom, for many in Lewin have tried to keep the old industries alive, and though linen weaving is no longer central in our lives, and even the mill has closed, there is a comfort in doing things as they have always been done.

There are not so many who will still plant and harvest the fields of flax that once surrounded us, but old techniques of treating the fibres and the spinning have not been forgotten. There is talk that embroidery will survive, and that they may even build a school in Lewin to teach this skill. Clearly times are changing, and new ways of life will come. I sit as I weave lengths of linen to take to the markets, though these tawdry little affairs are so sad compared to what we once knew. They tell us that fifty years ago there were near on 300 looms in Lewin; today the few of us who still spin know that there will be little profit made. We have watched people in the town no longer able to feed their families, and calling on the public purse for support.

I bless the fact that we do at least have land and some livestock; it is all that sustains us in these hard times. Hard they are, since Otto's work is gone. This is, I think, the worst that could have happened to him. All that passion that he had for the railroads, all his confidence that one day even our tiny Lewin would have its own tracks and station and engines ... well, it may yet happen. I believe it will, but he will not be a part of it. What use is a man with only one arm in the world of the huge mechanical beasts he loved to tame?

As I sit and spin I can understand the dreadful harm that has been done him. No matter that the accident was his own fault. Had he not been so many hours drinking in the alehouse in Glatz, would he have been more cautious on his way to the lodging house? Would he have been so stupid, so befuddled by liquor, as to have sought his way home along the railroad tracks?

The irony of it, that he, who loved the iron monsters, should have suffered under one!

'Would I were dead,' he groaned in those first awful days. For a time it seemed that he might indeed not survive, but he has always been a big man, a strong man, and by some miracle he lived.

'We cannot save the arm,' the grave-faced doctor told me. I shivered, for I knew what this would do to my husband. While there was no love left in me for him, I could feel pity. He was the father of my children, and there had been moments of tenderness between us – hard to remember in the seven years we have endured since his maiming.

For a time the company gave him some work in Glatz, but it was clear this could not last. Such work, for a man of his sort. He who had driven the huge machines, who had fed the ravening beasts with coal and watched the flames in their bellies, to now move among the pasty-faced little men in the offices and do their bidding. Perhaps he drank even more to blot out all that had happened, so I was not surprised when, outraged and resentful, he came to us in Lewin with news that he no longer had work.

'Thrown away like a dog!' he raged. 'I have worked for them near twenty years, and this is all I get. Those bastards ...'

As his language became more immoderate, I turned away, glad that the children were at school. I wondered what would become of him, no longer able to satisfy the lust for power I had always known was the deepest part of his being.

Well-founded fears, for these years have been unhappy ones for us all. Work in our field is of little interest to him; even with the animals he must often ask our help. A missing arm is more than just a limb gone. It is a deep change in a man's image of himself. I found him looking at the photographs taken in those first heady years of our Iron Chancellor's rule, and the desperation on his face as he saw the man he had been was pitiful to watch. I turned quickly from the door, because I know that my pity is unbearable to him.

If not pity, what else can I give? Not love, for there never has been love. Now we are locked together more than ever before. His time in Glatz made our lives possible; that relief is gone. I see the rage building in him, and I know what will come when it reaches – like one of his great boilers – an explosion point. He goes to the alehouse with the coins we so desperately need, and I wait, anxious only to shield the children.

The old days of softness for Hanna are gone, and even she

has felt the swift blows from his strong right arm. It is as if he must use double force to compensate for the missing limb. It was good for her when she found work in the town, for this too brought us money for what we needed.

At thirteen she was ready for her confirmation, the main moment of transition from childhood to adulthood. I would have wished her to wait another year or so but she was yearning to be free of this house. So we allowed her to join the class that Pastor Schirmer was holding each Sunday after the first service for the day. She had been through the earlier years of instruction, so there was no problem facing the examination given to her class.

Otto and I sat, he according to custom in the left-hand pews in our local church, though his church attendance, never frequent, is rare indeed since the accident. Whatever God there is has treated him unjustly, he is sure. Ten-year-old Kurt was with me on the women's side, but he understood the importance of this public testing, and fidgeted nervously; soon, I sighed, he would be old enough to join the men.

Hanna does not become nervous; her thoughts were, I was sure, on her first long-skirted gown for the confirmation ceremony on Easter Sunday. From this time she would be officially a woman, allowed to go to dances, allowed also to think about a future spouse.

It was as she wished. From that time she went each day to the house of our Bürgermeister, to do the cleaning and the washing that his wife, a sickly lady, found more than she could manage with her eight children. There has been talk each time she is again with child, and the boldest in our town have much to say as we sit together over the looms. Frau Schmidt, who knows about these matters, casts her eyes heavenwards and makes crude gestures when she talks of him.

I feared for Hanna when she found a place in that household, but she was eager to leave us and make a new life for herself. Otto was no longer the father she had known. At first she was perplexed, confused by the changes. The dark brooding silences that could explode into sudden rage – both children learned to watch for these.

For Kurt it was easier; he was accustomed to his father's rages. He had always known the need to keep clear of the man who would lash out at the slightest cause for anger – or even without cause. Back then Otto had seen it as his duty as a father.

'He needs to learn to fight back.' It was his justification in all those early years for the roughness in his handling of the little boy.

'See the way he cowers! No son of mine is going to act like a frightened girl. He has to be taught to fight.'

Kurt would flinch from the upraised hand and run from the expected blow. Until he realised that escape was impossible, and to try it made the final beating more brutal. Better to endure than to run.

For Hanna, his pet, the change was bewildering. At twelve years one cannot comprehend the misery that can so corrode a person that even a beloved child becomes an outlet for rage. The first time he struck her was when she came late from the school so that her evening milking of the cow was delayed and the animals not in their pens. I had watched fearfully, knowing how long he had spent in the alehouse and his dangerous temper when he came. I had thought to do her work instead, but before I could reach the animal he was there.

'Get inside!' His voice was raised in anger and his words slurred. 'Let the little slut do her own work.'

He pushed me roughly into the house, and I watched apprehensively as she came, unawares, towards him. The sight of his face should have warned her, but her laughter as he stumbled and fell against the cow was all that was needed. There was no more laughter after he struck her across the face, his one good arm flailing wildly.

I could understand her readiness to take on any sort of work that would take her away from us, and the man who had so changed towards her. Even life at the Bürgermeister's house, with a fretful ailing woman and a house full of squalling brats, must have seemed preferable to this new father.

She was only sixteen when she came to tell us the news that she would marry. I could only hope and pray that she had found someone who would treat her well and feel relief that she had found a different life for herself. Franz is a good man, though much older, and the fact that his first wife died in childbirth made him, I think, especially tender towards Hanna when her time came. But that was later.

Those years in the Bürgermeister's house had taught her many things about life, and the ways of men. I gave thanks daily for her quick wit and, yes, the strength she had inherited from Otto. I am sure she needed both in that household where caring for one and escaping the other must have been a daily challenge.

We rarely talked. There had been the bond of birth between us, and that, I have now discovered, is by no means as strong a tie as is generally believed. I did not like the woman she was becoming, strong and ruthless. But love? Did I love her? Child of my body – there were ties there that did not break. The cord between mother and child is never completely severed, even when the midwife's scissors have cut it and clamped the little stub that remains. Invisible it may be, but still alive and strong. It was there, even though I found it so hard to show her love. And God knows she had seen little enough of it between Otto and me. Why would she have expected love to be a part of marriage?

I listened with concern as she told us of the marriage that would take place and wondered whether her new husband's age had led him to believe that he would be master in their home.

'He is fifty,' she declared. 'A good age for a husband. Why, he is older than you are, *Vati*, but seems younger than you.'

It was a cruel thrust, but accurate. Otto did look older; the years of drinking were taking their toll and the strong body of his working years was flabby and weak. The great stomach that hung over his low belt owed little to my Sunday rouladen and dumplings; more to the strong potato beer that he drank daily in the town.

I looked at Franz in his wedding suit, the new waistcoat bright and fashionable, and I saw the spindly legs that could not be concealed by tailor's art. I wondered what my daughter had done. It was her doing – that she had made clear. A man her father's age to replace the father she had lost, perhaps. It made sense. His house and land were substantial; that too must have been a great inducement, to get away from the drudgery of the Bürgermeister's household. But to sleep close to that scrawny aged body. To feel it press against her, to enter her, the very thought was repellent. Would there be children, I wondered.

It seems that Hanna had taken this into account, and assured herself of his abilities ... I did not question how.

'Where did you meet?' I ventured the question when she came with her news.

'He was often a visitor at the house,' she explained. 'I knew his eyes followed me when I served at table, and his hand lingered on mine when I served the afternoon coffee. He came often – it was very proper. My mistress is his sister, after all, and she is so ill.'

'Even so. You were a servant. And so much younger!'

'Many chances to brush against him in the passageways as I brought him in and out of the house. Many chances to be surprised when he ventured a touch ... and to make it clear that I was virtuous. Still, not too easy to bring him to the point.'

'How then was it managed?'

'For a time I did not know, but then I took a risk.'

'So?' By the time she told me I was even more impressed. My daughter indeed, in some ways. I doubt that Otto, smart as he had been, would have given her such initiative.

'One day I wept and said I would have to leave the house. That my honour was at risk, but I could not tell my mistress because the knowledge would have killed her.'

'Surely he would have spoken to the man?'

'That was indeed the hard part, to prevent that happening. I said I did not want to stay there but wanted no scandal. What was I to do? Where to go? Tears are so powerful. Soon he had thought of the solution – it fitted his wishes well, and once he saw that he knew I would be willing.'

'But marriage! Surely there will be talk?'

'*Mutti*, talk does not count when you have the marriage cap and ring, and the money to support the life you want. Nor does the husband.'

She smiled when I shook my head, but it was not a pleasant smile.

Although Otto gave his permission readily enough when Franz came to ask for Hanna's hand, we could not give them the wedding that the new husband would have wanted, so Hanna was forced to ask him to provide. He was happy to give funds for the feasting after the simple service in the Lewin church. The civil ceremony was, after all, a formality. But the wedding proper was to make clear his standing in the community.

I was pleased that they did not want to follow the new English fashion of the bride in a white gown. I recalled the Countess telling me of this, saying that the English queen had made this fashionable, and that so many brides were following this – a symbol of their purity perhaps? Or their hypocrisy!

We chose instead a dress of dark green, cut in a style that all admired, for in the town Hanna had learned to study the pictures of the new clothes great ladies wore. I had watched Lydia's interest in dress during the years we had been together, and when she heard that my daughter was to be wed, she had offered to make her a gift of the bridal gown.

We see each other but rarely. Lydia does not often come to the Chateau, though her father still brings hunting parties, but when we are together the years that have passed seem to fall away. For a brief time, we are young again. We talk of past times, of that summer of Gustav and Kurt, and how little we knew of life in those days. We do not talk often of our present lives. Festering sores are better left untouched. If they cannot be healed, at least they should not be poked into life.

But our times together are, I think, a comfort to us both.

'How I once envied you,' she confessed to me one day. 'You

and Mama – all that you shared. Not that I wanted it. All that reading! But I knew how she loved you.'

'And I you,' I replied. 'I would have so wished to have had her as my mother.' But even as I spoke, I felt the familiar twinge of guilt. My mother had known this, and it had hurt.

It does not surprise me that Lydia has had no child. Her way of life offers no place for children, and her aged husband gives her freedom to live life as she wishes. And the money to do what she wants. But she takes an interest in both Hanna and Kurt and would, I think, try to find a way to help me if she could. She has offered money, but that I cannot accept. A payment for my supervision at the Chateau, yes. Her father's payment does not degrade me, but I will not accept Lydia's charity.

Yet the wedding gown for Hanna – that was a gift we could both enjoy. She had brought it for the girl from Berlin, and its high neckline suited the girl's long neck – swan-like, said Lydia approvingly.

'You have your mother's neck! She too has the same long and graceful neckline. See how her collar sits.'

I confess I felt pride at her words. It is rare these days for anyone to compliment me, and I valued Lydia's words. Hanna looked at me in surprise, not expecting her mother to be praised for her appearance. As I approach forty years, I do not expect it either.

The dress was indeed beautiful, with only a hint of a bustle. The green silk taffeta of the skirt with its long line of bows trailed down the girl's back from the frill-trimmed jacket. I was glad she had chosen not to have a long train, just a simple addition to the skirt. How little chance would she have had to wear a formal gown. Lydia's other gift in her dark hair, a wedding wreath with its wax buds and orange blossom – no veil.

I take little interest in fashion and dress, but I found myself so pleased to see my daughter properly attired as a bride. Perhaps a substitute for my wedding to Otto, no joy there, concerned only that my simple dress should not betray the swelling stomach that I had to conceal.

Was this marriage any different from mine? No love, more an act of convenience. I could only pray, as I knelt in our church listening to their wedding vows, that it would be happier than mine. I looked to where Otto, mercifully sober for once, stood behind his daughter, the daughter whom he had once so adored, and wondered how he felt about these missing years.

Now she is gone, to the home of her new husband in Mittelwalde, and already there is a child. Otto laughed crudely when they brought news that soon he would have a grandchild.

'More life in the old man than I'd thought,' he jibed. 'More than in me, anyway, eh Anna?'

It was true. There has been no coupling in our lives for many years now. I wonder often whether he misses the woman I know he had in Glatz, or whether the drink has taken away all such needs. I think of Macbeth: there the porter knows what he is about, when he reminds his hearers that *while drink provokes the desire, it takes away the performance!* I doubt that for Otto it even leads to desire, and certainly there is no performance! At least, not with me.

There is little happiness in his life. I at least have Kurt and the years we have enjoyed. My son, in every way. A reader and a dreamer. But Otto's son as well, and with the same fascination for the new worlds opening around us. Is it a matter of inheritance, I wondered. They tell us that each parent contributes, so why should it surprise me that Kurt has found a passion for steam and for what can be done with it?

From the start I watched it with fear, sensing the threat it posed. There has been such pleasure for me to see the success of his schooldays, but no surprise. Otto once had intelligence, and has always known how to get what he wants. In our little Rauschwitz school he was clearly brighter than the other children, and his years of technical training in Glatz were a success. What life has made of him is not because of a lack of wit, but of something more important – understanding. Kurt has both: he is intelligent and is also a thinker. His schoolfellows know this. He is the one they turn to in trouble, his advice can be relied on and his suggestions followed. Perhaps it is this that so maddens Otto.

It was as I had hoped. This child is more my Kurt's son (as I still think of him) than Otto's. This is the son that Kurt and I should have had; the son who died that terrible night in the snowstorm. How I have valued watching him grow and develop. But the qualities that I love in him are the qualities that enrage Otto.

We have learned to keep out of his way when he returns from the inn, his wits addled by drink and his temper roused by the sight of our companionship.

'Why do you stay?' Hanna often asks, when she visits with little Theo. But this is rare. She comes only when she is sure her father will not be here.

'Why do I stay?' I reflect on her question. 'But where would I go? How would I live?'

'You could come to us. Franz would welcome you in the house; he knows what help you would be.'

I could foresee my role in that household. A servant, working for my lodging. I had little contact with their child, and there were few bonds there.

'There will be another child this year. I am already three months gone. I know how much I will need your help.'

'But I could not leave Kurt alone with his father,' I protested.

She smiled and spoke with some bitterness. 'Of course you would not leave Kurt. I should have thought.'

When my boy came to tell us he had won a scholarship to the technical school in Glatz, my heart sank. I knew how empty my life would be. Yet there was some relief; he could at least come home at the end of each week.

'This is your doing, *Mutti*,' he said with pride. 'If you had not always urged me to work, to study, I would not have reached this point.'

'This is your doing, Anna,' said Otto, accusingly. If I had not insisted on the hours spent reading, on teaching him the love of languages instilled in me by the Countess. If I had not encouraged him to apply himself so whole-heartedly to his books – then perhaps we would not be losing our son to another world.

'What is there here for him, Otto?' I asked. 'Do you want him to follow in your footsteps?'

The years have taught me cruelty, and the pity for him that once softened my words is long gone.

The day Kurt left, his portmanteau packed with the new clothes he needed, he took the one bright spot in my life.

CHAPTER 7

Lewin, Silesia 1886

Did I not say how hard it was when Kurt left me four years ago to study at the technical college in Glatz?

At least there I could visit him, and he could see us if there was a carter coming our way on a Sunday. Those days in Glatz were happy times for me. Our new pastor often travelled the seventeen miles and when he and his young wife were happy to fit an extra body into the trap with its spirited horse I accompanied them.

Only a few hours with my dear boy, but such an opportunity, if he had no classes, to explore the city and hear of his progress. Though I confess tales of his studies left me bewildered – both the theory of his work in science and the complexities of the mathematics. I was delighted to find Kurt still reading as avidly as when we raided the bookshelves of the Chateau.

Exploring the city of Glatz, so many times larger than our town, was a delight, its Roman relics from days when it was an important stopping place on the old Amber Road. So much history and, like life itself, so many ups and downs. We dwelt on the changing allegiances – the times when it was part of

Bohemia, of Austria and Prussia, times of war, siege, plague – but now more than 13,000 people live here in the peace and prosperity of the new German Reich.

Otto did not come. I confess I would not have wanted him, and it was worth facing his anger when I returned late in the evening, the minister's trap leaving me at our gates.

'I left food ready for you,' I protested. 'You were sleeping when I departed.'

'The fire had gone out, and the oven was cold.'

I fought my irritation. 'You could surely have started it again.'

I knew he would have gone instead to the alehouse, full of complaints against the wife who had left her duties.

'What do you do when you are in Glatz?' he asked once, when not so far gone in drink.

'I walk around the town, sometimes with Kurt if he is free to join me, or on my own. Sometimes Frau Muller from his boarding house will join me.'

We had become friends, the older woman and I. She loved her town, and never tired of showing me all its beauties. The old city walls were almost entirely gone, but parts still reminded me of times when the gates, now long demolished, had closed each night securing the lives within.

'It is a beautiful place,' I told Otto. 'I can see why you were happy to be there during those years.'

He scowled. 'I would not wish to go back again. Not like this.'

I could understand that. Frau Muller had told me as we walked along the banks of the Neisse River one day, of Otto's reputation in the town.

'He was known for his strength,' she said with reluctant admiration. 'At fair time, he would win the trials of strength and few would take him on in the wrestling ring or at the axe chopping. It was terrible – what happened to him.'

'Yes,' I admitted. By now we were on close terms, calling each other by the familiar terms. 'It was terrible, and it changed him.'

'But I think, my dear,' her voice hesitant, 'that he would never have been an easy husband.'

I nodded. 'He was always dangerous to provoke. And I have a gift for rousing his anger. I did not mind that he spent so much of his life here. Mine was a cold bed for him.'

Berthe nodded comprehendingly. 'But now?'

'Now he is shackled in Lewin and feels he has lost everything. It drives him to fury, to lashing out at whoever is within reach. Usually me.'

'The children?'

'I have tried to protect them. It has been worst for Kurt because he felt he should protect me. Many a beating that got him. I think he knew there would be bloodshed if he stayed. That it would be easier for me if he was not there.'

'Was he right?'

'No,' I confessed. 'With Kurt here at school and Hanna married and gone, there's no one else to lash out at. But I stay. Where else can I go?'

'It is indeed sad,' Bertha agreed. 'He was highly regarded here. Not just for his work, but in other ways.'

She told me of the floods of recent years, when the placid Neisse, for twenty-five years tranquil and easy-flowing, had burst its banks. We stood together on the Gothic bridge, looking over at the peaceful tree-lined waters. A beautiful spot, and a beautiful bridge.

'They say,' I ventured, 'that this bridge is famous, almost like the lovely Charles Bridge in Prague.' Kurt had told me that on one of our walks through the town. 'It is hard to imagine it in flood, and dangerous.'

'What year ...?' she ruminated. 'Yes, it would have been six years ago – in 1879. And then again, two years later, and two years after that.'

'But what has this to do with Otto?'

'He had warned us,' she explained. He had looked at the flooding patterns of the last centuries, and had predicted more. Before his accident, he had tried to get big banks built, the sort they have now in other lands with flooding ...'

'Like Holland?'

'Yes. Also in the northern parts of our land. He read of it and gathered a group of men, strong men, to begin work. But then, his accident. And after that, nothing more.'

I was impressed. I had always guessed that Otto could have been so much more than the drunken shell he had become.

'When the next floods came, several years after he left us, people remembered his words. But nothing has been done. We will live, as we have always lived, with the Neisse holding us in its power.'

I had thought to tell Kurt of this the next time we were together. Instead I found myself on a seat overlooking the river listening to him in dismay.

'My teachers here have suggested that I need a bigger school, a college where I can learn much more than they can teach here.'

'But you are happy here! This is such a lovely place.'

I did not add what was in my heart, that he could still come home. That I could come to him and talk to Berthe about his life. I looked at the Marian Column in the town square, where we were seated. Mary too had known what it was to love and lose a son.

'They've suggested I transfer to Breslau.'

'But that is so far.'

I knew he could hear the misery in my voice, I made little effort to hide it.

'No, no, *Mutti*.' He put a comforting arm around my shoulders. 'It's not so far. It's only sixty miles from our home, and already you have come to me in Glatz.'

'Ah, but my son, my dear son, it is not even twenty miles, and here I have had the good Pastor Heinrich and his wife to bring me. Breslau will be very different.'

'Come,' he said, and drew me to my feet. 'Let us walk a little along the river.'

'I had always thought that some day, when your studies are finished, you would find work in this area. That you would be able to visit us often.'

'Us?' There was bitterness in his voice. 'I would be coming to see you. Why would I return to be abused and struck? I had more bruises than you ever saw. I have trouble with my hearing. The doctors here have said it was caused by the blows to my head – '

I felt my hand go, of its own volition, to my mouth.

'Your father struck your head?'

'There was much you did not see, for all your care and protection. And I knew that to speak of it would make your life worse.'

I saw the truth of his words. I had known that Otto disciplined the children according to his own rules, but not that so much had happened that was outside my ken. Only now was Kurt willing to tell me more.

'But when? How did I not know?'

My son looked uneasy, then shrugged. 'Ach, *Mutti*, it's all in the past now, and I'm away from it.'

We walked in silence for a while.

'Christmases,' he reminisced. 'Do you remember the Ruprecht?'

I nodded. Every German child knew that story, and most had experienced it. Before Saint Nikolaus came at the beginning of Advent with his bag of sweets and small gifts, in our area Knecht Ruprecht would come, masked and threatening, with jangling bells and a big stick.

So frightening. I could remember my childhood, and the way we children would run from the sound of the bells. Yet often he would find us, and the distorted booming voice would ask ... ask? Demand! Interrogate!

Had we been good children? Had we said our prayers? Anyone too slow to give the right answers would feel the stick around their legs. And then the monstrous figure would move on to the next farmhouse and the sound of the bells would fade away. Saint Nikolaus following, with his sack of toys, was scarcely a compensation for the terror we had felt.

I had wondered how the village leaders chose the actor to play Ruprecht, as we called him. Now it did not surprise me that Otto had been given the role. What I had not known was how often Kurt had been singled out for special attention, and the punishment he received each year had made Christmas a nightmare for him.

'But, Kurt, there was also happiness, surely?'

'I truly enjoyed the Advent wreath on our doors, and the lighting of the candles each Sunday. And yes, both Hanna and I loved opening the twenty-four windows on the Advent calendar. But ...'

'But?' I urged.

'But the threat of the masked figure each Christmas loomed over me. The fear and the beating I knew would come.'

'I am sorry,' I said simply. 'I did not know.'

'When we brought home the Christmas tree and added the candles and small ornaments, when we put the tiny crib at the foot of the tree and placed the wooden animals around it, all I could think of was the Ruprecht and fear that he might, as he had threatened, come back for me.'

'I did not know.'

'What could you have done? I know how often you were his victim. So many nights I hid behind our bed curtains, away from the sounds of his blows and your sobs.'

I had always known that Kurt feared his father, but not how deeply he had been hurt. There was nothing that would change this.

'I cannot forgive what he has done. I want only to get far away. The further the better. I cannot return to Lewin. Glatz was a start. I will go to Breslau, though it hurts me to be away from you. Then further yet.'

'What do you mean?'

Now his eyes shone with enthusiasm. 'I want to work with steam, *Mutti*. It fascinates me. We have not yet explored all its possibilities. It will change our world even more.'

'Are you talking of rail? I have seen how the new lines travel further and further. Soon they will crisscross our land.'

'No, no. These are impressive, it's true. But other things too. Ships. Huge ships are now being built that can cross oceans in half the time of sail ships. I want to find out how far the new power of steam can take us.'

I could see how this boy of mine was also Otto's son. His eyes had shone in just the same way when he was captured by the new world of rail. But Kurt's words frightened me.

'Breslau is on the river, and there is a great deal of shipping traffic there. But you are talking of more than that, aren't you?'

Kurt did not reply but took my arm and turned me towards the river. 'See how beautiful the light on the water is.'

We did not talk further that day about his future, but a fear had been planted in my heart. I was right to be afraid.

CHAPTER 8

Lewin, Silesia 1886

Glatz had been a start; Breslau was the next stage in my son's escape from the past.

'It is not so difficult, Mama,' said Hanna, when I told her. She had dropped the familiar *'Mutti'* of childhood, and now used the more fashionable *'mama'* when she spoke to me.

'Breslau is easy to get to now that the train goes from Glatz. Without the children I would accompany you, but there is no way I could leave them with Franz.'

'Is he kind to you, child?' I asked.

'Oh yes, he is not Papa!'

I winced. I knew what she meant.

'But he is old – and at times he seems very like an old man. But a kind old man. I cannot complain. I knew what my life would be when I married him. Though I have been surprised at times. I did not foresee that he would want more children. Or be so demanding of the marriage bed.'

We did not talk intimately. She had always rejected discussion of such matters and I found talk of them difficult.

'Would Papa not go with you to Breslau?'

'I doubt it.' If I examined my heart I would have admitted I did not want his company. 'Perhaps Frau Muller would accompany me,' I suggested. Though I knew I did not want a third person intruding on my relationship with my son.

'Anyway,' Hanna continued, 'it will be good for Kurt. He is too tied to your apron strings, even in Glatz. Perhaps in Breslau he will meet more young people. Maybe even find a girl who appeals to him.'

I found that thought oddly distasteful. 'Many years for that. He is only nineteen.'

'Mama, at nineteen I was married with a child. He is not too young!'

'He has many years to study and explore the world before he thinks like this,' I said decisively. 'But I will think about Frau Muller.'

I had always found her a pleasant companion, and never more than on our visit to Breslau. For we did travel there, in spite of Otto's gibes. It was a year before I could find the money for the travel, many long hours of knitting, selling vegetables at markets – and safeguarding the coins lest they find their way to the inn.

'Let the boy get away from you. He's been in your swaddling clothes too long!'

I believed Otto was concerned for his well-being and I was prepared.

'Frau Schmidt will bring you food every evening. That is, of course, if you are here and not drinking yourself stupid each night.'

Breslau was a window on a new world, an experience like my life at the Chateau. I began to realise just how much more there could be to life than my years in Rauschwitz and Lewin had shown me.

I could scarcely believe our good fortune, when Berthe told me of a friend in Breslau who would give us rooms in her house. It was a small boarding house, but clean and comfortable and Melita Noske's welcome was warm and enthusiastic.

'I am so happy to have you here, dear ladies. I know you are tired from your journey, but when you have rested and unpacked, there will be *Abendessen* in the front room below, and you will meet the other guests.'

We looked around with approval at the room we were to share. It was small, certainly, but with a big bed and heavy feather quilts and the window looked over the snowy square below. The winter days drew in to darkness early, and the chill in the air made the bed look inviting. But outside the Christmas markets were set up, even though Advent Sunday was just past, and we were full of anticipation.

Frau Noske's house was popular, and she preferred to treat her lodgers as guests. When we came down the narrow stairs, two gentlemen were already seated at the table, and Frau Noske's face beamed as she made the introductions.

I warmed at first to Herr Holstmayer, with his broad red face and huge curling moustache.

'He looks like our Chancellor,' I whispered to Berthe under cover of the table chatter.

She nodded, for Bismarck's luxuriant moustache was almost his trademark, no longer the carefully shaped beard of his early life. This was more imposing.

'Herr Holstmayer works at the new railway station,' our hostess explained. 'And Herr Stieglitz has work with the Postal Service.'

'My son has told me about the new station,' I commented.

'He says it is a wonder, and the pride of Breslau. I thought it very imposing when we arrived, but scarcely had time or energy to take it in.'

Hans Holstmayer's smile broadened even further, and his chest expanded. 'I should be proud to show it to you, ladies, if you would care to visit one day. The platform hall is one of the biggest in Europe.'

'Oh yes,' added Frau Noske. 'It is indeed wonderful. There is a restaurant and waiting rooms – all very beautiful.'

'But of course, for first, second and third class passengers there are separate waiting rooms – no mixing of the classes here,' added Herr Steiglitz truculently.

The others looked embarrassed at the younger man's comment. He was a spotty-faced youth, in his early twenties, I guessed, with weak eyes behind thick glasses, which almost obscured the jagged tufts of red eyebrows.

Herr Holstmayer interpolated smoothly: 'Our young friend has advanced political ideas. He claims to be a student of politics and would like to reform society.'

Herr Steiglitz flushed unbecomingly. 'One day there will be many more who are concerned about these matters,' he muttered, and Frau Noske turned the conversation swiftly to our presence in Breslau.

As we talked of Kurt and his studies, the older man nodded in approval.

'Your son has come to the right place. Friedrich-Wilhelms University is a fine institution, and its traditional faculties have been highly regarded for almost two centuries. But we are – ' he smiled benignly on us all, especially Herr Steiglitz, 'we are indeed a truly progressive society, and only a few years ago the

Technological Institute was added. It is another jewel in our crown. We are famous for our scientific faculties. Oh yes, if your son is interested in steam, this is the place for him to learn how to harness this force for our greater good.'

I sighed and studied my plate. Friendly and warm-hearted as he was, the man's pompous manner was now beginning to annoy me. But we would see him only at mealtimes, and I could endure his company for the sake of a visit to the station. Little did I think that one day that building might be of more relevance to me.

Frau Noske kept a good table, and by now we were hungry from our travels, so Berthe and I ate well of the various breads and wursts – Leberwurst and Teewurst, Blutwurst and Weisswurst – and an array of cheeses, gherkins and onions. There was no way we could have remained hungry, but she was apologetic.

'We still have our main meal in the middle of the day, ladies, for the two gentlemen come home for the *Mittagsessen*. I hope this will be convenient for you.'

'This will suit us well, for I want to spend time with my son ...'

'He will be most welcome to join us for meals,' she put in.

'That is a kind invitation, which I am sure he will be happy to accept. But when he is busy with his studies, there are many parts of Breslau we wish to see.'

The suggestions came rapidly. Not only the station and the university, with its fine library and observatory, but the famous parts of the Old Town and the Opera House.

'Another of our prized places, ladies. It was built over forty years ago but has had additions in the last decade and is even more splendid.'

'Oh yes, another treat for those who can afford the ticket price,' it was of course Herr Holstmayer who interrupted the older man, and I could see that most of our dinner table conversations would go the same way.

'But you must also wish to spend time at the famous Christmas markets, I imagine?' asked Frau Noske quickly.

We agreed enthusiastically. I had heard of these markets, even Glatz had a version. But the big cities, like Breslau and Berlin, Nuremberg and Cologne ... there the Christmas markets were so splendid that visitors came from all over our country, and others as well. So we had carefully timed our visit to see this famous market, and I had come with commissions from Hanna as to what I was to buy for the children and for their family Christmas. I looked forward to doing this.

Our visit to the new station was a revelation. I had taken little notice of it at our arrival, my mind a confused whirl of impressions. The trip by train, a fearsome experience for one new to it, and the flurry of people all blurred my picture of the place.

Now, with Berthe on one side and Herr Holstmayer as a guide, I could admire the spacious platform, known as one of the finest halls in Europe.

'A triumph,' boomed Herr Holstmayer as he ushered us through. 'One of the most distinguished works of Herr Wilhelm Grapow, the famous royal Prussian architect, as you would know.'

We nodded, although I was sure that neither of us had heard the name before.

'And let me show you, dear ladies, the luggage lockers and the new telegraph facility – we have all modern inventions. Also the waiting rooms – they are extremely fine, but best of all is the special room and hallway for VIPs.'

They were indeed beautifully furnished, though I was sure, as I whispered to Berthe, that Herr Stieglitz would not approve.

'But now,' our guide continued, 'let me take you for a little *Kaffeetrinken* in the restaurant.'

I could have happily bypassed this coffee, especially as Herr Holstmayer had tucked his arm under mine to guide us through the doorway. Splendid as the restaurant was, and excellent as the coffee and the cakes he insisted on ordering, I was not comfortable with the way he looked at me. Or with the pressure of his arm.

'You have made a conquest,' Berthe said to me that evening. 'He admires you greatly.'

I blushed. It seemed so long since I had thought of myself as a woman. 'Tut, Berthe. You are teasing me. I am an old married woman with grown children. Berthe, I am past forty years old! That is all long in the past.'

She smiled knowingly and told me I was still an attractive woman. I was careful not to be alone with Herr Holstmayer in the evenings in Melita Noske's drawing room.

The few days in Breslau became a true holiday – the first I can remember having. The contrast was poignant. Instead of the dull and dreary routines of life at home, with only work to look forward to each day and Otto's drunken return each night, I had freedom. Above all, I spent time with Kurt each day. Somehow he arranged his work so he could spend time with us exploring Breslau.

We marvelled at what we saw. Although Berthe had been in this city earlier, she said it was like a new place, and with Kurt as our guide we went to parts she had not seen before. But she also wished to have time with her old friend, so Kurt and I went alone to the Shambles, that ancient slaughter yard, in among the medieval houses that lined Jatki Street.

'Look, Kurt,' I exclaimed, as we rounded the corner and caught sight of the wooden market stalls from olden times. 'What did they sell here?'

'Geese, goats – oh, all sorts of meats, hare, pigs, roosters, hens. Remember that this street was once the abattoir for the city. All animals were slaughtered here. Look over there.'

I followed his pointing figure to a picture painted on one of the wooden stalls. It was Reznik, the butcher gnome, axe in hand, contemplating his waiting victims. I shivered. The look on the little man's face was uncomfortably familiar. We glanced at each other, both aware we were thinking of Otto.

'Do you have to go back?' he asked softly. 'Could you not escape? Live here, even?'

'How would I live? Your scholarship is barely enough to keep you. It took me many hours to earn the money to pay for this visit here, even just these few days. In any case, I could not do that. I made marriage vows, and I will keep them.'

'Empty words in a church when you were young and did not know what you were doing.'

'No. In spite of everything, what I have said before God is still most important to me.'

He looked disbelieving. 'Still? Although my father gives you nothing, abuses you cruelly?'

'I made those vows, and my faith has kept me going all these years. That is the great comfort of my life. How could I take communion before the altar if I broke my word? That, and you and Hanna – you are the bright moments in my life.'

'You keep the vows, even though he has driven your children away?'

'That's what hurts,' I admitted. 'The loss of you – and Hanna of course. Though Hanna I do see at times. But you here, so far from me ...'

Kurt glanced quickly at me, then looked away. 'It's possible,' he ventured, 'that I might go even further.'

The weather was cold, but it was not why I shivered. 'What do you mean?'

He tried to reassure me. 'There is nothing certain yet ... in fact these are only faint possibilities, but my professors have said I might need to go elsewhere. Further yet. For Breslau does not focus on ships, and that is where my real interest lies.'

This was no surprise. Each time he spoke of ships, his face came alive. I said nothing.

'The new steam ships they are building. The Dampfschiffe. These are the future – and I want to be part of it.'

'These steam ships. They're for sea-going, I think, not river travel.'

He nodded, unwilling to put the next thoughts into words.

'There are no seas in this part of the world. Not in Silesia.'

'Ah, but in the north. In Prussia, and now we are all part of one German Reich. There in the north, in Hamburg, in Bremen – in those cities there are some of the greatest shipbuilding companies of the world.'

I turned away. 'I don't wish to think about this today. Let's just focus on the happiness we have. Tonight, the Christmas Market – I want to enjoy this time.'

I think there was relief on his face. He knew the subject

had been opened, and he too wished to delay the inevitable discussion that would have to come.

But as we wandered around the markets that evening, fascinated by the colour, the lights, the profusions of foods and drinks, the variety of crafts and ornaments, I found it hard to drive away the thoughts.

I tried to focus on the sights around me. Stalls of Christmas ornaments, the straw stars of every size, the Christmas angels, the carved wooden figures. And the foods, with their wonderful spicy fragrances, especially the Lebkuchen with its pervasive aromas of ginger, cinnamon and nutmeg. The Magenbrot and the Stollen ... and the drinks. Everywhere stalls of Gluhwein, and the heady perfume of the spicy mulled wine and the egg punch.

Such goods for the children. I bought the requested nutcrackers that Hanna had ordered, with their colourful carved figures that would please my grandchildren. But the real delight were the cribs, the intricate nativity scenes with their carved wooden stables and mangers, their tranquil Marys and brooding Josephs (well might he brood, I thought – he too had faced a wife pregnant with a child who was not his). I marvelled at the ornate costumes of the three kings from the east and the faith that had led them to follow the guiding star – that star still poised on wires above these stables. Beyond them, the heavenly hosts, with angel wings carved into protective folds above the kneeling shepherds.

But, most of all, the animals around the manger: cautious cows with the dumb bovine look that all cows seem to have (was Frau Schmidt milking my Hermie each day at home, I wondered. Yes, she would be reliable in what she had promised); the placid compliant sheep dutifully following their shepherds to the crib side; the big-toothed donkeys waiting to bray at the sights; the little lambs, no longer frisking in the fields but gravely waiting their turn to see the small figure in the manger.

I would have so wished to buy one of these scenes to take back for the children, but my precious store of coins was almost spent. Hanna's Franz would have to purchase nativity scenes for that family.

Then Kurt was at my side again with something hidden behind his back.

'Close your eyes, *Mutti*,' he ordered. 'And hold out your hands.'

I felt the hardness of the wood and when I opened my eyes it was to see the small Christmas angel he had bought, on its face a look of sweetness and wonder that made one marvel at the craftsman's skill.

'I saw you admiring these when we passed that stall, and I wanted so much to give it to you. She reminds me of you.'

Tears pricked my eyes. 'But you should not have done this. I know how little money you have, even for what you need.'

'Ah, reason not the need,' he quoted to me, one of my favourite lines from the Shakespearian play I had read, first with the Countess, then with the son to whom I had tried to pass on what she had given me.

'You remember that?' I whispered. I could not speak.

'I remember everything you have done,' he said. 'And I want you to keep this.' The fear clutched at me again. It was too like a farewell gift.

So it proved. Soon he came back, briefly, to say farewell. Not to us; he would not come to this house where he had been so unhappy. Instead to Hanna's, and Franz came to Lewin to take me to her. I knew what this visit meant. He would go to Bremen, to work there in the shipyards.

That night, I rose from the bed where Otto lay snoring and looked at the shelf beside me in the moonlight. I cradled in my hands all that I had left of my son, and the carved angel gazed inscrutably back at me.

CHAPTER 9

Lewin, Silesia 1887

I will not pretend that I found that time easy. It seemed to me that the walls of our little house were closing in on me inch by inch, foot by foot. Where was the joy in life? The time in Breslau seemed a dream.

The house seemed like my life, empty. It had been bad enough when the son who brought such happiness had left me. First to Glatz; then to Breslau – ah, how hard that had been. But I had found pleasure there, and the kindness of Melita Noske and my dear friend, Berthe.

Now Kurt was moving himself further away from us all, from Lewin, from his father – and from me. He was abandoning his scholarship and his life in Breslau. What for? I railed to Hanna. This dream of ships. Where had it come from? There were no sailors in our family. No one who had contact with the world of ships, of sea faring.

'It isn't the shipping, Mama,' Hanna explained patiently, yet again. 'It's steam. Kurt is fascinated by the potential that it unleashes, what can be done with steam power.'

'But it is wrecking our lives, child. How few of us can find a living from what we make in the home. Now it is all factories and mills. This is where things are made.'

'Mama,' she spoke gently. 'You have always taught us that change is inevitable. You cannot now wish to stop progress.'

I winced. 'You call this progress. Look at your father. This is where your progress leads. Steam engines destroyed him.'

Hanna shrugged. There is a hardness in her, a robust sense of truth. 'It was not steam that lost him his arm. It was his own weakness, and the drink. You know it.'

I could not deny it.

'Nor is it steam or trains that make him what he is today,' she continued. 'It is something in him. Why do you think I come to you so rarely? And Kurt not at all?'

There was nothing I could say. Already, although it was barely noon, Otto was at one or the other taverns in Lewin and would stay until the *Mittagessen* closing. At best, when he came in to eat, he would be silent, sitting in brooding darkness of spirit. At worst, he would abuse me for the food, the drink, the coldness of the house, the warmth, whatever he could find to criticise.

'On a good day,' I defended him to the young woman, 'he will work in the field for a time.'

'Until the taverns open,' she retorted.

That too was true.

'Does he harm you, Mama?'

I sighed. 'There are times when a sort of fury enters him. His life is nothing, it is over, and he knows it. And sometimes it maddens him to the point where he must lash out and release the fury on someone else.'

'And that's you. You can't deny it. We've seen it, remember?'

It was strange to find Hanna my champion. All these years I had seen her as Otto's daughter. Now it seemed there were still bonds that tied us. It was almost disconcerting; I had become so accustomed to an old familiar alienation from my daughter.

'Let's talk of happier things. There is a new letter from Kurt.'

I pulled it from the pocket of my apron and laid it on the table before turning to take the bread from the oven. They were loaves of the dark rye bread that Hanna and Kurt had always loved, and I planned to give her a loaf to take home to Mittelwalde. I knew that her Liesel and Hans looked for 'Oma's bread' that I would send them. These little ones I saw only rarely, for Hanna came dutifully every four weeks, but always alone.

She had made no move to pick up the letter, so I unfolded it to read to her.

'He has found work in a huge shipyard, he says. It's called Norddeutscher Lloyd. He writes that it's one of the biggest companies in Bremen. It's well established, too – Kurt is very proud of this new work. He gives a lot of detail about the firm.'

I persevered, in spite of Hanna's lack of interest.

'Actually, he says it was started back in 1857, but in these thirty years it has grown to be the largest in all the German Reich. Think of it, Hanna. How well Kurt has done, to join such a company.'

The girl yawned. 'Oh, Kurt will always do well,' she commented, with a touch of bitterness. 'He has charm.'

I looked at her in surprise. 'But he has not had it easy, Hanna. Life here was not happy for him.'

'No, not with *Vati*, true. But you more than made up for it.'

'Someone had to,' I retorted, perhaps a bit more harshly than I had intended. 'After all, you got away from it.'

Her face took on that mulish look that so reminded me of her father. 'Yes, well, there was little for me here.'

I chose to ignore the comment. 'Let me tell you a little more of what he says.'

'If you wish ...' her tone was indifferent.

'He seems impressed by the company and what it does. Already in the first ten years it had fourteen steamers, eight on the voyage to America and six to England. And it gained the mail-carrying rights – that was a big achievement. He says that in spite of a few problems in the years when we were at war with France – they actually blockaded our German ports for a few months – the company has gone from strength to strength.'

'But what does he actually do, Mama?'

I frowned. 'He doesn't clearly say. The letter is all about the company. He is full of praise for its reputation for safety and reliability, but now they are making speed of travel their priority. In the last seven years they have been constructing fast steamers – he talks about a future with twin-screw steamers ...'

'Do you know what he is talking about?'

'No, it means nothing to me. But he seems impressed by the foresight of the founder of the company, a Herr Meier. I think your brother is working with the steam engines, which is what he wanted. He says it is in Bremerhaven – that's where the shipyards are.'

'So Kurt is not actually in Bremen itself?'

'No, it seems to be about forty miles and on the waterfront.'

'That would be logical, wouldn't it!'

In spite of her sarcasm, I continued. 'He says seven years ago the first fast steamer was launched – probably because Englishmen had built one three years earlier – and since then in Bremen they have added more. It seems like a competition. Kurt is going to post us a photograph of the *Kaiser-Wilhelm II*, a new ship they are building as we speak.'

'The next thing, Mama, will be that he wants to sail on one.'

'Ach, *lieber Gott*, I hope not. These ships are now going, he says, not only to New York but also to South America, and to countries far away across the Pacific, even to Australia!'

At last Hanna looked impressed.

'They are really crossing the world. I can see why he would be excited to be part of this.'

She sat down again at the table and took another piece of cake.

'But does he tell you anything about himself? What does he do in his leisure time? Even our hard-working Kurt must have some free time!'

'No ...' I admitted reluctantly. 'He writes mainly about his work and how excited he is about it.'

Hanna shrugged. 'That's our Kurt.'

I went on. 'He's proud of the company. The Imperial Post that they carry has been important. They say these new ships have increased exports to all these countries, because their cargo space is so much greater.'

'That would be profitable,' she said thoughtfully.

'It must be. They are now building more cargo steamers. And they're planning to deepen the Weser River, so that the new ships can carry their cargo as far as Bremen itself, rather than having to unload at Bremerhaven and transport goods there.'

'I would think the new ships might be for people-carrying also. Franz tells me there are many men in Mittelwalde who are packing up their households and families and emigrating.

Mainly to America, but some are also going to Australia.'

I was not surprised by her words. 'It's so hard to make a living from the land, and those who go to the cities say that conditions are hideous. Not enough work, nowhere to live, and they cannot get used to the cramped dirty city life.'

'Franz says that as Bürgermeister he has had to complete many documents for the emigrants. Some just close their cottages, even farms that have been in their families for generations, and walk away. There is no one to buy them.'

'But to leave your home and your neighbours – that is an act of great courage.'

'It is indeed a long way to go. They say it takes many months.'

'And such a dangerous journey. What makes them think they will be any better off in a new land?'

Hannah shrugged her shoulders. 'Who knows? Someone goes, and then sends letters back, saying there are great opportunities. Hans Dichtermeyer went, and now six other families are planning to follow him to Australia because his letters have made it seem so attractive.'

'Such courage. Or is it stupidity?'

'They sell everything they can to raise money for the passage, then set off for Bremen or Hamburg in the hope of a ship to take them. But to what?'

Kurt's letter had been forgotten as we talked. I scanned it again quickly.

'There is little mention of the work he does, but he tells us about the lodging house he has found; it's one where many emigrants stay while they are waiting for a ship. He seems happy there, and that is the main thing.'

'Will you go there too, like your Breslau adventure last year?'

I laughed. 'Oh, my child, too far, too difficult. Where would I get the money for another such trip?' I hesitated. 'Also, I am concerned for your father.'

She looked up curiously. 'What do you mean? Concerned?'

'More than usual, I mean. I look at him, and I fear sometimes. No, not of his blows – ' I forestalled her response ' – but for him. I think there is something wrong.'

'There would be no surprise in that, the way he drinks.'

I folded the letter and put it away, then packed the bread, some eggs from my fowls, and biscuits I had baked for the children before waving her farewell from the front doorstep. She walked to the pony trap that Franz had brought back, his business in Lewin completed, and they drove away.

I was always regretful when her rare visits were over, regretful that I was not sorrier to see her go. Regretful that so much of our time had been spent with me talking of Kurt. Sad that our time together was stilted and awkward, and our conversations formal and constrained. Had it been Kurt, how different the hour would have been.

But that was a thought to dismiss. My son was in Bremerhaven, and I was in Lewin. Time to think more about Otto, and what was happening there. Perhaps, I mused, I should have been more honest with Hanna, and let her see the level of my concern.

It was hard to look at him; even harder to remember what he had been. I had given up all efforts to stop his drinking; years of failure had left me exhausted and defeated. What more could I have done?

If my days were dreary and joyless, at least they were not filled with the nightmares that seemed to accompany him. He seemed shrunken, and the yellowing of his face alarmed me.

Even the violence in him had waned, and that, such irony, alarmed me even more.

'There are doctors in Glatz,' I urged, after I had seen the blood spots on his clothing. 'You are not well, Otto. You need to see someone who can help.'

'God damn it, wife. What do you care?' His voice faded into confused muttering as he lurched toward the bed.

Yet, I did still care. For all the years of wretchedness, we shared a past. Days in the little village school, before I had gone to the Chateau and separated myself from him. The two children he had given me, his tenderness with Hanna when she was a little girl – I wondered if she could recall those days.

I had kept a cold home for him, and I could not be surprised that he had turned to other satisfactions. It had not been a good bargain that he had made in agreeing to marry me, and we both knew it. Did he sometimes feel that the empty flapping sleeve was a punishment on him? Or was our marriage even more the punishment ... for us both?

Now I looked at his face where he lay, yellowed and sunken, and the great mass of his swollen belly. Frau Schmidt's words came back to me, for our neighbour had been brutally honest with me that day.

'Anna,' she said, for her age and our closeness had given her the right to call me by my name, 'your man is doomed, I fear. I have seen it before. It is the drinker's fate, and I would not wish it on my worst enemy.'

'I have begged him to go to a physician in Glatz, but he will not listen.'

'It would be pointless. When it reaches this stage, there is nothing that can be done. His innards are rotted.'

Frau Schmidt looked at me with pity. 'I know about this disease. I have seen it before, and the symptoms are the same. Have you not noticed the bruises and the dark marks on his face, or the yellow of his skin and his eyes?'

I could only nod.

'It is in his gut, his liver,' she shook her head, and then did something strange, uncharacteristic. She laid her hand on my arm and, with the other hand, made the sign of the cross upon my forehead.

'You will need to be brave before the end, my child.'

I wondered, should I have told Hanna of this conversation? Should I write Kurt to come home? Home to the house he had said he would never set foot in again, to see the father he so hated? Perhaps a chance to make some peace between them?

But before I could do that, Kurt's letter came, and I knew it was too late.

Hanna had known her brother all too well, and I berated myself for not listening to her. He will want to sail, she had foreseen, but I had refused to believe her. How right she had been.

'*It is a rare opportunity,*' he had written to me. I think I knew, even before I opened the envelope, with its Imperial Reich stamp. Up to now, I had blessed our new postal service, and the fact that I could at least hear from my son each week. He had been so good about writing regularly to me. I think he sensed how I lived for those letters.

But not this one. It was like the doomsday bell, which still rang out over the township for each funeral.

He would take this rare opportunity, a chance to sail on one of his beloved steamships. They would give him the opportunity to experience firsthand just how this ship performed. It was, he explained, the *Hohenzollern*, a ship built in England fourteen years earlier. Now, after further work and many voyages, they had decided to ready it for the new run to the Far East and Australia.

My heart sank. Not even the more regular crossing to America, but this time a much less predictable voyage. Australia. What did I know of it? Nothing. A strange southern continent. My reading had not prepared me, and I was heartsick at the thought.

He would go as a seaman, a sailor.

'They classify us as "firemen",' his careful handwriting explained.

> It will be my chance to see a steamship in operation, under all sorts of conditions on such a long journey. I am so fortunate that I get this opportunity, so early in my time here.

They must, I thought cynically, be anxious to take on extra crew, if they will take such an inexperienced lad. But then, he has studied in this field for many years.

I read on.

> I will have no chance to see you before we depart, as the ship sails in February, and there will be little time to prepare. But I promise you, dear Mutti, that I will be sure to come straight to you on return. Then I can tell you all that happens.

It seemed that I would have to hold close to myself the happy times at the Christmas Market in Breslau; they already seemed so far back. I would not see my son again for many, many months.

CHAPTER 10

Lewin, Silesia 1888

I have wondered so often if it is a good or a bad thing that we cannot see our futures: a blessing, or a curse?

The year that has gone is one that I would not wish to bestow on an enemy, no matter how I hated him. Losses, only losses.

For scarcely had February come and gone, the knowledge that Kurt's ship had sailed lying like a heavy weight in my heart, than I knew that Frau Schmidt had been right. I would soon lose Otto.

Almost Hanna too. She was filled with fury when she discovered her father's condition and, as always, unleashed it on me. Her father's daughter, yes.

'You should have told me how bad he was. You had no right to keep it to yourself.'

This was the week before he died, when I sent messages to her to come. I could have pointed out that if she had not deliberately avoided seeing him these last years she would have known. That it was a situation of her own making.

I swear I did not say it like that, but she recognised the message, and it made her even angrier. We could find no comfort in each other's presence, even at Otto's deathbed.

It was not an easy death, and I was glad to have had Frau

Schmidt's warning. Death is never pretty, and I have seen enough of it, both man and beast, to have been prepared. But it is harder when the body that is writhing and disintegrating is one that you have joined with, whose seed has been planted in you, whose children you have borne.

There were times that he was conscious, and toward the end the pain abated a little and his mind was clear. There were no deathbed reconciliations, and who would believe in those anyway? But he seemed to soften towards Hanna, more like the father she had known as a small child, so at least her memories of him will be more tender than otherwise.

We talked, in his moments of consciousness, about Kurt, and I told him of his son's love of steam, and his voyage to Australia. For a moment a spasm of regret crossed his face. But still he blamed me.

'You made ... milksop of boy.' His speech was thickened, slurred, but the meaning was clear. 'Wish,' he tried to moisten his lips, and I reached for the wet cloth to put on his mouth. He could no longer drink, only take some moisture squeezed out for him. 'Wish ... different. Tell ... him.'

The words came slowly, haltingly, but I understood. 'You want me to tell him you are sorry?'

They were the last words he spoke, and with a final gagging croak he was still. Frau Schmidt closed the one eye that was open, that still stared blindly up at us. Only Hanna sobbed.

After we had buried him, I found I was very tired. Days went by when I did little but sleep. There would be few changes in my life, that I knew, save that the small money I made from my linen weaving – pitifully small now that machines and factories turned out goods more swiftly and cheaply – or from selling at the weekly markets the vegetables I still grew, would now be at my disposal, and no longer funding the taverns in Lewin.

'You could come to us in Mittelwalde,' said Franz. But there was little enthusiasm in his voice, nor in Hanna's half-hearted seconding. I swear they looked relieved when I said I would stay in the house that had always been my home.

I went only rarely to the Chateau during these weeks, though the payment from the Graf still continued, as it had all these years. I doubt he knew of it. I was sure that it came from Lydia, who, for all her frivolity and love of pleasure, had her mother's warm and generous heart. They still kept the Chateau for the hunting that he had always enjoyed, and at times Lydia joined him. When she did, there was always time for me in her life. I valued those brief times with her.

She had written to me on her distinctive personal paper with its flowers and crest when news was sent her of Otto's death. She did not come to the burial.

'I do not like funerals, so I will not be there. But you are in my thoughts, and in a few weeks, when you have had time to adjust, I will come to you. Is there any news of Kurt?'

Although we did not keep in close contact, we did communicate more often than I would have anticipated after her marriage. I knew that she was glad there were no children in her home, but it pleased her to take some interest in mine. I had not forgotten her kindness over Hanna's marriage, and her gift of the wedding gown.

But her question about Kurt opened the worry that filled my heart no matter how I tried to keep it at bay.

There had been the promised letters. Not many, it is true. But how could there be, I told myself firmly, when his ship was on the long sea run. I had taken books from the Chateau library and followed his course closely. It made me feel closer to him to know a little of the places where he would be.

When the first letter came, it was brief. Just to tell me the ship had departed, as planned, on the thirteenth day of February, and that he was settling into his crew's quarters with a group of others, most of them from different parts of our land.

'But only a few foreigners', he wrote.

> You would be interested in the scenes here, dear mother. The crowds of emigrants arrive, some of them from far away. Already they are weary, for they have many children and chests of household goods brought by barge or on the trains that bring them to Bremen. Then often they must wait here while the ships load, and sometimes also for good weather conditions. Though it is not like the old days of sail, when the clipper ships depended on favourable winds for departure. This is another of the benefits of steam power ...

I smiled when I read that. He missed no chance to praise the new way of life that steam had brought. It reminded me of Otto, and his passion for the coming of the railways. Yes, he was Otto's son too. I read on:

'It is a scene of such turmoil and activity. Ships' agents race from group to group, organising their departures, and checking that they have their visas, for they cannot depart without this clearance if they wish to emigrate. I am fortunate, because as a sailor I am cleared to depart. I am not an emigrant, but a worker. But my heart is troubled for these people. Already the mothers look exhausted, and they little realise how long and hard the voyage will be. They have great courage.'

I shook my head. Or great desperation, I thought. Years of bad harvests, the memory of the potato famine, the ever-present threat of military service (how I rejoiced that Kurt had missed this!) and now another time of economic hardship – it was not surprising that so many felt their only hope lay in a new land.

'There are still some,' his letter continued,

> who say they seek greater religious freedom. These are the Old Lutherans, the ones who held out against the coming of the State Church. Even though the time of persecution is over, they still wish to find a land where they do not feel under threat that one day they may be forced to give up their traditions and join the Emperor's church.

I nodded when I read this. Even here in Lewin there had been bitter debates in the church, and many had left rather than compromise their ways. It had seemed of little importance to me. Surely it was not a matter of great concern. These issues of doctrine were matters for theologians, and our young pastor was happy to be part of the State Church. God, he said, is interested only in what is in our hearts. That is what counts. But doctrines had divided our people, and many left to worship according to the old ways. For Otto it had been unimportant. He did not often set foot in the church for Sunday worship, and Kurt and Hanna and I had walked unaccompanied to the town.

Kurt's letter remained folded in my apron pocket for many weeks. He had found it possible to send mail from Antwerp, where the *Hohenzollern* stopped briefly to take on more cargo. I knew I would not hear again for many weeks.

A letter from Aden, where the time dragged as they crawled through the new waterway of the Suez Canal. His letters were short, and I worried. He was not happy, that was clear, and relations on the ship were strained. *'Much depends on the captain'*, he wrote,

> *and we are not fortunate in ours. There is unrest among the passengers, and there has been illness. We have had four burials at sea, and these are sombre affairs. Two have been children, and to see the parents' grief is awful. It reminds me of the importance of family, and how much I miss you, dear Mutti. It reminds me also of my own childhood, and how much I wish it had been different. Perhaps one day I may be able to forgive my father, but the memories are still too raw. I wonder if he will ever change.*

Oh Kurt, I thought, if you could see the broken old man he became, and how he suffered, you may well feel differently. But there is no way to tell you of it.

The next letter he posted was even more desperate. It came from Colombo, where they had stopped to take on coal, but the men were not permitted to go ashore. He wrote of passenger anger and dissension, and a captain who was drinking heavily and concerned only with delays that ship repairs had created.

> *He is worried about the owners, I fear, for his payment depends on meeting the conditions of the contract. Already we are behind time, and he tries to push the boat beyond what it can do. We have tried to talk to him, to explain that there must be limits on what we demand of the engines, but he refuses to listen. He is a violent and intemperate man – he reminds me much of my father – and yesterday he struck our first officer. I fear what may happen. Among our crew*

there are some hotheads who speak of mutiny, but this is something not to be considered, surely.

It would be an act of great foolishness, for our ship carries not only passengers and cargo, but also a great troop of naval personnel. I think I have not mentioned before that we are transporting almost 300 men, both officers and ratings, who are on their way to Sydney to relieve the men on the three German ships stationed in that harbour. I am sure that the marines on the Olga, the Bismarck and the Sophie are waiting their arrival with great anticipation, for our ship will then take them back to Hamburg. I had not known that we had such a squadron on the other side of the world, but with these disciplined troops on board any act of rebellion would be madness.

For a long time, no word. And I had no way of telling him of the gravity of his father's condition. Then finally, another letter. My heart sank as I read.

Dear Mother, I will post this letter to you from Australia, that vast southern land we have known only through stories in the books we shared. I remember well all that we have shared, and I look back so fondly on our time together.

What I must tell you will be of concern and regret to you, I know, so I hesitate to say it. I have left the Hohenzollern. Not happily, and not with a peaceful dismissal. I have told you of the captain, and the problems, which became worse as we came closer to land. He is a drunken fool. The ship is overloaded and his demands on it were excessive and dangerous. I could no longer accept his orders. We had reached Adelaide, in an area they call South Australia, on the southern coast of this huge continent, where we needed to stay for repairs. But he forced us to push on against all advice, to make haste for our next stop, to the east, a city called Melbourne, before the destination of Sydney. The naval officers are impatient and press him to meet deadlines. His orders defied all reason; he wanted the steam dampers closed and the ship pushed beyond its limits. If we had screwed down the safety valves as he wanted the boiler would have been increasingly unsafe. But I had no choice. To disobey would be, he told me, mutiny and I would be imprisoned on board and charged on return to our country.

The man is mad, I truly believe, and I cannot believe that this ship will ever see northern waters again. I do not want to die at sea! A number of our passengers left the ship in Adelaide, and over a hundred more disembarked in Melbourne. A great number of the naval seamen were given a few hours shore leave – and were even told they could travel free on public transport if they were in uniform, a concession they much appreciated. So I have managed to depart among them, even though I did not have shore leave.

In Melbourne, I made the decision not to return. Do not worry about me. It is easy to disappear in this city and not be found. Many have told me of the opportunities in this country for a young fit man, and also of the German communities spread throughout the land. In the north, in Queensland, one of my fellows has friends in a township where he is sure we would find work. He himself left the boat, 'jumped ship' they say, in Adelaide to walk north to find this place. Would I had gone with him. It will be a long journey from Melbourne, but I am about to undertake it. I

believe I can find work along the way and when I reach there
I will write and tell you where I am.

I could scarcely read the rest of his letter. All very well to tell me his only regret was the concern I would feel, that he would depend on my prayers, that he loved me – oh yes, all this. But all I could think was that my son was now wandering in a wilderness on the other side of the world, and I had no idea where or how he might be. And I had no way of telling him of his father's death.

CHAPTER 11

Lewin, Silesia 1889

Two years.

They tell us, wise men and scholars, that time is relative. They lie. Time is a slow dragging of one day after the next while one's life is whittled away, like the wood my father and brothers used as they carved spoons in my childhood home.

With Otto's death, at times I saw my family again. I have wondered over the years why we have not been closer. Otto had no wish for close family living. His childhood home had been unhappy, and his main wish was to break away from all that reminded him of Rauschwitz and our early days.

I had always felt separate from my family. My years at the Chateau had set me apart, and after my early marriage we had little contact with my brothers and sister, for Gertrud had never been to me what Lydia was. My father's death had brought my mother closer, and the naming of my daughter for her had been a sort of bond. But she did not like Otto, and he barely tolerated her presence.

I would have been shamed if she had known just how bad my marriage was, and in some ways her death came as a relief. I no longer had to pretend. But now, with Otto's death, we gathered at Christmas for a family meal. Not comfortably. I was still seen as the Chateau 'lady'. I would never lose that image. I was more at home with Lydia than my own flesh and blood. She was my only confidante. I could never open my heart and share my desperate unhappiness with Berthe Muller.

And I heard nothing of my boy. He was not cruel. Young and sometimes thoughtless, but I could not believe the cruelty of this long silence. Was he alive? That was my agonising concern. If he had died, if he had been hurt, would anyone know to contact me?

I woke each day, sick at heart. Each night I went to my solitary bed in frantic prayer. Prayers that became less and less trusting as first the weeks, then the months went by. There are no words to describe the desolation of that time.

'You should not worry,' said Hanna, when I tried to talk to her. 'Kurt will be fine. He is young; he is adventurous. He is enjoying his freedom.'

I looked sharply at her, reading the hidden message. 'You think I tied him too closely?'

She was cautious in her words. 'Sometimes I think he loved you very much and knew how you depended on him. You were perhaps too close.'

'You had your father. You were always his daughter.'

'Perhaps. When I was small. Not in later years,' she added bitterly. 'All I wanted was to get away.'

'Kurt too?'

'Yes, but he had to look after you. He needed to break free from that too.'

'But not like this. How can I rest not knowing where he is?'

'Well, you can scarcely go after him!'

Words spoken in jest, but they began to fester in my mind. Go after him. It was a preposterous thought. Impossible. At my age. At forty-five I was old, a grandmother. I had never been further than Breslau, never even to Berlin. The very notion was ridiculous.

Yet there it was. My son, whom I loved so dearly. So long without word. How else would I learn what had happened to him?

'But Lydia,' I said, when I told her of this wild notion, 'where would I start? It would be impossible.'

'Difficult,' she agreed. 'But not impossible. Where was he last known?'

'The letter from Melbourne,' I told her. 'But he said he was about to head northward. To somewhere called Queensland where people had told him of a settlement by our countrymen, people from Silesia.'

"So you have a starting point. And you have one other great asset.'

'What do you mean?'

'All those years my mother made us learn both English and French – you would have enough of the language to communicate.'

'True,' I admitted. 'And Kurt too. I had tried to pass the language on to him.'

'Well, perhaps not quite impossible?'

'But I could not afford such a venture. The money that you pay me – yes, I am sure it is through you, not your husband or your father that this continues – '

Lydia shook her head but did not deny my words.

'This payment to care for wellbeing at the Chateau, it's been so important to me. You know where Otto spent all my other earnings, so there's been no chance to save from it. It has spared us total poverty, and I have been thankful for it.'

'Then let me do this one further thing. Kurt is my godson, let me send you to look for him.'

'Such a fool's errand. I could not let you do it.'

'Even for the sake of our old friendship? Even for the memory of my mother, whom we both loved?'

I wavered but shook my head. 'I cannot do that. But I am so grateful to you – you and the Chateau and your mother. You and my memories of the past are all that I have to keep me going in this world. And my daughter, of course.'

I did not tell Hanna of the conversation. I could imagine her reaction.

It seemed an act of the God I still believed in, an answer to my prayers, when the letter came. It was crumpled, and the envelope was blurred and smudged and dirty, but my heart leapt as I saw the writing.

I write to reassure you, dear Mutti, that all is well with me. I think you will have been concerned for my wellbeing, and it grieves me that you will have been so distressed. Indeed for a time I too ill to send mail. A beating in the streets left me almost for dead – I am sure a punishment for deserting the ship. He could not afford for me to get away without some outcome. But do not worry. There is a strong German society in Melbourne, and when they found me I was cared for and am now fully recovered, except for greater deafness in my right ear. A small price to pay for freedom.

I am now travelling northward again, working on farms

as I go. I stay for a time and expect soon to be in the border area between this state, Victoria, and the next, New South Wales. I have heard of many German settlements in this area, so it may be possible to find work for a time. It will be a long, slow journey. It is hard for you in our homeland to envisage just how enormous this land is. Do not be concerned for me. When I reach a destination in Queensland, I will write to you of my whereabouts.

I breathed deeply and thankfully. He was alive. His letter concluded with loving messages to me, and to Hanna and Franz and their children – and a greeting to his father. The father no longer alive. I knew it was an omen. I should go. But where?

When I told Lydia of the letter, she was wholehearted in her support.

'Indeed, you must. You will need a ship to take you to Melbourne – your starting point. I will see shipping agents in Hamburg and find a passage for you as soon as possible.'

'Lydia, how can I let you do this for me? How will I ever repay you?'

'Anna, dear Anna. We have been like sisters. I am simply doing what I know my mother would have wanted. And I will give you her big travel chest for your clothes. She would have wanted you to have it for such a journey.'

'One day ...' I said firmly. 'One day I will return what you are giving me.'

'One day ...' she agreed lightly. 'But now you must organise a passport for your departure. I am sure that Hanna's husband can do that for you.'

My daughter was aghast.

'You must not do this, *Mutti!*' It was a measure of her feeling that she had slipped back into the childish name. 'You are an old woman, and you have never travelled further than Breslau. This plan is insane. I cannot believe that anyone of sense would countenance it.'

'Lydia is in favour – and will provide me with the money for it.'

'What of us? I need you here. I had not thought to tell you yet, but I have a third child coming, and I need you to help me with the household during the months before the birth, and with the other children afterward.'

It interested me that for the first time she had found it desirable to have me with them. A new development indeed.

'If Kurt has been ill, and is in a strange land, he needs me too.'

Hanna set her lips. 'Oh yes,' she said, her voice bitter, 'if Kurt needs you, no one else will count. Not even your daughter, facing her third childbirth.'

The sad part is that she was right. It was true.

I lived those last months before departure in mingled terror and anticipation. How could I, from this little town in Silesia, travel alone to the other side of the world? An act of madness, it was agreed. Neighbours and church people were free with their advice and warnings; few supported me.

When the wooden travel chest was packed, Frau Schmidt's husband came with his wagon to take me to the railway station at Glatz. I said farewell to friends and neighbours, among head-shaking from all those around me.

Hanna did not come to say goodbye.

Part *Two*

CHAPTER 12

Departure from Silesia 1889

They are right. This venture is madness. For all that I sat in the church and prayed, harder than I have ever prayed before, for guidance on what I should do. I still did not know.

A lie, anyway. My strongest prayers, my most desperate ones, were not for guidance but for my boy. All that time with no news. The waking every morning sick at heart. The uneasy sleep filled with nightmares. The days when I could push thoughts of my son out of my mind as I busied myself with the animals, with the small crops kind neighbours helped me to harvest and thresh, with my work at the Chateau, my weaving in the Lewin hall ... yes, then I could forget for a time. But as soon as my hands were free my mind would leap to Kurt, and the blanket of fear would settle again.

These had been my most fervent prayers and, see, they had been answered. He was alive. But now. Was I right to take on this journey? A woman of my class, my age, to travel alone across the world. Such terrible doubts.

'*A prey to saucy doubts and fears ...*' I could hear the Countess reading those lines as we sat in the library, the volume of Shakespeare's plays between us. It comforted me to think of her. She had confidence in me. What would she have done?

How could I tell? But there were signs, and I depended on these. From Mittelwalde, Franz told me, emigrants were about to leave for America. I would join them for the first part of the trip and be less alone. They too would go to Hamburg for their ship. That gave me comfort.

'I still do not approve of this wild venture, Mutter Werner.' He was adamant, and I knew that Hanna had instructed him to stop me. She would be furious that he had given even this assistance. There was no doubt who ruled that household.

She had even brought the children to beg me not to go. But Liesel and Theo were more excited at the idea that I would be travelling on a big ship than concerned over my departure. They had seen too little of me during these years to have formed a close bond, and I could not wonder at their lack of feeling for me.

'How long will you be on the seas, *Oma*?' This was Theo, who had resisted all Hanna's efforts to make him call me Grandmother and kept to the simple childish name I preferred.

'If the sea is rough and there are big waves, will you be sick?' asked Liesel, who had clearly overheard her parents talking.

'I don't know, child,' I answered firmly. 'I will have to trust in God.'

'And the ship's captain,' Theo suggested. My trip had been much discussed in his schoolroom in Mittelwalde. With emigrating families, many knew the hazards of these voyages.

'But steamships are fast,' he added knowledgeably. 'Before they had motors, it took a long long time.'

'If the winds didn't blow the sails, the boat got stuck and couldn't move,' Liesel contributed.

'My goodness.' I was impressed. 'You do know about this.'

I was not naïve enough to ask if they would miss me. I was scarcely a part of their lives, though I wondered if I were to stay, to help Hanna with the coming baby, it might be different. But no, I had made my decision.

Secretly, I was glad I would not set off alone. At least for the first days of my journey I would have companions. Lydia had given me the promised sea chest and helped me plan what I would put in it. I valued her advice, even while firmly rejecting her wish to equip me with the clothes that she, still a society lady far out of my sphere, would have wanted.

We planned for the hot weather that she warned me the tropics would bring, and the rugged weather of the early weeks of colder climates.

'Simple practical dresses, my dear friend. Besides, I can't afford to buy fripperies I don't need. No, do not say it – ' for I could see she was about to offer me her purse. 'You have given me already far too much, and I can't take more.'

It was a measure of how desperate I was that I could accept so much from her. She had found an agent in Hamburg and arranged for my lodging and voyage, so that when I arrived there all would be organised. I was so grateful.

'But you can't set off without sufficient resources for the trip and for your arrival,' she scolded. 'Even if you sell the cottage,' for that was what I was planning, 'you may not have enough for such a trip.'

I knew the truth of her words, but it was not easy for me to swallow my pride and accept money from Lydia.

'I have more money than I can spend on dresses and jewels and fans and trinkets. My husband is generous with money. I think – ' her lip curled in a way I did not like, ' – I think it is compensation.'

I did not ask for what. There were parts of her life, like mine, that we did not talk of.

'But it's hard for me to take money from you, no matter how close we are.'

She understood. 'It is not from me, Anna. You have been a part of my family since childhood. Think of it as from my mother. If she had lived, this is what she would have done.'

Tears pricked my eyes. It was an argument I couldn't counter. I could not set off penniless, and I did not want to sell the cottage that had been my wedding dowry. With that gone, I would have nowhere to return to. Except Hanna's. No, that did not appeal.

So somehow my departure was organised. Frau Schmidt would take my cow, horse and hens. The pig I had let go many years before; I could no longer depend on Otto for the slaughtering and sausage-making, so that had been abandoned when Kurt left for Breslau. Once the hearth fire was out, the cottage would be cold and dark while I was gone. For who knew how long before I returned?

'But what of the Chateau?' I fretted.

'The servants there are reliable.' Lydia, once feather-headed, was now the practical one. 'I will visit more often. All will be well.'

It was as I had suspected. My work there had been more a way of helping provide for my children than meeting a real need. My pride had not let me pursue the thought.

It was a sad farewell in the cold early morning at the station at Glatz. Frau Schmidt had come in the wagon with her burly husband, and I was glad of his strength when my big chest had to be loaded on the train. Glad also to see that my fellow-travellers included some strong youths. A woman making such a journey on her own would face problems, I could see so well. As the Schmidts said their goodbyes, I felt already the separation from all I knew. The older woman pressed into my hand a small canvas bag.

'Food for the journey,' she shook her head in worry. 'I do not know what provisions there will be, so here are cheese and sausages, and good black bread. You will need to eat.'

I was glad of her thoughtfulness; the others who waited with me had come with bags and crates, and hampers of food for the days on the train. I had met them only once in Mittelwalde but found their advice most useful. But for them it was different; they were making their ways to a new life in a new world, and they carried with them goods and equipment to establish homes and farms. And their destination was different. They had chosen America as their new homeland.

There were two families. The men were brothers and one could see the resemblance at first glance. Both Gottlieb Schramm and his brother Christian were big men, but it was clear that Gottlieb was the head of the family. He and his wife Magdalena spoke for the group; how did Christian and Emilia feel about being in second place, I wondered. It was different with their sons, for the two young men seemed less willing to follow whatever their uncle ordered. I watched as they gathered our goods in a neat pile ready for swift loading, while their mothers tried to keep the small children from dashing around the railway station.

The arrival of the train stunned all into silence. I had made this journey only once, to Breslau, but that had been a different affair, travelling with Berthe and taken at arrival straight to our lodgings. This time, as the black monster pulled into the Glatz platform and we hastened to get our goods aboard, it felt like the loss of my known life; a journey to an unknown future.

What must it be like for these two families, farewelling the land that had been home all of their lives? But the engine belched steam and a loud whistle rent the crisp wintry air, and there was no time for idle speculation.

'Why the choice of America?' I asked Emilia when we had settled ourselves and were sharing the simple food. She looked at me, a trifle bewildered.

'Gottlieb said it was the best choice.' She did not seem to know the reason, but her sons were anxious to put another point of view.

'We would have preferred Australia,' the older youth, Hans I think, spoke decisively. 'But *Mutti* and Papa wanted to follow Uncle Gottlieb.'

'As always,' added his brother. 'They wouldn't listen to us.'

'What did you want?'

'We wanted New South Wales. There are good opportunities there for young men willing to work. It is easier and cheaper to buy land. Too many people are flooding into America.'

'But why emigrate at all?' The question fascinated me. There were so many people leaving our homeland.

'Why stay? There is no money to be made in farming; the landlord's rents keep rising, and it is impossible to save enough to buy your own land. It is no wonder that many our age simply walk off the land and look for work in the cities.'

His brother joined in. 'But that is almost worse. In the last years it has been hard to find work, and there is always the danger of military service again.'

'Have you not seen these?' Hans asked, pulling sheets of paper from his pocket.

I took them and looked with interest. They were posters and handbills, and they showed the attractions of emigration to the new worlds.

'Where do they come from?' I asked.

'The shipping companies put them out – they tell us everything that is wrong at home and all the opportunities we will have if we travel.'

'Can you believe this? Surely they are just trying to gain custom.'

'So our fathers said. But then we read all the letters from others who have gone. Seven families from Mittelwalde have left in the last two years, and they all write that if one is prepared to work, it is possible to buy land very swiftly.'

'Imagine,' agreed Johan. 'At home we could never do this. No land. No chance of work, even if we go to the cities.'

'But the mills and factories that have taken over production – surely there is work in these.'

'For low pay and in truly terrible conditions. We had hoped that the Chancellor was going to change this. He has tried to bring in a pension scheme, but nothing seems to help. And when the workers try to organise and protest – well, you see what happens to them.'

'What do you mean?'

'Ten years ago we thought we had an opportunity with the new Social Democratic Party – but look at how he crushed that. No workers' parties for our Iron Chancellor. You can see why he is called that.'

I had lived with Otto for too long to let this pass unchallenged.

'But hasn't he also done much for the workers? I have read about his measures for workers who become ill, and didn't he just a few years ago provide a scheme for those involved in accidents? There's even talk about state money being provided for workers over seventy. Surely all of this is good?'

'Just attempts to keep the socialist movement down, Frau Werner. He's a ruthless man, but clever. But we had better stop this discussion. Uncle Gottlieb is coming. Mention socialism and he will explode.'

The train journey to Breslau interested us all. We watched familiar countryside disappear as Glatz was left behind, and rolling fields gave way to forests and lakes. Our small local train stopped at little townships while goods and travellers were loaded and unloaded. Strehlen fascinated me with its granite buildings, so different from our own area. But soon we approached Breslau and the first big challenge of changing trains; our trip to Hamburg was not a simple matter of getting on a train at one end and off at another. I could see the famous fortress as we neared what we thought of as a big city and pointed it out to the others. They gasped at the sight of the station as our engine pulled us to a halt.

For me, familiar territory. I recalled my tour of the station under the guidance of Herr Holstmayer and wondered if he was still there. Indeed he was, as was Melita Noske who had come to see me and wish me well for my journey. Though they invited our group to join them in the station restaurant, Gottlieb Schramm would have none of it.

'We have our food with us, and must save our money for the voyage,' he announced truculently. The rest of his group looked on enviously as I left with my friends for coffee and kuchen in the comfort of the dining room.

Herr Holstmayer was vocal in his disapproval of my coming trip. It was clear that he and Frau Noske had spent many hours ruminating on my foolhardiness in undertaking such an enterprise, and dire in their forebodings of disaster. While it had been kind of them to come to the station to see me, I could not help feeling that they were providing an ominous start to my travels.

'It is surely not too late,' he said with urgency. 'You can still abandon this enterprise, this foolishness. What can you expect to do when you arrive, a stranger in a strange land?'

'How will you speak to the people?' Frau Noske chimed in. 'Will they speak our language?'

'I learned to speak English in my early years,' I tried to reassure her. But in truth their concerns troubled me deeply.

I was not sorry when it was time to board our next train, this time to Berlin, and a delay of some hours. Again I was glad to have the company of the Mittelwalde group and the help of the young men with my goods. It annoyed me to find that I was not self-sufficient, that although I was strong and fit and could manage everything else, the wooden sea chest was beyond my capabilities and I needed help. There is something in me – there always has been – that dislikes being dependent on others, and I looked forward to this part of my journey being over. But then, I thought, what will it be like when I arrive at my destination? I need to steel myself for this.

The hours to Berlin passed quickly. Even the children were fascinated as we watched the passing countryside from the windows of this bigger train. They moved from side to side of the carriage, and passengers smiled indulgently as we steamed through villages and stopped briefly in cities I had only heard about. Liegnitz, with its parks and gardens, and from there to Gorlitz, where the train waited while many passengers took the chance to buy food from station vendors.

The Schramms smiled smugly as they portioned out their supplies of bread and cheese. I ate some of my bread and wurst, thinking with gratitude of Irmtraut Schmidt's forethought, but would have preferred if there had been time to leave the train and look around a little. After we crossed the Neisse River I knew my homeland in Silesia would soon be behind me. All very well for Bismarck to have united us, all parts of this new German Reich, but for most of us we were, if not Silesian, at least Prussian.

We could see in the distance the flattened top of the Landeskrone, the mountain that overlooked the city sprawled below. It was good to stroll along the platform, free to move for a short time, and I caught sight of the famous Reichenbacher Turm, that massive four-sided tower that looms over the Old Town. I knew it was regarded as one of the treasures of this place. I turned impulsively to Hans, who had established himself as my escort on this platform walk.

'It would be so good to have time to explore these towns. There is so much history here.'

He was not concerned for the past. 'Where we are all going,' he commented, 'there will be little history. We are going to new worlds.'

Our train was speeding north now, for there were still many hours of travel before Berlin, our stopping place for the night. Through Forst, but not, I was sad to find, to Cottbus, that famous town with its pyramids in the centre of the lake. Cottbus lay to our west and our train forged on, uncaring of the wonders bypassed. Soon we were skirting the Spreewald, with its forests of alder trees and pines, and the flat-bottomed boats on the canals we could see from the train windows. The children, tired and now bored with the journey, were sleeping, but for the rest of us it was all too new to allow for sleep. Except for Gottlieb Schramm, whose head lolled back against the high seat, and whose open mouth gave forth a high-pitched whistling snore.

The day was passing rapidly, and as we journeyed north it became colder, in spite of the coal-burning heaters at the end of the carriage. Still we travelled near the water. At Frankfurt the river was no longer the Neisse, our new friend, but once again the Oder, for this tributary had rejoined its mother river on its journey north from Breslau. We were more and more removed from home and the familiar.

I could not tell you how depressing our arrival in Berlin was. The main station, the Hauptbahnhof, was huge and cavernous and the night air chilly. There was a hint of snow in the air, and we knew we had the rest of the night to get through before the early morning departure to Hamburg. Although the children were fretful and difficult, and their mothers tired and harassed, I was glad to be with others. To have arrived here at night and alone would have been worse.

Yet soon I will have to face this situation. As so many times before, I wondered if I could cope with what I had undertaken. Beyond the platform, and the waiting room where we settled for the night, the sight of lighted streets and shop windows was enticing. I sighed. Oh, to have been with a man and see a little of the city. Instead we bundled the soft bags together to make up beds for the children and sent the men out to buy fresh food for our evening meal.

Gottlieb Schramm grumbled. 'We have brought food, mother!' he insisted. 'Why do we need more?'

Magdalena was clearly used to him. 'We will need what we have for tomorrow's travel. See if you can find a delicatessen. Hans and Johan will tell you what to buy.'

I envied them their foray into the streets, but not their having to deal with their uncle in the shop. It would not be pleasant. Yet they managed, returning with bowls of hot noodles and dumplings, and warm sausages. It was amazing how heartened we were by fresh hot food, it had been a long hard day.

'There are people in the streets,' Hans and Johann reported. 'Many little shops are still open, and we saw people in fancy clothes going into theatres.'

'A bad place,' their uncle's voice carried across the waiting room, and travellers turned to look at our small group in surprise. 'There is great sin in this place. I have seen it. It is a Sodom and Gomorrah.'

I caught sight of Hans winking at Johann. 'Our uncle did not approve of the women's clothing,' he explained.

To our surprise we slept until the grey light of a cold Berlin morning crept into the station and children awoke, needing trips to the lavatories and something to eat, as well as warmer clothing pulled out of bags. There was much activity before we set off once more, loading cases, bags, chests onto the Hamburg train.

Spirits were higher now. The end of this stage of our journey was in sight. Once the slow creaking exit from the Berlin station was over and the railway yards behind us we travelled through different country.

'See all the trains!' marvelled the children, for these little ones had never seen sights like this. Neither had we, I reflected, though by nature we were less likely to exclaim with the same innocent delight.

So we looked out, amazed at the junctions and bridges, fascinated by the broad flat plains of this northern land, dotted with villages, each with its church steeple rising above the steep-gabled houses, the mills and factories in the larger towns.

It was the excitement of knowing that, as the train sped on, we were drawing ever closer to Hamburg, to the sea, and to the next stage of our travels, whatever they might bring.

CHAPTER 13

Hamburg, Germany 1889

Nothing I had read or heard prepared me for the chaos of our arrival in this vast city. Our train clanked to a halt, with a final belching of smoke from the engine funnels, and we stood on the platform, a small bewildered group, our boxes and chests stacked behind us in the midst of a seething mass of people.

Chaos everywhere, as porters raced for custom and shipping agents struggled to find their clients. The thin frosty air of this winter day might otherwise have been bracing, but we just shivered in dismay. Even Gottlieb Schramm was silenced as he listened to the counsel of his brother, urging them to find their shipping agent.

'For once,' Hans muttered to me, 'I could wish we were Jewish.' I looked around and saw what he meant. Our train had been packed with emigrants, among these many groups of Jews, clear from their dress and their appearance. Everywhere the babel of foreign tongues, for there were groups of refugees from the east, all eager to leave behind the wave of anti-Semitism that was once more rife.

'Most of these, I think, are Russian,' said Johan. 'Life there has been very hard since the Czar passed many laws against them. I hear that they come to Hamburg, to start their voyage to a better future in America.'

'Or so they hope. But why do you envy them?'

But as I looked around, I understood. They were being greeted and taken away. Where? I wondered. Later I discovered the many relief organisations for their support, and big hostels established for their care until sailing dates. Yes, it might have been easier to arrive here as a Jew.

Men dashed through the crowds with offers of steamship tickets for those lacking them, goods that emigrants would need, or places in lodging houses. In future days we came to know of these men, the Litzers, who worked for the shipping companies and touted for custom. Even now, we knew enough to be wary of them, for many were frauds, and the tickets they sold to naïve emigrants proved useless when they tried to embark.

'With whom do you travel?' I asked Gottlieb Schramm. He pulled from his small case a sheaf of papers, relieved there was something he could do.

'We are with the HAPAG,' he informed me. 'Their agent came to us in Mittelwalde and we bought our passages there.'

'The HAPAG?' I queried. 'Not my company. Who are they?'

'The biggest company taking ships to America.' He was filled as usual with self-importance. 'Their name is the *Hamburg Amerikanische Packetfahrt-Aktiengesellsschaft*. First we must go to their offices to discover what to do now.'

I forebore to point out that his brother had been urging just this.

'We will need wagons to transport our goods, husband.' It was Magdalena, who was always practical. 'You boys, go with your uncle to hire a wagon from here to the shipping office.'

'But what of you, Frau Werner?' asked Hans, always concerned for my wellbeing. I had grown fond of the lad; in many ways he reminded me of the son I was seeking.

'My company deals with travel to Australia, I believe. It is new, but an agent is to meet me here. I think I see him. He has a sign with my name.' Indeed, a small fat man was bustling toward me, a porter hurrying behind him.

I was sad to part from the Schramms. Losing them, I knew, would be the end of contact with the past. I would be completely alone. In the bustling city and waterfront I feared we might not meet again, so we said farewells with many good wishes. In fact, it was premature, for we lodged together for the next days.

Lydia, whom I no longer saw as a frivolous socialite, had organised well for my trip, finding a company to sail to the Far East and Australia, unlike the swelling masses of American travellers. It was, she had told me, a new company, the DADG.

'The what?' I had asked.

'I have it written down.' She hunted for the scrap of paper. 'Such an imposing title, the *Deutsch–Australische Dampfschiffs Gesellschaft*. The German–Australian steamship line. It has only just begun, but already has seven ships; they hope for a bright future with this new trade route from Germany.'

She had arranged with the company for an agent to meet me at the railway and take me to lodgings.

'But where is the sea?' I asked Herr Solomon as we made our way through the streets that led from the railway yards towards the city. 'Is this not the place where the ocean-going steamships start?'

'You are right, *gnädige Frau*.' He was anxious to please. 'But here we are on a mighty river that takes us to the sea. It is some sixty-five miles to the North Sea. You will soon see the Elbe, your lodging house is close to the wharves.'

'How long will I need to wait for departure?'

'Your boat is the *Elberfeld*, a fine new ship built in Newcastle – that is in England, you understand.'

I nodded, somewhat amused that he assumed me ignorant.

'She was launched some weeks ago and it was a fine launch indeed,' he said. But there has been a delay in bringing her to Hamburg. Strikes in the shipping yards and now the captain wishes further adjustment to the engines.'

'Is the ship here?'

'Not yet, but soon. She is on a trial run in the North Sea; Captain Sass is a man well known for his care and caution.'

I thought of Kurt's experience and breathed a sigh of gratitude. But Herr Solomon was still talking.

'And then, of course, after her arrival here there will be cargo loading. That will take some days.'

'Is she not a passenger ship though?'

'Truly. There will be several hundred passengers, but there will also be a big load of goods for the colonies. So there will be some time yet before she departs, I suspect.'

I was glad of the money Lydia had pressed on me. Emigrant housing had been set up in many big disused warehouses and was not expensive, but there was food to be bought, however cheaply, and I wanted to save my precious store of coins and notes.

The Schramms did not have so long to wait. We discovered our lodgings were close together, and it was pleasing to explore Hamburg with company. Magdalena and Emilia rarely moved further than the nearby shops, but Christian's two sons were eager to see life in this city, and happy to escort me. At times, laughing and talking with them, I could forget that I was moving toward my fiftieth birthday, for they treated me as a friend, an equal, not an old woman to be cared for.

We walked often among the wharves, fascinated by the crowds of emigrants from so many different lands.

'America will soon be over-populated,' the boys laughed. 'We should be coming with you to Australia.'

We were intrigued by the huge warehouses for the Jewish emigrants, not only from Russia, but from Galicia and Romania, even from persecution in Austria–Hungary. Their numbers grew each year and accommodation was running short, but the Jewish emigrants who were waiting departure were allocated to licensed landlords. We were impressed by the organisation: lodging houses were supervised and inspected by a Board of Emigration.

This business was a revelation. In this very year, they were quick to tell us, there were forty licensed lodging houses, and people coming and going all the time. They needed a board to control transit and provide security for ships. But they also looked after thousands of emigrants, making medical checks to prevent epidemics, and providing travellers with information. Most important, I thought, were the authorities' efforts to protect them from fraudulent practices of the so-called Litzer.

The boys had been talking to others their age in the big warehouse lodgings. I had never heard of Litzers before, but now they told me about them – I could hardly believe what was being done. The Litzers worked for the clerks of the shipping companies, landlords, for special stores selling useful and useless utensils for the voyage, and for money changers. It was no wonder they worked hard. They were paid a commission on each customer they brought, and many emigrants were cheated out of their small stores of money with worthless tickets or unnecessary goods.

'It is evil,' thundered Gottlieb Schramm, when his nephews explained the role of the Litzers. 'God will surely punish them for the way they exploit the poor!' It seemed to me that they were prospering, in spite of this threat of divine retribution.

The warehouse district too was a revelation, beyond my comprehension. In the last three years they had demolished huge areas and moved over 20,000 people from what became known as City of Warehouses. Huge waterfront storage areas, built on timber-pile foundations, and interlacing canals had made this Speicherstadt the biggest warehouse district in the world. Understandable, for this was a customs-free zone, where goods could be freely transferred. One might enter from water or land – it was indeed an amazing concept. We walked among these new buildings filled with pride at the achievement.

Hamburg brought other pleasures. The weather was warming now, a cold spring had given way to a glorious summer. The waters of the Alstersee were no longer frozen, the winter skaters now joining boating parties to enjoy the late afternoons before the sun went down. The trees grew fresh and green, and gardens from the homes of the wealthy curved graciously down to the water's edge.

'See how these people live,' marvelled the boys as we walked around the lakeside paths. 'It is no wonder the Social Democrats wish to change the world.'

'Hush.' I was nervous with such talk. One did not know who might be listening. I did not wish to jeopardise my departure by falling foul of the police. Too much depended on emigration papers.

'No matter,' said Johan. 'Where we are going, we too will buy homes like these. All the letters say America is a land of great opportunity.'

The young men visited the huge Exhibition of Trade and Industry, and even Gottlieb and Christian accompanied them for this display of German production to the world. I had little interest in such matters. It would have been different if Kurt had been with me, his passion for engineering would have me seeing it through other eyes.

For me, the joy lay in the splendid public buildings.

'You must come,' I begged Magdalena and Emilia, using our familiar names even though we had known each other such a short time. 'Please do come with me to see at least the St Michael's church. And the Opera House.'

I had selected two I thought might appeal. In my lodging house there was discussion of what should be done during this time of enforced waiting. I felt nothing but scorn for those who simply sat each day, waiting for their time of embarkation.

So with Magdalena and her sister we explored the famous church that all had told me was the key sight of this city. We could see why. The steeple, that landmark for ships as they came up the Elbe, soared above the city, its copper covering glinting in the sunlight. I could not induce my companions to climb the more than four hundred steps to the viewing platform, so they remained below in the pews to pray for safe passage on the journey.

Possibly they also prayed for my safety as I climbed, but the view over the city was so spectacular that it was worth the hazards of managing my long skirt as I toiled upwards. There below me Hamburg spread, second only to Berlin in size and wonder, but we had not seen Berlin. My memories of that great city were of an uncomfortable night in a station waiting room. Here I knew I would never forget sights, like the enormous bronze statue of the Archangel Michael conquering the devil that guarded the entrance to this church.

'But is it Lutheran?' Emilia asked fearfully, pointing to the statue. 'It has a Popish look.'

I assured her that this gold-and-white splendour was no Roman Catholic building, not even one that had been converted to Protestantism from its origins. This had been built for the Lutheran faith, making it acceptable to my friends, and they marvelled at the beauties of the marble baptismal font and the crypt with its burial places for the wealthy of this prosperous city. I smiled to myself as I thought of the comment her son would have made about this further sign of privilege. It might be as well that those youths were going to a new land.

My friends were less impressed by the Opera House, which I could understand. The square plainness of the old building was being redecorated; I could see that the added columns and pediment might soften the Spartan look – but such matters were of no interest to my companions. Nor was the fact that the full Ring Cycle of Herr Wagner had been performed there only a few years ago – I doubt they would have heard of this man with his strange and stirring works.

But at least they had been induced to see a little of this great city, beyond the fish markets and shops, and I knew when they had gone I would now be confident to explore on my own.

Their departure date approached. We had all been occupied in discovering what conditions would be like on their boat. They had been fortunate indeed, for they were ticketed for the *Augusta Victoria*, a new HAPAG acquisition.

'It was named,' they assured me with pride, 'for our Kaiser's wife, although,' they added sadly, 'the name was somewhat mistaken at the launching.'

'How do you mean?'

'They named her the *Augusta* – not, as it should have been, the Auguste – ' she put heavy emphasis on the last letter, 'the *Auguste Victoria*. They say this will be changed in the future.'

I smiled to myself as I listened to the pedantic fussiness. It was typical of so many of my countrymen. Once again I sent up prayers of thanks for the Countess who had changed my outlook on the world. Without her I too might have been as concerned with trivia as my friends were. Yet they were good people, kind hearted and practical. I shook my head at my own petty criticisms even as I made them.

We had walked past the boat where she lay in the quay, with loading continuing every day. She was claimed as the first German express boat for this voyage, making the crossing in under ten days, including the routing via Southampton.

Compared to the weeks for this voyage on the old clipper ships, this seemed an impossibility, but the men had seized eagerly on details of its structure, with talk of twin screws and steel hulls and triple expansion engines. I thought again of my son with longing, and his passion for these matters.

We heard people exclaim at the promised average speed of

eighteen to nineteen knots, and the impressive sight of her three funnels and three tall masts. For sail was still there – a safeguard we could believe in, whether used or not.

'*Gott im Himmel*, she is so big!' exclaimed Gottlieb the first day we saw her.

'Ach, *Vati*, remember how many people she must carry,' said his son. 'I have spoken with the agent, who told me there is accommodation for four hundred people in first class, and more than a hundred in second. We will be with near to six hundred third-class passengers.'

'Do not forget the crew,' Johan pointed out.

'That would be bad,' Hans laughed. 'Yes, they say the crew will be another two hundred and forty-five.'

His mother was aghast. 'But that is over a thousand people!'

'Which is why the ship must be so big.'

'It is also why,' practical Magdalena added, 'we can now see them loading so much foodstuff.'

'I think it will be better than the old days. It would have to be.'

'Why do you say this, Hans?'

'Ach, there is so much talk in the quarters where we live. One man had a paper about the old clipper ships, an advertising paper from the old days, and it listed the food they could expect. It was not good!'

'Tell us,' said his little sister. I had noticed what a greedy girl she was, food always an interest to her.

Hans was keen to share his knowledge. He pulled the flyer from his pocket.

'He gave it to me. It says,' and he began to quote in pompous official tones:

*there will be sustaining and nutritious food such as salt
beef, salt pork, herrings, peas, beans, pearl barley, oats,
rice, sauerkraut, butter, plums, pastries, pudding, etc., all in
sufficient quantity and of the best quality. Coffee is served
in the mornings, and in the evenings tea and ship's bread
with butter.*

'Well, that sounds quite good.'

'True, but that was on paper. They didn't actually get that.'

'I heard,' Johan added, 'that by the end of the voyage the
bread was mouldy and anything fatty was rancid. Bugs in the
flour, the water almost undrinkable.'

'By law they had to provision the ships for ninety days.'

'But that is over twelve weeks!' Emilia was aghast.

'The sailing ships sometimes took that long, but generally it
was six to nine weeks, depending on wind and weather. We are
fortunate that steam ships are faster – and this *Augusta Victoria*
of ours is to be the fastest of all.'

'They say we will sail in two days,' Gottlieb sounded confident.
'We must be ready to board early in the morning.'

I watched from the deck as their departure began, with ship's
agents calling the names of passengers and supervising their
loading. Our farewells were sad; we had come to feel almost
like family during these days. Although they were travelling in
steerage, at least these days it was no longer the rat-infested
filthy area of the earlier ships. I knew they would have separate
compartments for single men, for women and for families. But
that number of people! The scenes at the quay were chaotic and
it seemed to me a miracle that eventually all had mounted the
narrow gangplank and made their way to the deck for allocation

to their quarters. There was a final wave towards me as they set off down below.

The next day I stood on the pier as the *Augusta Victoria* began its stately progress down the Elbe towards the sea. Plumes of black smoke billowed from the mighty chimneys, and I knew I was truly alone. A crazy woman, setting off to an unknown destination. And for what? I did not know.

It was July before my ship, the *Elberfeld*, was ready to sail. Delays, delays, delays. But her North Sea trial run had been successful, and I had no argument with a captain who was anxious to check and double check all aspects of this new craft before the longer and more hazardous route she was to undertake.

My ship, I could see from the quay, was no *Augusta Victoria*, but a much smaller affair, with only one funnel and two masts. Unlike the Schramms' boat, with its two screw engines and capacity to take a thousand people, the *Elberfeld* was single screw and slower, eleven knots said the gossip in our lodgings.

We were becoming quite knowledgeable about these ships. I puzzled over the word 'screw' that all seemed conversant with, until the men explained kindly that it was simply the term for the propeller. Little did I know then how important that piece of machinery was to become as the voyage proceeded.

Other emigrants brought back reports as they watched the loading of the ship, and there was discussion of iron hulls and double bottoms, of steel decks sheathed in wood, of steam winches, steering gear and windlasses. They smiled patronisingly when I tried to join the discussions, a way of feeling closer to my son. These things were his life, and I began to understand the lure of steam.

Our small community waited for the departure. There was talk of what was happening, most of it untrue. The captain was a drinking man, they said, who could not sail until he had sobered. The owners were not happy about the crew, who lacked experience. The new ship still needed to be fumigated before we could leave. Passengers did not have their passports, young men did not have their military clearance, more reasons for delay. So many stories, and most of them simply idle chatter from people who should have known better.

I was eager to leave the emigrant lodging house. The food was not attractive, or wholesome, and the bunk beds in our compartments were crammed close to each other in long rows. Smells and noises in the night would have made even a comfortable bed unpleasant, and these were by no means comfortable!

We had learned more about the ship that would take us to the other side of the earth. While much smaller than the *Augusta Victoria*, it was still large. There was accommodation for over three hundred people in the third class, and just a handful of first-class passengers' cabins. I was glad I had resisted Lydia's wish to get one of these for me, and fortunately all were taken before she began negotiations for my ticket. The people for those cabins, I was sure, would be waiting departure in big Hamburg hotels, not lodging in our emigrants' quarters.

In the time we waited, I had explored Hamburg, walking the streets and visiting many of the splendid churches and galleries. It was a revelation to me. Scenes I had read of in books now unfolded around me, and I was glad of the purse that Lydia had insisted on giving me. No matter how frugal I was, and how simply I chose to live, money had to be spent. If I had seen a way of working and earning money, I would have taken it, but work permits had to be applied for and took time, and were restricted to residents. I found myself, for the first time in many years, without the burden of daily toil, and free to spend hours in the library. I could have spent all day in the Stadtsbibliothek, with its rows on rows of shelving. Books! More books than I had seen before. And I had thought the Chateau library extensive!

I wandered the Old Town, the Altstadt, and round the canal area, fascinated by the Deichstrasse, with its rows of tall narrow houses, built in the Dutch style. People were quick to tell me that fifty years ago a fire had devastated the area. I marvelled at the sense and thoughtfulness of those who had rebuilt these beautiful buildings from an older gracious way of life in the middle of a bustling port city, thronged with emigrants.

Still we waited, but finally Herr Solomon came for me, with news that we could board next day. I was glad to have his help in getting my goods aboard, and his advice of keeping only what I needed for the voyage with me; my big chest could go in the hold. The compartment I had was small, with four bunks and little storage space. I waited in some trepidation to see just who I would be sharing this voyage with.

As the *Elberfeld* slid past the wharves and warehouses that lined the riverbank, I waved a reluctant goodbye to the lodgings where I had learned I could be alone and happy. My homeland and all that was familiar slipped away, and the open sea and the unknown lay ahead.

CHAPTER 14

Aboard the *Elberfeld* 1889

This time, instead of watching a ship depart, I was aboard it. The world passed by us, as the pilot boat took us on our dignified progress down the Elbe towards Cuxhaven, where we knew the final formalities would take place. The last check of papers, and final medical inspections. No captain wanted the chance of a sickness outbreak on a voyage of this length, and I had heard he was less than happy that three of his passengers were in advanced pregnancy.

Probably, I thought wryly, so were they, for while there was a ship's doctor and a small hospital room, I doubted any woman would want to give birth on such a perilous journey. A pity that they could not have had first-class cabins, though there were few of these. The *Elberfeld*, Herr Solomon assured me with pride, had not planned to have a first-class section, but to provide good conditions for large numbers of emigrants.

Yet we looked with envy at the top deck, with its well-appointed cabins and comfortable saloon. My travel companions were impressed.

'They even,' Ida was breathless with excitement, 'have lounges to rest on during the day and proper beds for the nights.'

I looked with resignation at our tiny cabin. Two double bunks either side, and only enough space in the middle for one of the four of us to dress at a time. Already my companions had strung strong ropes along each of their bunks to hang their clothes each evening. At least behind these shrouds, there was some privacy, and most of us quickly learned how to dress in modesty. Even if using the washbasin at the end of the cabin was a public event.

The *Elberfeld* deserved its reputation as a new and modern boat, and we wandered around it marvelling at what it offered.

'We would not have had this in the old days,' I commented, looking at the walking area available to all who travelled on this boat, for the poop deck extended from bow to stern, and we were free to use it instead of being confined below decks.

'Nor would we have had lighting,' Margarethe added. 'There's electric light all through the boat.'

'It is practical,' Herr Solomon explained. 'It is not only for passenger convenience, but it means they can continue loading during the night as well as daytime.'

'And ventilation!'

The little man was as proud as if he had constructed the vessel himself.

'*Ja*. A very powerful ventilator so there will always be fresh cool air, even during the voyage through the tropics. And fresh water always available – there is a powerful condenser installed that distils a large quantity each day.'

I was glad that on this boat there were, even for third-class passengers, lavatories and bathrooms and a common area in the saloons for us to sit and eat the food brought to us from the galley. Though I confess I sighed as I thought of the tiny restaurant on the upper deck, with its table linen and fine china.

A small blessing, to have this four-bed compartment, so different from the old days of sailing ships where ship owners crammed, like cattle, as many bodies as they could fit into the big common area. Steerage, the English call it. Or *Zwischendecke*, that space built in under the main deck when they realised the growing trade of transporting people to the new world. These days regulations specify how much space we 'between decks' passengers must have, and the horror tales of previous times with vomit and faeces slopping around the floors in bad weather and hatches battened down so there was no air or light were, I hoped, well and truly over.

Now, although the cabins were tight and cramped, at least there was some privacy, and the divisions were strict. Single men at one end of the ship, in the middle the married couples and families, and at the other end, the single women. And a matron to make sure there was close supervision and morality upheld.

I heard Ida and Margarethe discussing the bunks.

'Perhaps we should give Frau Werner a lower one,' they agreed. 'She is an older woman. To climb that ladder might be difficult for a woman her age.'

'True.' Clara joined the conversation. 'We could take turns in sleeping in the other bottom bunk, to make it fair.'

'No need,' said Ida. 'I am quite happy to be up above. It will be less shut in, up there.'

I could see her point. It was claustrophobic in the tight area below, especially with our makeshift curtaining. But I was touched by their consideration, though a little insulted that they should think me so elderly as to need it. After all, I am not yet fifty years.

To them, I must seem old. There were not many single women on this boat, and the matron should have an easy time. Ida, fresh-faced, with her irrepressible curls refusing to be confined in her tight cap, had thoughts only for the man she was about to marry.

'We have waited three years,' she confided to us all in our first night in the space we were to share. 'I have known Klaus since our schooldays, and when he planned to emigrate our thought was to marry and go together. But my parents said no, and that we should wait to see what would happen, that I was too young.'

I listened with pangs of memory. So too had I been young in those far-off days when I had loved Kurt and married Otto. Younger, much younger than Ida, but no thought of delaying that necessary wedding.

But now this girl was hurrying to a lover who had made his way in a new land and was waiting for a bride to come to the home he had built for them in wine-growing country in the southern areas. Barossa, she had called it, and her Klaus was working in vineyards and planning to plant his own vines on the land he had purchased.

Margarethe was perturbed. 'But you are travelling without a chaperone. Surely you cannot just travel across the world to marry with no family to care for you.'

Ida giggled. She really was very young, I thought. 'You do sound like Papa,' she said. 'He was not happy about it. But he knows Klaus's uncle and aunt, who also live in that area, and I will live with them until the wedding. And Papa was most reassured that there was a matron to care for us on the voyage.'

We had met Frau Schroeder, the third-class passenger matron, as we stowed the baggage in our room. She was the sister of the captain, she told us with some pride, as if this conferred a special status on her. I did not warm to this gimlet-eyed vinegary little woman, with her grey hair tightly screwed into the bun beneath her cap. She had given sharp instructions on the need to keep our cabins tidy and goods stowed under the bottom bunks, and our times to eat in the saloon common areas.

'The men's area at the other end of this deck is restricted access, just as this end is. But you may walk and take exercise on the open areas and I would strongly urge you to do so often. It is important to keep good health in the coming weeks.'

Her tone was that of a schoolmistress with a class of potentially disobedient girls, though she looked uneasily at me. A woman of my age travelling alone was less familiar territory for her, and she was not quite sure what to make of me.

'I am sure you are right,' I agreed.

But she was not to be disarmed. 'Hmph,' she sniffed, and left us to go to the next cabin, where the four women were already bickering noisily over use of the shared space.

'Well,' said Margarethe, 'I think we have our orders.'

I immediately liked this young woman with her frank open face and friendly manner. Her voice was particularly appealing, clear and melodious and I found myself listening to it with pleasure. She was a little older than the other two, closer to thirty I estimated, and I was interested to hear why she was making this voyage.

She volunteered information with no reserve.

'I have been a teacher for some years in Berlin, but most of my work has been as a governess in families who wished to have their daughters privately educated.'

Clara was impressed, but Ida had reservations. 'Did they make you feel like a servant?' she asked.

A somewhat crass question, I thought, but then, the girl was very young. It did not bother Margarethe.

'On the contrary, I was always made to feel like one of the family, I have been very well treated. *Always*,' she emphasised.

'So why are you now going to the new world?' asked Clara.

'My last post has just finished, because Graf von Steckhold is taking his family to a new diplomatic posting in the East and his daughter is past the age for a governess. They asked if I would like to continue as her companion and travel with them, but it did not appeal.'

'You see yourself as a teacher, I suspect,' I offered.

She nodded. '*Genau!* Exactly. So when they said that they had friends in Australia whose daughters had lost their governess, it seemed a good opportunity to do something different with my life.'

'What happened to the other governess?' Ida was a curious girl, keen for information.

'She met someone in their city and has married and left them. They asked the von Steckholds to find a new governess for them. They wanted someone from home.'

'Doesn't it feel risky,' asked Ida, 'to be going to a family you don't know in a strange country?'

'No riskier than travelling to the other side of the world to marry someone you haven't seen for three years!'

Perhaps Margarethe's tone had been sharper than she intended, because the younger woman flushed.

'But we have written so often to each other. We know each

other better than we did before.' She was clearly defensive and Clara, the peacemaker, stepped in quickly.

'Of course this is so. You can get to know someone really well through letters. And Margarethe, I am sure your previous family would not have sent you anywhere that would be less than happy for you. What do you know of them?'

'The father, Herr Bauer, is in import-export trading and is, I think, a wealthy man. They have sent photographs of their house, which looks very fine, and of the two daughters. He wants them to have a German education rather than going to an English school in their city.'

'Which city?' I had wondered where these three were going.

'Melbourne, capital of the south-eastern colony, Victoria, is large and wealthy. The name they call it, Herr Bauer's letter said, is Marvellous Melbourne.'

I felt a sense of relief. At least one of these women was also travelling to Melbourne. I would know one person there.

A bell sounded, our summons to dinner, so we smoothed skirts and patted our hair into place before making our way to the dining area. By now the ship's rocking was more pronounced, and I found myself swaying from side to side as we progressed down the corridor.

We found ourselves spaces at the long benches that edged the trestle tables and waited with interest to see what we would get. With relief I saw the typically German meals, sauerkraut and dumplings with boiled pork that might have come from my own kitchen in Lewin. I was surprised by the homesickness I felt as the food was ladled from buckets onto plates and passed down the tables. Our boat was superior to the old times, with a pantry provided where we could make tea and coffee and water stations where we could get dippers of water to take to our cabins for washing in the washbasins provided. In all, better than I had expected.

We were now well on our way, and the gentle rocking that had calmed us earlier was no more. We lurched our way back to a time of misery in the cramped space, and I was glad to be in a bottom bunk close to the basin and the bucket as bile rose and I competed for space to retch and vomit. Harder for those in top bunks, who had to swing their legs over the railing and climb down before disaster overtook them.

'Will it be like this all the way?' moaned Ida.

'No,' Clara assured her, between bouts of retching. 'It's just this part, until we get into the open sea. We're now into the North Sea and it's very rough.'

As if to prove her right, the *Elberfeld* bucked and rolled, and nausea overtook us all. Only lying perfectly still in my bunk made life bearable, and I found it hard to accept that this would not be my whole voyage, prostrate in misery. I believe that if I had had the chance to listen to my friends and advisors and change my mind, to go quietly home, I would have seized it. They were right, Hanna, Pastor Liebelt, Frau Schmidt, Herr Holstmayer, all those who had told me I would regret my actions. Oh, they were right!

But when, almost as if by a miracle, several days later the ship stopped its wretched rolling and bucking, we were able to climb wearily from our bunks and even face breakfast in the dining area. Life improved. Happy just to walk, I pulled on the warm, thick mantle Lydia advised me to take and found my way with Clara to the main deck, where the aft area formed a promenade for the *zwischendecke* passengers. I wondered how the ship's movements had affected those in the first-class cabins, but there was no way to know; they kept to themselves for walking and recreation. Did they, like us, come out now into the pale sunshine like troglodytes from their caves, as relieved as we were, or had their voyage been more peaceful?

After Antwerp and the loading of cargo, our contact with our old way of life was over. We entered a strange existence, almost as if time had stopped and we were caught in another world. For the *Elberfeld* had its own laws and expectations, and a mini-society for our three-hundred *zwischendecke* inhabitants. We learned the times we could go for meals and walk the decks, and soon social groups were established.

With weeks to live together, trapped in this new existence, people found others of like mind. Families tended to form a separate world, with care of children as its focus. Mothers banded in small clusters for sewing and sharing experiences. Music lovers found each other, and music-making groups sprang up. So too did the card players, and the deck game enthusiasts – even an artists' group, whose members gathered outside in good weather to sketch the ship and endless seas.

I had been lucky in my companions. Not all cabins were so harmonious and there were all the problems that enforced intimacy could bring. I sometimes wondered if the Sunday worship services that Captain Sass held on deck for those who wanted it gave people time to think about the bickering and tensions of the week. It was good to put on bonnets and Sunday clothes and to make our way into the sunshine to listen to him read from the good book, while one of the first-class passengers gave a short address. Almost like normal living for an hour.

'I like these Sunday observances,' confided Clara, as we made our way up the stairway to the upper deck. Thank goodness the old days of rope ladders for steerage passengers on clipper ships were over.

'It is more like being at home,' I agreed. 'But I have noticed that you spend much of your time on study of the Bible.'

'It is my life,' she said simply. 'It is the work that I plan to do when we arrive.'

Up to now she had given little information about herself or her reasons for the journey. But then, neither had I, and tact had prevented us all asking too much about each other. Except for Ida, who had no reluctance about asking direct questions. Up to the point where a certain stubbornness made one unwilling to be interrogated – it certainly had that effect on me! I had evaded her questions, as had Clara.

'Would you like to tell me about your plans?' I hesitated, lest I should seem as inquisitive as Ida. But Clara was happy to talk.

'I have spent the last years in our church's mission training centre near Nuremberg, a place called *Neuendettelsau*. It fits people for mission work in various parts of the world.'

'But you are not Catholic, I think.'

'No, this is a Lutheran mission. I have been called to work with the native population at Hermannsburg, a place in the middle of Australia – perhaps not the middle, but well inland from the coastal settlements. It is still very new: only twelve years ago two missionaries went there, but it is growing. The hope is it may expand and they can introduce schools for the children.'

'This is a brave undertaking, my dear girl. I would find it daunting.'

'Oh, so do I, Frau Werner. But I believe, I really do believe, that this is what God wants me to do with my life. And I will not be alone. The missionaries have their wives and children with them.'

We had reached the upper deck where people were gathering. The singing of the old familiar hymns from home, most of them known to me from childhood, was comforting, and I looked at the young woman beside me with a sense of wonder. To dedicate her life to a strange land and such an enterprise ... it made my journey, foolhardy as it was, seem almost trivial in comparison.

'Commit thy way unto the Lord,' intoned Captain Sass as he read the lesson for the day, and I listened to Pastor Krause, one of the upper-deck passengers, expound on the text. It seemed so apt for the journey I was on and my mind wandered again to thoughts of Kurt and the task I had set myself in finding him.

Or, a thought had begun to haunt me, what if he did not wish to be found? What if, as Hanna had hinted, this was a way to abandon his former life? And me ...

Others' attention was also wandering, I noticed, for as our ship progressed southward the weather grew hotter. Oppressively so, and a chair was brought from a stateroom for a pregnant woman who had swayed, near fainting, during the sermon. Soon we would reach the tropics, and we had been warned that the weather would try us. We did not know how far off that time was going to be. Or how much longer our voyage would last.

CHAPTER 15

At sea, *Elberfeld* 1889

The next Sunday at the end of the service people were gathering near the noticeboard on the corridor walls. They were reading, with occasional laughter, the week's broadsheet of ship's news. I had heard of this little paper put out several times each week, for information and entertainment, but I had not seen it before.

'An excellent idea,' I commented to Margarethe, who stood beside me. 'A wonderful way to keep people interested in the life around us.'

'Forgive me for joining your conversation,' said a man's voice, 'but that is exactly the purpose of this little bulletin. I'm delighted that you think it a worthwhile venture.'

'Oh, I do!' I said enthusiastically as I turned to the man beside me. 'And I like the range of these articles – some funny, others thought-provoking, all well-written and interesting.'

'Might I introduce myself, ladies?'

Margarethe answered for us both. 'Please do.'

'My name is August Eberhardt, and I am the editor of this little newspaper. A small group of us work on it each day, excepting of course for Sunday – a day of rest for us too – and post it here for people to read.'

By now I had guessed that this small group must be drawn from the nine staterooms and their well-educated first-class passengers.

'How do you produce it?' I asked, intrigued.

'I have brought a typewriting machine with me. They are being made in America, by a company called Remington, for fifteen years now.'

'And you have one!'

'I purchased one to take with me to the colonies, so this is a chance to practise with it while on the voyage.'

'But how do you make copies?'

'There is another American firm, Underwood, that makes carbon paper enabling us to produce a number of copies.'

'That is so impressive. You are to be congratulated, Herr Eberhardt.'

'But we are limited. We know nothing of what is happening among the majority of passengers. We have often said it would be good to have representatives from those who travel ...' he hesitated, uncertain how to make his point without being insulting, 'from those who travel in the other areas of the *Elberfeld*.'

'It would certainly give you a broader range of viewpoints and events, I agree.'

'I wonder if you ladies might be interested in joining us. Am I being presumptuous in suggesting this?'

The idea had immediate appeal. Years of reading had given me a passion for words. It would be a chance to be in contact with others interested in ideas and writing, and even to try my own skill in the field.

'Margarethe?' I queried, turning to her.

She nodded. 'Yes, I think we would both enjoy that. If you think we can be of use.'

So began what was, for us both, the most pleasant part of this shipboard life. Our daily meetings with the production group were, for a time, somewhat intimidating. The others knew what they were doing; we were inexperienced. And they were first-class passengers. As we entered their cabin area we felt conscious of differences in status, and diffident about contributing to discussion.

But that soon wore off, and I told myself sternly not to be ridiculous.

'You are,' I said firmly to my reflection in the little cabin mirror, 'as well-read as any of these others, as is Margarethe.'

It was an entry to a new world, and I looked appreciatively around these very different surroundings. Room to move, was my first thought, for the cabins were spacious, with large beds and comfortable chairs and day beds. Their washstands were beautifully fitted, with large ornamental basins of flower-painted china.

The two ladies in the group looked a little askance as Herr Eberhardt explained our presence, and I had the feeling we were not entirely welcome. But the three men were affable and happy to have extra hands for the work, it seemed. They were also members of the social committee, involved in producing the musical evenings that were held occasionally on the main deck. Another group, we found, had been formed to organise games meetings and sporting matches for passenger entertainment. Captain Sass, they told us, understanding the dangers of boredom in the weeks that we would be confined, had called a meeting of interested passengers and asked them to form these committees.

We were our own little world, a floating world, but it was surprising how many people were willing to contribute short articles to share in our pages. Many had interests or areas of expertise, and Herr Eberhardt proved himself an excellent editor. Not surprising, for he had been a newspaper man in Berlin, and was going to a similar role in a German publication in Sydney.

Sometimes Captain Sass joined us for a few minutes in Herr Eberhardt's stateroom, providing an update on progress or information about the ship and the crew. Frau Wandel proved to have a talent for writing pointed and witty verses about life on board, and most issues would feature a poet's corner for her offerings. I noted that she and her sister, the other lady of the newspaper committee, had become a little more friendly when they perceived we were not planning to challenge their rights to the male company in the group.

Gathering material for the little newssheet proved an interesting exercise. Others became involved as we moved through the different areas of the boat looking for scraps of information about daily routines and personal lives that might give us a paragraph or two. Production of a few copies of this collection several times a week became a highlight of the voyage, not just for those of us who were responsible, but also for the readers who waited its appearance with real enthusiasm.

It was good to have had this diversion, for the novelty of shipboard life swiftly paled, and as the time passed and the weather became less and less bearable we needed something to occupy our minds.

I worried about Ida. Clara had her studies and her constant preparing for her future work on the mission station. She seemed to relish this time of freedom, for apart from the rostered cleaning sessions, which we all endured (and then rejoiced when the decks were clear, and our living areas freshened) she was free to continue her reading and learning. Margarethe and I had our work on the newspaper, and the times we joined in deck games or watched the card players at their whist. But Ida? Her days were long, and who could blame her wish for company her own age?

Frau Schroeder, in her matron role, watched like a hawk over the young women. Woe betide the girl who lingered too long over the bland breakfast serving, for the sight of the young men approaching was ample cause to delay over the bread and butter or oatmeal porridge, or that last cup of coffee. Easy to brush against a young man's arm as he took his plate to the stewards to have the midday soup ladled into his bowl, or to eye each other as the beef and potatoes were piled on his dinner plate. Surely it was only civil to stop and chat for a moment, though it earned sharp looks from Frau Schroeder and a warning talk later in the cabin.

'There is no harm in being polite,' Ida said sulkily when we remonstrated with her. 'The old cat is just jealous because we have friends.'

'I think it is more that she feels responsible for you. To both your father, and also to your fiancé.'

'Klaus would understand,' she was adamant. 'He knows I like to have a bit of fun. He knows I belong to him.'

'But would he really be happy about you dancing on the deck yesterday afternoon with Sigmund?'

Ida pouted. 'No. But then he won't find out, will he?'

Too easy, I was thinking, on a hot tropical night with

the bright orange moon above, to forget about the future and the real world waiting. It took me back to those days in the pine forest with Kurt and the seductive slipping into an all-consuming intimacy. I could still feel its lure. Even now, almost thirty years on, I ached for those days.

Such foolish thoughts for a woman my age. A widow, a mother, a grandmother. And most of all, a woman searching for her son.

But soon there were more serious things to fill my mind. The *Elberfeld* had made good time in her progress south, and Captain Sass proved that his reputation was well earned. He seemed never at rest, checking on the wellbeing of his ship and crew and friendly and attentive to his passengers. Not only considerate of the cabin dwellers, but all of us – especially the mothers with children.

'It is a long voyage. The children need an occupation and their schooling should be continued.'

He knew that both Margarethe and Clara had teaching skills and experience, so soon had drawn them into the small school that was set up on the poop deck five mornings a week. They seemed happy to have an occupation and tried to draw Ida into their work. Without success. She was much more interested in joining in the deck games with the young men. I smiled. Frau Schroeder would find her chaperone duties more time consuming than she had expected.

Despite our age differences, the four of us were good companions. Ida too, flibbertigibbet as she was. But there were things we didn't talk about. They knew only that I was planning to visit my son, and I had been vague on his whereabouts.

No surprise in that. I did not know where I was going, and it was starting to weigh on my mind. Until now I had been able to push aside the inevitable questions, the necessary questions, but they were beginning to loom darkly. Yet I could tell myself it was a long way off, that there were other matters to think of for the time being.

Perhaps it was the work on the newspaper, and my greater knowledge of this huge floating castle that we inhabited. It had become a regular feature of our production – each issue some aspect of life on board. I could see why Herr Eberhardt would be such a skilful editor of any newspaper; he had a sharp sense of what might be of interest, and how to go about it.

The men were sent to investigate the engineering of this vessel, and all the various jobs that kept us afloat – all three hundred passengers, and the hundreds of crew members – from the Captain's role down to the youngest cabin boy. While we, Margarethe and I, interviewed the stewards and stewardesses, and looked at the kitchens and storerooms, talking to those who were responsible for feeding this army of people. Meanwhile Frau Wandel and her sister Ursula discovered how the medical care on the *Elberfeld* was organised and run.

I saw the way the ladies' eyes lit up. More contact with the doctor. Single. Available? It would be a task to their taste. They continued to view me with a coolness I found disconcerting.

'You do know why, don't you?' asked Margarethe.

I was genuinely puzzled, and she could see it.

'Frau Wandel thinks that Herr Eberhardt likes you too much.'

'You are teasing me! Aren't you?'

'Not at all. I'm sure she had hopes that this long voyage might lead to something for her. After all, he's a widower; she's a widow. What could be more comfortable? As for her sister, if you watch her with the doctor, I think you'll see what I mean.'

I could feel my face flush. 'That's absurd. She couldn't think that.'

'And why not? You're also a widow, and just as available. And he clearly likes you very much.'

'But our only contact has been over the newspaper. No, you're quite wrong. He's just being courteous and friendly.'

'Mmm.' Her tone was sceptical. 'You're younger than she is, too. And much more attractive.'

Whatever the reason, Frau Wandel obviously did not like me, and I wondered how I had managed to antagonise her. I could not accept Margarethe's idea. In fact, I was so unused to thinking of myself as a woman that it bewildered me that anyone could see me in this way.

Our pleasant routine was soon disrupted, and my days of happy work on the newspaper with new friends and hours spent reading – so many emigrants had books among their baggage that we had created our own ship's library – were sadly interrupted. It was the first of the disasters on this maiden voyage. One could only feel for Captain Sass. He had been so careful, so attentive to all aspects of the workings of the ship – but there was nothing he could have done to prevent the loss of the propeller off the Portuguese coast. A devastating blow, on a brand-new vessel. He was mortified.

Not that his apologies stopped the complaints, particularly from Frau Wandel. I was beginning to feel a distinct aversion toward this arrogant woman. Any suggestions I made for our little paper were met with something close to contempt.

Irritations grew with the disappearance of the propeller. The first decision was to be towed into port at Lisbon. But no repairs could be achieved there. We must return to Cardiff, decided Captain Sass and the owners, so a steamer was sent to tow us there.

'But that is in Wales,' shrieked Ida, when she heard. 'I'll never get to Klaus. We had a wedding date planned.'

There was general dismay when the decision was announced and we realised how many weeks this would add to our voyage. It took every bit of Captain Sass's tact and charm to manage the tensions, and he enlisted the aid of Herr Eberhardt to help explain through our newspaper just what was happening.

'Try to reassure them,' he begged. 'This is most unfortunate, but it could not have been foreseen. We will make good time afterward.'

Not an accurate prediction.

It was as everyone had warned me. Sea voyages are risky. It was over four weeks since we had left Hamburg, and nearly five weeks before a new propeller was fitted and we sailed out of Cardiff. A second start. All breathed a sigh of relief, and even Frau Wandel's cartoon for the paper had an optimistic note, with a cheerful grin on the bow of the *Elberfeld* and a joyous smile on our Captain's face.

Past Gibraltar and on, but not so happily. We grieved for the young mother whose baby was born dead, and who watched, tears streaming down her cheeks, the small body, wrapped in sailcloth and consigned to the deep as Pastor Krause read a funeral psalm. I spent time with her, understanding what it was like to endure the pains of childbirth without the joy that should have followed. I could talk to her as one who had also borne a dead child, and we wept together. The pain for me was as fresh as nearly thirty years before, for that dead son would now have been twenty-seven. No, I told myself. I could not lose another son.

But we were, as promised, making good time, though unable to compensate for the time lost. I remember little of the Mediterranean, except for the distant sight of Malta, because our lives had turned inward. It seemed that this world, this floating world, encompassed all we had ever known and all we would ever know. I could believe in Herr Wagner's Flying Dutchman, doomed to sail the seas forever.

I could talk of these things with Herr Eberhardt and, while careful to give no cause for offence to his friends, it was good to have someone who would discuss books and music. And yes, if I am honest, it was good to feel admired, perhaps even desirable, for now that Margarethe had opened my eyes, for the first time in many years I thought of myself as a woman.

I examined myself carefully in the cabin mirror. My skin was still clear and unlined, my dark hair not yet shot with grey, and the eyes that Kurt had admired were bright and alert. The long neck that Lydia had so surprised my daughter by admiring had an elegance that surprised me. It was many years since I had taken an inventory of my appearance, and now I found I wanted to look as good as possible. The sea air was putting colour in my cheeks, and I blessed Lydia for the care she had taken in selecting clothing for this trip.

But for what? Or for whom? I laughed at myself, worse than those silly vain young things. Not for Herr Eberhardt, good friend as he had become. And not for Captain Sass, though he had taken to speaking to me with a sort of gallantry that was enjoyable. Nor for the doctor, who was a frail-looking character, subject to fits of depression, and clearly reserved for the first-class ladies. Anyone else in my age group was firmly attached to wives and offspring. It was no wonder that Frau Wandel and her sister Ursula were so proprietary about the few available men.

We had settled into a harmonious way of life, and as I joined in deck games and watched the dances at night, or promenaded with Margarethe in the late afternoons on the poop deck, I realised with surprise that I was happy. A feeling I had not known for a long time.

It was not to last. Captain Sass had explained our route. We, like the mail steamers, would be travelling through the Suez Canal, that miracle construction that had so shortened sea journeys.

'The costs are high,' he told us. 'But the time saved, especially for ships with mail contracts, justifies the expense.'

Good in theory, but not for the *Elberfeld*. We had no swift efficient journey through the Canal. As we reached Port Said, one of the screw propeller blades broke off and disappeared into the waters. This time it was retrievable by the divers employed to find it. But Port Said had no docking facilities to enable repairs so once more we were towed, now to Suez where repairs could be made.

'A new propeller has been ordered,' boomed Captain Sass. 'It will be sent to Sydney and the whole unit will be replaced. Meanwhile we continue!'

More delays, and this time the ship seemed to seethe with discontent. There was no chance of going ashore, unlike Cardiff where it had been possible to visit the town and feel again the strange sensation of walking on solid ground. There, the repairs to the *Elberfeld* had seemed almost a brief holiday time, and we had explored the flourishing coal port.

'Research for our newspaper,' decreed Herr Eberhardt, as he escorted our group through the city centre and the ancient Cardiff Castle, built over the ruins of an early Roman fort.

I found so much pleasure in talking to this man, who knew about these places and was willing to share his knowledge. I wrote under his guidance, and took pride in finding my accounts of our visits and explorations in print. I had never known that writing could become a satisfying activity – I was learning new things about the world and myself.

The stop in Suez was different. Unlike Cardiff, where even the most impatient grumblers could find activity to compensate for the lengthening of their voyage, at both Port Said and during the Suez repairs we were confined to the ship.

'Too dangerous.' Captain Sass was decisive. 'There have been cases of cholera in these ports, and I cannot afford an outbreak on the *Elberfeld*. There will be no shore leave, and we will take precautions with contacts during the repairs.

So we watched enviously as swarms of little boats circled our ship and eager faces tried to sell us grapes and watermelons and lemons. Meanwhile our refuelling took place at Port Said, with coal shovelled from the barges by men who ran up and down planks, their brown bodies glistening with sweat under the loads they carried. During the scorching nights, many of our young men slept on deck. Captain Sass, always inventive, had a swimming bath erected on the deck, and after dark even ladies could swim on our allocated nights. It gave some relief, but not enough.

Our closed world now seemed a prison, in which the steamy heat of midsummer became a breeding ground for resentment and hostility. Frau Wandel's cartoons assumed a vicious streak, and the children complained and whined through their daily lessons.

In our cabin, Ida's petulance drove us to seek other areas of the ship. Even the most casual of remarks could lead to a tirade of annoyance, and she took the fact that we were confined to the ship as a personal affront. In many ways, she and Frau Wandel made a good pair, for neither could brook delays or the curbing of what they wanted. I wondered if Klaus would have the patience to deal with his new bride. Even Clara's tolerance was tried, and Margarethe and I would glance at each other and roll our eyes in exasperation.

'This will be a swifter repair,' Captain Sass assured us. But some muttered that disasters came in threes, that there would be yet another breakdown, an ominous idea. Because we had taken in coal at Port Said, there would be no need to put in at Colombo, as ships on this route so often did.

Clara sighed. 'I had hoped that we might see something of the native life there. I have read about it – it seems most colourful.'

Ida could not resist a comment. 'Oh, you'll be seeing enough native life where you are going, I should think. You don't need to start so early. You'll get enough dark-skinned people before long!'

I could see Clara biting back a sharp retort. A peacemaker by nature, she had the right temperament for the way of life she had chosen. Or the way of life that God had chosen for her, as she explained to me. I found her simple faith touching, envious of the certainty of her belief.

'Too much reading,' my father had said, when I tried to talk at home of some of the doubts that troubled me. When I tried to involve our good Pastor in discussing matters of faith, the sheer panic on the good man's face had left me unwilling to distress him. Now I felt the same with Clara. I did not want to raise issues that might lead to trouble between us or, worse still, infect her with my doubt.

At least with Herr Eberhardt I could talk honestly, knowing he shared many of my concerns and would not be shocked. With him I learned of the problems of varied translations of texts that had puzzled me, and of ways of considering the contexts in which the scriptures had been written.

'Metaphor?' a perturbed Pastor Liebelt had shaken his head. '*Ach nein*, Anna. Such thoughts will lead you astray. One must have simple faith in every word as it is written.'

It was good to find that there were other positions between Otto's blanket denial of all that religion stood for and the blind accepting faith of my family. But I did not speak of these things to Clara, for I felt that she would view me as on a primrose path to damnation. There it was again – *the primrose path to the everlasting bonfire* – and I was back once more in the Chateau library, reading *Macbeth* with the Countess.

Spirits revived as we steamed out of Suez, the canal now well behind us. Through the Red Sea, and as I recognised places with familiar names my thoughts turned swiftly to biblical lore and the stories from my childhood of fleeing Israelites and pursuing Egyptians. Soon the Red Sea too was behind us, and before us lay the Gulf of Aden and at last, again, the open sea – and then the vast Indian Ocean.

Early in the morning we could see the peaks of the far-off island of Socotra, and another small island behind it. We knew, from Pastor Krause and our captain, that this isolated place, with its fierce heat and strange and wonderful plants, would be the last land we would see for many days. The morning prayers on deck that day seemed a feeble effort to propitiate an uncertain deity.

For a moment, a sense of panic seemed to wash like a wave over the *Elberfeld*. We were such a frail vessel to be setting off across this expanse. What matter our carefully repaired propeller and our double bottom with its seven watertight steel bulkheads? What value our steam winches and windlasses and steering gear? (By now I had a fair understanding of the vessel we were on, and all its features!) More relevant, at worst, would be the six boats we carried in case of disaster ... But we did not wish to think of such things. It was mid September, and we knew we had at least another five weeks ahead on this perilous sea.

CHAPTER 16

In the tropics, *Elberfeld* 1889

Captain Sass had been right to keep us occupied. Little had he realised that this apparently straightforward voyage on a new ship would turn into a wandering of the seas to rival opera! A month longer than anticipated, already. And even though I wondered about the pressure mounting on our supplies, the food continued to maintain the standards set when we left. There had been much re-stocking at Suez, for even the animals on board would not have been sufficient for our needs with these delays. Without refrigeration life would have been more difficult.

How grateful we were that our craft had been equipped not just with the generator for electricity but also the water condensation plant, ensuring our supplies of fresh water. We had all heard the stories of the drinking water on the old clippers, so foul by the end of long voyages that it was nearly undrinkable, and the way in which disease, once unleashed on these sailing ships, could run rampant. And of the daily funerals, especially when large numbers of children were on board.

It was harder for the children. Even though there was ample space on the promenade decks for children's games, and space made in the saloons for their schooling, once we reached the tropics the high temperatures led to many problems. The hospital rooms were often crowded. Frau Wandel and her sister saw less of Dr Menz than they had hoped for; the poor man was kept busy with children's fevers, debility, diarrhoea, jaundice and all the other ailments that now seemed rife. The doctor, always a gloomy man, now seemed permanently harassed and miserable.

He conducted the regular musters of children on deck, and carefully checked throats and ears for signs of disease, while counselling mothers on the need to bathe their little ones each week and to make sure that the children, like the rest of us, drank their daily ration of lime juice. Examination over, he would give a rare smile as he doled out sweets to the children he had seen. I was amused to see that he had refused Fraulein Ursula's offer to help with the sweets distribution – she was not volunteering assistance with the medical checks.

Our funeral for the newborn off Gibralter was the first, but not the only sad ceremony. We grieved most, I think, at the funerals of children, and Clara and Margarethe took hard the sight of two of their schoolchildren consigned into the waters after brief farewell services. There was no laughter in our cabin those nights, nor when the mother of one of those little boys could be found nowhere on the ship one morning and we came to realise that she must have joined her young son.

'I should have foreseen it,' wept Clara. 'I knew how hard it was for her. She said, she actually told me, she would be happier to be with him.'

'But you could not know what she meant,' I tried to reassure her but she would not be comforted.

'No, the way she sobbed. It was more than just grief. She was brokenhearted, I should have seen what she had in mind.'

'Even her husband did not know – how could you?'

'He is a man. I should have known.'

I was surprised at how deeply Captain Sass felt for the loss of life during the voyage. It was, I suspect, almost a personal reproach to him. He consulted long hours with Doctor Menz, especially when two sailors who had been in Suez sickened with symptoms that were worryingly like typhoid fever.

'It was expressly forbidden,' the doctor assured the captain. 'They were told to eat or drink nothing while ashore.'

'It may not be the typhus,' Captain Sass ruminated. 'But they do show red spots – and some other familiar symptoms. We must keep them isolated.'

When they died there was a hasty disposal of their bodies without the usual ceremonies, and only Pastor Krause was on the deck in the early hours of the morning to speak a rushed prayer before they went to the deep. If it was indeed typhus, it did not spread.

It was different when two elderly ladies died. Both of them matriarchs of their families, both of them widows, and one as much feared as loved, I suspected. But this voyage and its seeming endlessness had taken its toll on aging bodies. Even with the air ventilator, so much the pride of the *Elberfeld*, the steamy heat of the equator left us lethargic and irritable, and older people at greater risk. Their families wept as they said their farewells in that sad week when both left us. Our captain took these deaths deeply to heart. You could see him thinking that if the voyage had gone to plan, they might well have survived the trip. His ship; his responsibility. Without the delays, they might have reached the new land their families sought.

The middle cabins were quieter those days, and noisy children were hushed and sent to play on deck. Even that was to prove hazardous. As we moved south, we steamed steadily towards the South East Trades, hopeful there would be no further mishaps. No one had warned us of the impact of these freshening winds on our journey.

'It is the English name for them,' Herr Eberhardt explained to me. We were walking, with some care, bracing against the gusts that came. 'Trade. It comes from an old English word meaning a path or track.'

'Why a path?'

'It was how the sailing ships found a way across the great oceans. Without the winds they would be becalmed. Unable to sail on. The Portuguese sailors who opened the new worlds understood this. We have all learned from them.'

'But today in English that word, trade, has a different meaning?'

We had slipped into a pattern that we both enjoyed, of speaking English together in preparation for our own new world, ignoring Frau Wandel's scathing comments about the ugliness of this language.

'True – but the meaning of 'trade' today comes directly from that past. The trade winds made trade possible, trade with the new lands across the seas.'

He was, as always, formal and at times irritating in his pedantry, but I valued the wealth of knowledge he brought to all topics. I valued also, I confess, the sense of being cared for and admired by this man. What woman would not have been flattered?

So when I stumbled in a sudden gust of wind, I was not offended by the protective arm he placed around my shoulders, even though he removed it the next moment with careful apology.

'Forgive me, Frau Werner. I did not wish to see you fall.'

'Or even,' I said, laughing, 'be blown overboard!'

But we sobered quickly at the memory of all the bodies already departed by that route.

'Thank you for your care,' I added quickly. I did not want to admit, even to myself, how pleasant it had been, even that brief moment of a man's arm around me.

'We should indeed be grateful,' he pointed out, 'that our ship is steam. In the old days we could have been becalmed for days, even weeks, near the equator in the doldrums.'

I looked up with interest. This was a new word.

'That is the area where trade winds from the south-east meet the trade winds from the north-west; where they collide the air is forced upwards. So there are few surface winds, and ships have no way to move.'

'And these are the doldrums.' I rolled the word experimentally on my tongue.

'It has come to have a more general meaning in English. It means a state of apathy, of misery. Like being becalmed in life, unable to get free.'

'I think my life has been like that for a long time. In these doldrums. It's useful to have a word to describe it.'

He glanced at me quickly. 'I would hope that your future life may be well away from the doldrums,' he began, but I cut him off quickly, suddenly afraid where this conversation might go.

'Oh look, Herr Eberhardt, Fräulein Margarethe is coming to join us.' And so the moment passed.

We had worked together so closely that at times I was tempted to ask him to call me Anna, but such a degree of familiarity would have raised the eyebrows of the others in our group, so we maintained the proper distance that custom decreed.

Since Margarethe's warning I had been careful to give no occasion for gossip, or for rekindling the hostility of Frau Wandel or her sister. But I was honest enough to admit the enjoyment I had in the company of a man whose interests and values were so similar to my own, and who gave me the sense of being appreciated. Did I want more than that?

Our deck walks were no longer possible as the winds increased in intensity, and swelling seas made even short promenades hazardous. Violent waves could come with unexpected force, as we found one day. The boy was only seven, but Gunther Kowald was often in trouble. Somehow he had managed to let a chicken out of its coop, and was now fearful of punishment. As well he should have been. No wonder he tried to chase it across the deck and back to its quarters, but when the ship bucked at a sudden onslaught he was hurled to the side.

'He could so easily have been swept over,' reported Clara, who had heard it all. 'But one of the crew managed to grab him before the next wave and pull him back to safety.'

'But the boy was screaming, wasn't he?' asked Ida.

'Well, that was understandable. But it was just then the First Officer came by and thought the man was maltreating the child. He knew what the Captain would have said and wouldn't listen to a word but clapped him in irons in the hold to wait for punishment.'

'Surely the child could have said something?'

'He was frantic, just sobbing, and his mother whisked him

away, shouting abuse at the sailor as she went for what he had done to her son.'

'How totally unjust!' Margarethe was flushed with indignation.

'No, it was cleared up,' Clara continued. 'One of the passengers at the other end of the deck had seen it all and went to Captain Sass to explain. It's been sorted out.'

'I think the mother should apologise, don't you? After all, he probably saved her son's life.'

'To a sailor?' said Ida dubiously.

'I doubt it.' Margarethe was regretful. 'You know how some of those cabin ladies view the sailors.'

But she was wrong, and an emotional Frau Kowald brought Gunther to thank his rescuer in front of the whole crew at the next Sunday service. I was left wondering the next time eggs appeared at our breakfast whether the chicken had also been saved.

'Write it as a story for our paper,' suggested Herr Eberhardt, ever the editor. 'That could be your ending for the tale.'

The long journey continued, and as the heat of the tropics abated after the equator had been crossed a new spirit revived among the passengers. It was still not calm travelling, for now the force of the westerlies had hit us, but this at least was bracing weather, rather than the enervating conditions we had endured. Even when swells were large and seas heavy, it was more bearable.

We now had respite; our south-east course and easterly winds had brought us a peaceful sea and warm sunshine. We stood on deck and watched the enormous numbers of flying fish, a diversion with their antics. It was almost like a show for our entertainment, and a welcome relief from the games and concerts we had contrived for ourselves.

In our cabin, like many others, tensions quietened as we were able once more to spend time above deck. Though our uneasiness grew over Ida, who ignored us and spent time with her new friends from the aft end of the boat. Frau Schroeder's lips tightened every time she looked at the girl, and we tried to warn Ida to be more careful.

'Why should I?' she retorted. 'She's not my jailer. Though this feels like a jail. How much longer before we can get free?'

'We still have some weeks before we reach Australian waters. You'll be with Klaus soon. Don't do anything to jeopardise that.'

Ida's face reddened. 'Just because I enjoy being with Siggi, it doesn't mean anything.'

'It may mean something if you let it go too far!' I could not keep the sharp comment back.

'You're not in a position to lecture me. We've all seen the way Herr Eberhardt looks at you. And you're always together.'

'There is absolutely nothing between Herr Eberhardt and me. And we are usually with other people. Working together. That is very different.'

The look on her face was disbelieving. 'Are you sure?'

But I was not confident enough to answer.

The first engineer had recommended to Captain Sass that we set course for the distant land, the Chagos Islands, to pick up coal and, anxious as he was to make up some of the lost time, I think there was recognition that all would profit from a chance to leave our floating home.

We watched, fascinated, as the *Elberfeld* was manoeuvred with care through the narrow channel to a bay, where an English coal ship lay anchored about a thousand feet from shore. Further on a settlement lay, in among dense green trees.

Some of us chose to be transported across by natives in their small boats for a few hours exploration of the island. It was a surprise to me that so many refused the experience. Mothers with children – that I could understand – but the ones who gazed dubiously at the transport offered and decided to stay on the familiar territory of the ship? That amazed me, so eager I was to experience something new.

'Ah, but you know they tell us that prisoners learn to love their chains,' Margarethe murmured as we were helped across the planks to the waiting boats, more like large canoes. Clara had come, interested to find what sort of religious practices might exist on these islands, and Ida giggled as she lowered herself on to the cross benches in the boat.

I was less amused when, as soon as we had landed, I saw her disappear with Sigmund and his friends on a private sightseeing expedition. But this was soon forgotten in the fascination of the place, with its vast plantations of coconut palms, and the coco mill, operated by native workers with donkeys. Beside me, Herr Eberhardt was taking notes in his small black book, and I foresaw several newspaper articles emerging over the next weeks.

We gazed up the fifty-foot coconut palms, with natives scaling the trunks to collect the fruit from the top. Almost dizzying to watch their agile scrambles up and down. And the fruits! The oranges, dates, bananas, the ground with its melon vines – so sad that most of this fruit was not ripe, but at least we could try the coconut juice, when natives bored with sharp knives into the three small soft points of the shell after the husks were removed.

'A sort of paradise,' whispered Clara as we walked to the

settlement with its houses and store and animal enclosures, as well as the hundred native huts.

'Even,' pointed out Herr Eberhardt, 'an oil refinery. One could live here very comfortably.'

'But the isolation?' I queried.

'It does not seem to bother the Frenchmen who own this island,' he replied. 'Perhaps they prefer the solitude to sociable life.'

'It would not do for you,' Margarethe laughed. 'You would have no newspaper.'

'There are more important things in life than a newspaper!' he retorted.

As we neared the Australian coastline, I sensed a need to sort out my feelings. We were still producing the paper twice a week, and contributions came readily. Everyone seemed to enjoy seeing themselves in print, a feeling I could relate to.

'You enjoy this work, Frau Werner,' Herr Eberhardt commented one afternoon as we completed an issue.

'Yes,' I responded frankly. 'I have found it very satisfying. To see the words I have written in print – and then, best of all, to watch the reactions of others as they read them. I could not have believed all these years that I enjoyed reading how much pleasure the writing also gave.'

'I have very much enjoyed working with you. I have wondered if there would be any possibility of continuing our association after landing.'

'Are you offering me work on your newspaper, Herr Eberhardt?'

'That too, if you wish. But I had hoped there might be a

chance of a closer connection. Anna – might I call you Anna?'

It had come. The moment I had felt hovering for many weeks. And still I did not know how I felt about it. This good man, for he was a good man, a man I liked and respected so highly. But more? Was liking enough?

'Herr Eberhardt – ' his face clouded as he recognised the implication in my use of his name. 'We are such good friends, or so I see us.'

He nodded. 'We are, and I had hoped we might be more. Since my wife died, and that is now five years, I have known no one I felt I wished to share my life with. I had not expected to feel this again – '

I broke in. 'But you know I have made this voyage for one sole purpose, to find my son.'

I had told him the story of my search, though little of my earlier life. I think he had sensed that my marriage was not happy, but had tried not to pry. Equally, I had the feeling there was much left unsaid about his own.

'Perhaps in the future, when you have found your son?'

I did not wish to leave him with false hopes.

'Can we not remain just as we are? Good friends, who care for each other's wellbeing? I think that is all that I can offer you.'

'I understand what you are saying. But please do not close the door on this matter. Perhaps one day, Frau Werner, you may feel differently. I would like to feel that you might contact me again in Sydney. I am a patient man.'

'I would not wish to lose a dear friend. Can we be as we were?'

'Of course. And I would like to offer you my help in your mission. If I can assist you in any way ... What do you know of your son's whereabouts?'

I told him more fully of Kurt's experience in Melbourne, and the beating he had received. Of the help from members of the German Club, and his plan to work his way to Queensland.

'But you thought he was making his journey through the border with New South Wales – perhaps that should be your first field. That, and the German Club.'

'I plan to take lodgings in Melbourne and begin from there. I have a little money – enough to last a few months – then I must seek employment.'

'I will check the local newspapers. If there are regional publications, that should be your start.'

'You mean an advertisement?'

'Yes, they will be certain to have a column for seeking missing persons. I will be able to help in Sydney, where I am based, if he has come that far. Let me check what newspapers are in the border area for you.'

We had slipped back into easy conversation, and the awkward moment of his avowal had passed. I knew I would value his help.

That night I lay awake a long time, pondering the day. Had I made a mistake I would regret for the rest of my life? I seemed to be rather good at those. What more did I want in life? He would have helped me with my search for Kurt, and I would have had the security of life with a man I could live with happily.

My thoughts ran in circles. But I am still young! On this voyage I had come to see myself with new eyes, and realise the promise of life ahead. I still had yearnings, and I could not accept that the feelings I had shut down in all those years with Otto would never have the chance to live again. I wanted more. More than a comfortable growing old.

In this clear weather, the nights too were lovely. We walked on deck, and gazed at the starry southern sky. Clara pointed to the bright stars forming a constellation.

'They call it the Southern Cross,' she informed us. 'I have been told that where I am going the stars are peculiarly brilliant. I look forward to that. It makes me feel closer to God.'

Margarethe was more interested in the two white clouds that seemed to consist of many small stars. She pointed to them for Clara, who nodded.

'The Milky Way. See, in the middle there is a round dark-blue spot where not a single star can be seen. Like a life without faith.'

'You are really going into the right work for you,' Ida's tone was spiteful. 'Every word you say you bring God into it.'

Clara was unperturbed. 'Because he is,' she said serenely.

I envied her this quiet certainty about her life. My own was far more troubled. But then, Ida's life was less sure than it had been. That night, I listened as she slipped out of her lower bunk and dressed hastily in the dark. I wondered what to do. As she reached the door, I called softly.

'Are you ill, Ida?'

'No, just going up on deck for a breath of fresh air. This cabin is too hot at night.'

'Alone? Let me come with you.'

I knew this would not be acceptable, but I was half out of my bunk before she could respond. The other two slept on.

Her voice was sulky. 'I won't be alone. Siggi has asked me to come and see the stars with him.'

'Come here, child. Sit down with me a moment.' She did seem no more than a child. She was younger than my daughter.

'You are going to lecture me, aren't you?'

'No, my dear, I'm not. I'm going to tell you a story. It is so easy on a romantic dark night, when the stars are shining and a man you like is close, to let things happen that later you regret.'

'You don't understand. You're old. I'm young and I've been cooped up here like one of the animals in the hold. And Siggi makes me feel alive.'

'I wasn't always this age, Ida. And I do understand. But I also know just how easy it is to do something that changes your life. Think about it.'

At least she was silent, listening.

'You are missing your Klaus. You are missing that feeling of being loved and cherished. That's something we all want. But don't look for it in the wrong place and risk losing what is waiting for you.'

I had not meant to tell anyone, ever, about the old days with Kurt in the pine forest. And certainly not someone like Ida. But I did tell her, about myself and my feelings, and even of the child I had lost. I found myself wanting to make her see just how a life could be shaped in unplanned ways. I will never know how much she really understood of what I was saying, but she did not go to Siggi that night. And in the days ahead she was less often to be found with the young men.

I had not realised that Margarethe had woken and heard, but some days later she spoke to me.

'Please don't be angry with me, dear Anna. I could not help overhearing you with Ida. You did so well to tell her your story.'

'I hope this has not altered your opinion of me too much. I value your respect.'

'The opposite. I was so struck by what you said of our need, all of us, men and women alike, to be loved and cherished. I think perhaps you did not have it in your marriage.'

I nodded.

'But perhaps you are finding it now with Herr Eberhardt?'

So I told her of our conversation, and my reluctance.

'It would be a good match, and I like him very much. We could live together so well, so comfortably.'

'But?'

'But I do not love him. Nor, I venture to say, does he love me. Not the way I want. He is ten years older – that is no problem. But I am only forty-five, and I still want what I have had before, so many years back. I want to love, and be loved.'

The younger woman's voice trembled. 'Oh yes, I do understand. But I have never had this. Ach, there have been men interested, some. But no one who ever made me feel alive. And yes, passionate. Are you shocked at my talking like this?'

'Of course not. I think this is what all women want, whether we admit it or not.'

'Not Clara, perhaps?'

'Clara has found herself with God, it seems to me. If she were in the Roman church, she would make a good nun. As it is, she has found a field of service that satisfies her. And who knows? She may find within it a man who shares her faith.'

'So what will you do, Anna?'

'I will go on as I have planned. I'll search for Kurt – that is my first priority. And one day I may search for myself.'

CHAPTER 17

Victoria, Australia 1889

The easterly gales off the Australian coast were so vicious at times that sailors on watch were tied to the mast. Waves lashed the decks and we were confined below closed hatches. Would this journey never end?

Then we were past Cape Leeuwin, sailing the waters of the Australian Bight. An air of anticipation seized us. Washdays on deck saw us preparing clothes for landing, chests were brought up from the hold and our tropical garments packed away, even though we knew we were heading towards the southern summer. It was hard to envisage, this reversal of the seasons.

'Fancy,' said Ida. 'It will be summer and we will be celebrating Christmas. 'Do you think we will have goose, like at home?'

'More likely turkey,' said Captain Sass, overhearing her. He seemed to be everywhere at once, checking all details on his ship before arrival. 'These are British settlements, and their tradition is more often turkey and ham.'

There was great excitement when we saw Kangaroo Island. We had learned about these strange hopping creatures, which could bound over long distances and fight each other like grown men sparring. The island appeared as a long blue stripe on the horizon late one afternoon. Children ran gleefully along the decks, hopping like kangaroos – Clara had taught them about the native animals that they might encounter in their new homes. I did not point out that she herself was more likely to see these creatures where she was going than children in Sydney or Melbourne, where most of our passengers were destined.

Very early the next morning we entered the Gulf of St Vincent. On the right, the wooded heights of the coast of South Australia loomed attractively. Land was so welcome a sight. At the Semaphore, we waited until the pilot could come on board, but the sun had risen so the waiting was pleasant. About 7 am we arrived at the small harbour town, Port Adelaide, where the shallow water made it necessary for us to anchor a half hour out. The city of Adelaide, we knew, was a further two hours away, but with a good rail connection, so now began the unloading of goods by light barges, which continued all day in the still, oppressive heat that had descended.

Here we would part ways. There were tearful farewells with Clara and Ida in the cabin. We had grown close during these months at sea, and we knew that the chances of meeting again were slim. Letters would endure for a while, then busy lives would take over and our friendship would become a matter of memory. Treasured memory.

Even Ida, who now, full of anticipation, prepared to board the harbour steamer that would take her to the landing point and re-unite her with her Klaus, was more pleasant.

'I wish we could have seen him,' I said, and her face lit up.

'Oh so do I. He is such a fine figure of a man. I can hardly wait to get there.'

All thoughts of Sigmund seemed to be gone, and we kissed her and wished her well.

With Clara, it was harder. No one could tell what her life would be like in the centre of this vast land, and we promised that she would have our ongoing prayers for her safety and her work. She waved from little steamer – it seemed so small beside the *Elberfeld* – and settled her sedate black bonnet more firmly on her head as the wind lifted its ribbons. Then she too was gone.

'You will miss your friends,' said Herr Eberhardt as we prepared the final edition of our paper. We had heard of English ships creating an obituary page in the paper for passengers who departed at each port. So now Margarethe and I concocted mock eulogies for Ida and Clara. We avoided any mention of Siggi ...

Captain Sass had invited members of the newspaper team to a farewell dinner that night in the cabin passengers' saloon, where we dined on the fresh sea perch that had been caught that afternoon by fishing lines over the side. The bakery had produced a celebration cake, but the mood of the party was clouded by the sense of ending.

'You have helped,' he said, toasting us in champagne, 'to make this very difficult voyage more bearable for us all. The ship – all of us, passengers and crew – owe you gratitude. You have helped unite us all, from the youngest cabin boy to the officers on deck, from the smallest children to the oldest travellers.'

In our minds was the thought of the bodies we had consigned to the deep, those who had not reached the end of our voyage.

We took more coal aboard and, once cargo was unloaded, set off in the mid-afternoon next day. At first fine weather prevailed along the coast and as we passed we could see the steep sandy hills and scattered farms of this new homeland. A few forest fires were visible.

'These are lit,' Herr Eberhardt explained, 'to expedite the clearing of the land for cultivation.' He pointed with unusual excitement. 'But look, see there.' Children were running to the deck railing with cries of pleasure, while anxious mothers rushed to pull them back, then stayed fascinated.

'There are pigs in the water,' a little boy called.

'*Ach, Schweinfisch*!' murmured the woman next to us.

And indeed they did look like pigs, with their soft grey snouts surfacing and diving, and the solid sleek bodies rising glistening from the water. They surrounded the *Elberfeld*, giving us an acrobatic display any gymnast would have taken pride in. I looked enquiringly at the man beside me.

'I think they are called dolphins.' He was hesitant. 'I have read of them, and I know they are found in these waters.'

We stayed, lost in wonder at these strange new creatures, not really like pigs as we had first thought, but playful and unafraid. Then light drops began to fall, and in the afternoon blinding rain began and lasted until we reached our destination. Melbourne. Here Margarethe and I were to berth off the Railway Pier at Port Melbourne as the cargo was unloaded onto lighters, and we would leave our now familiar home.

We sat for the last time in our cabin, and looked at each other apprehensively.

'You will, at least, be met by your employers,' I reassured her.

'But you, Anna. What are you planning?'

I did not want to confess to the sick feeling in my stomach.

'I had hoped there might be some traveller organisation to help me, the sort that Captain Sass tells me exists in London and New York. But the colonies do not have such assistance. I plan to find a cheap lodging, and Herr Eberhardt is finding the names of appropriate newspapers where I might advertise for news of my son.'

'Anna, I am in awe of your courage. This is such an endeavour. You must love your son very much.'

'I am glad you did not say "fool's errand" like my family and friends at home. And yes, I do love Kurt dearly. Finding him has become the most important thing in my life.'

'More than your own chance of happiness?'

'Ah, but was that happiness, or just comfort? I don't know.'

We were silent for a while. 'Perhaps I never will find what I am looking for, but I settled for second-best for too long. No more compromises, even for so fine a man as August Eberhardt.'

'Well, please don't leave him to Frau Wandel's affections.'

'I don't think there's a chance of that. I have far more respect for his judgment. And anyway, we will remain friends. As will you and I, dear Margarethe.'

I was greatly comforted to have at least one friend in this strange city. She had given me the address of the family she was joining, and I tucked it safely in my reticule.

That Captain Sass was concerned for me I had always known, and now I could see him consulting with Herr Eberhardt. A part of me resented the assumption that I needed their protection; another part was more realistic. I had not worked out what I would do on arrival, and now the moment had come.

'We will not be leaving Melbourne until later tomorrow,' the captain said. 'You should stay on board tonight, and we will try to find a contact for you. Someone who might be able to find you a lodging where you will be safe.'

It would have been churlish, and indeed stupid, to have refused this help.

'There is a very active German Society in Melbourne,' he assured me. 'I have had dealings with them on a previous voyage, when my ship was held up here by a dockyard strike. I will give you names of people there, and I am sure they will help you. Perhaps Herr Eberhardt can find them for you.'

They were as good as their word and by the morning they had arranged for two members of the *Deutsche Turnverein* to help me to a lodging. I suspect that Margarethe parted from me greatly reassured that I was not alone in this strange place.

Saying goodbye to both Captain Sass and Herr Eberhardt was a sad affair, for I had grown in respect and liking for them both. But at least with the latter I knew the contact would survive. He had pressed addresses and contact points upon me, and I was relying on his advice for my next actions.

So I had some starting points, but when I stood on the wharf at Port Melbourne with my wooden chest and my bags I wondered once more what I was doing. Herr Eberhardt, always protective, helped me find Herr and Frau Lindner, who eyed me with some concern. A woman, on her own, with no contacts. I knew they were somewhat shocked. But kindly.

In spite of onlookers, he hugged me warmly.

'Do not forget. If you need anything, you are to call upon me any time. The paper will always know where I am.'

'I cannot begin to thank you – ' I began, but he cut me off.

'No, please. But if you should change your mind and decide to come to Sydney, you will be more than welcome.'

I could not bring myself to look back as we set off. If I had, I would not have been able to hold back tears.

Part *Three*

CHAPTER 18

Melbourne, Victoria 1889

Such kind people, the Lindners. Even though they were surprised – no, let me be honest – somewhat shocked at my recklessness in travelling across the world to search for my son, they treated me with generosity and friendliness.

When I think of them now, I can see their faces clearly. She was round and rosy-cheeked, a little dumpling of a woman, always fussing over something. Was I perhaps hungry? Had I eaten a good breakfast before departing from the ship? Had I brought appropriate clothing for the warm summer climate, for soon the hot Melbourne summer would commence, even though today was grey and cloudy?

'Hush, Mother,' her husband, no taller than his wife, but a thin stick of a man, put a hand on her arm. 'Let Frau Werner get herself organised, and her goods onto the wagon.'

They had hired a carter and wagon to take me to the lodgings they had found, and as we travelled I tried to get a sense of this strange new place. Everywhere building and activity. Streets crowded with well-dressed people, all moving purposefully through the maze of houses and shops that bewildered my eyes. Smart new carriages and small traps, strange vehicles unlike any I had seen moving on tracks on the streets.

'Ach, you are surprised at our city. We have seen it grow so much and change.'

'But what are those conveyances?' I was marvelling at the number of passengers seated on the benches in the open areas of these vehicles, and I could see many more in the closed interiors. At the ends, top-hatted men stood at the open railings, and even one woman, her long skirt blowing slightly in the breeze as the carriage rolled past our wagon at a steady pace.

'They are transforming our streets,' Herr Lindner was happy to explain. 'They are cable cars, new to our city. This route will take us to Richmond, where the first of these was seen.'

'Yes,' cut in his wife, 'only four years ago, the very first one. A grand occasion. So many people there to watch when the first one set off. Such cheering. Ach, the noise of it.'

'Have you travelled on one of these contraptions?'

Herr Lindner shook his head. 'They may be changing our roads, but I will keep to our faithful old Fritzi and the trap. It will get us wherever we need to go. But the cable cars are useful for those who had to wait for the public coaches.'

I had thought little about what this city – this 'Marvellous Melbourne' – would be like, and I was astounded by its size and the broad public avenues with their imposing buildings.

'But what is that?' I found I was gaping like an ignorant country girl, even though I had now seen cities in my homeland. Well, in truth I had not really seen much of the world – though Hamburg had opened my eyes. But this was even more splendid ...

The Lindners' faces lit up with pride. 'It is indeed something special,' they agreed, beaming at the vast wedding cake of a building as if they had built it themselves. 'It was constructed for the splendid international exhibition held in Melbourne eight years ago. Such an event. Goods from all over the world, and people visiting from all countries. A magnificent affair.'

'So too was last year's!' Herr Lindner was not allowing his wife to tell the whole story. 'Just last August another International Exhibition was put on – even bigger. Like a huge trade fair, with the whole world's products on display.'

'Wonderful displays.' Frau Lindner could not contain her enthusiasm. 'A working dairy! Steam locomotives. A fern gully with a fountain, built in France – and even a German beer hall! More than forty countries sent goods and displays.'

'It went for months. There were over two million visits to the Exhibition – it is a great pity that it closed at the end of January, otherwise you could have visited it.'

But my mind had focused on the steam locomotives on display. How this would have interested Otto. Otto, I had hardly given him a thought. And yet he had been the centre of my life for more than twenty years. No, I amended the thought quickly. Not Otto. He had never been the real centre of my life. Always the memory of Kurt, my first love. And Kurt, my son, who had replaced him in my heart. How he would have loved such a display, with its show of steam power. And where was he now?

Strange the way that, in all these last months of travel and hardship, in all the new experiences that life had brought me, Kurt was always present. Had it not been for that would I now, yes right now, be travelling on to Sydney to a new destiny with Herr Eberhardt?

'But you must visit the building while you are here,' they were urging me. 'It is used for theatre performances and for concerts and displays – oh, and often for gymnastics.'

'Our German Club is called the *Turnverein*,' said Herr Lindner with pride. They must have seen the lack of comprehension on my face, for he went on to explain patiently – and at length – the principles behind this activity. And its history. So I learned about the 'father of gymnastics', the Turnvater Jahn, who had started a gymnastics movement in the early years of this century during Napoleon's occupation of Germany. A movement that had spread throughout the land, and now the world, with gymnastic clubs in every place German emigrants travelled to.

'You must tell her about the four *F*s,' put in his wife.

'These are the basic principles of Turnvater Jahn. *Frisch, fromm, froelich, frei!* I am not sure what they would be in English.'

'I think you could say energetic, respectful, cheerful and independent,' I suggested.

'Your command of English is excellent. It has taken me many years to feel comfortable in this language.'

'That is also why the Club is so important to us. It is a place to relax and speak freely in our own tongue. It is one of the biggest organisations in Melbourne,' said Frau Lindner.

'Well, among our countrymen.'

'*And* women. There is talk among the younger women of the need for a Ladies' Gymnastics section. Herr Beer has said he would be willing to organise this.'

I was not really listening as they debated the suitability of gymnastics for ladies, or was it ladies for gymnastics? I was still marvelling at the huge Exhibition edifice we had passed, with its enormous dome and lofty tower (the highest in Melbourne, they assured me) and the complex of elaborate and ornamented buildings spread over many blocks of land, surrounded by green lawns and lavish gardens. When the trees grow to full height, I thought, this would be a sight for future generations to marvel at.

'But the German Club does many things. We have held some outstanding events with other German societies – '

'There are eleven different German clubs in Melbourne – music and choral and skittle clubs, and there is for almost thirty years a Sick and Relief Society for our people – and we have enjoyed great celebrations and balls.'

'A masked ball,' Frau Lindner reminisced. 'The Governor came, and his wife and entourage. It was a splendid night.'

'We could not have done it without the ladies,' her husband added generously. 'Your role in these events has been valuable.'

His wife shrugged it off, but I could see she was pleased.

'But here we are. This is where many immigrants come when they first arrive. Not just Germans, but from many countries. There have been so many that the government established this hostel. The costs are moderate – Captain Sass told us you wish to be economical.'

I was grateful for this; the matter of money was beginning to disturb me. I had spent little of the generous purse Lydia had bestowed on me, but it was not a never-ending supply – much as I would have wished it to be like one of the beloved children's tales Jacob and Wilhelm Grimm had written, where supplies of gold appear by magic.

'That is indeed the case. I have been wondering about obtaining work here if I need to stay for some time. I would be prepared to do anything – I mean domestic work.'

'That will not be a problem. There are many local agencies to find employment for ladies. We can get you the names. And we will take you to the German Club to meet people – you may make contacts there. Many of our members are from wealthier families, who may well know of others needing assistance.'

'You are very kind.' To my dismay I felt tears pricking my eyelids. 'I have been truly blessed in the help that people are giving me.'

'We know of your search for your son. But we will talk of that later. Let us get you settled in the Coffee Palace.'

'The Coffee Palace?' I was taken aback.

They laughed. 'The name by which this hostel is known by those who live here. Officially it is Richmond House. Come – we'll show you.'

When I looked back on this early encounter with the Lindners I realise how fortunate I was in their friendship. Without it, my arrival in this strange city would have been challenging. But by evening, settled in my small room in the Coffee Palace, I felt that my search had begun.

It was a surprisingly impressive building, and I wondered what it had been before the government took it over. I studied its street façade, the two extra storeys of symmetrical windows with pointed arches above the curving verandah that protected the street-level windows; a small square tower over the elaborate carved pediment, its mini columns topping the central bay window on the third floor. Little chance I would get one of those front rooms; more likely somewhere in the depths of the large building.

Its confident assertive air was typical of many buildings in this main street of Richmond, a suburb near the centre of

Melbourne. I was glad to be a little out from the city, especially as it was an easy walk. Fifteen to twenty minutes, and I could be in the heart of Melbourne. Or the excitement of the cable tram, just up the hill in Bridge Road. Here, in Swan Street, I could look toward the city, and the new railway overpass.

An exciting and busy street, this Swan Street, with its mingled shops and taverns, and small workers' cottages. The constant clatter of carts and traps in the road, and pedestrians picking their way over the open drains at the road's edge. Heavy porticoed stone buildings, elaborately ornamented with carved garlands and shields, or decorative patterns. This too was Marvellous Melbourne, the years of prosperity at their peak. Little did we know that the crash would start by the end of the year, and the financial disaster that led to the massive Depression was just ahead.

But my street, in 1889, was in magnificent mode, and I looked along the row of shops, the overhanging verandahs with their elaborate wrought-iron lace frills and intricate balcony railings, and the windows filled with a display of goods that made me gasp.

Confectioners and pastry cooks, small goods shops (such sausages and cheeses!), ironmongers and household goods, painters and decorators ('*We have the largest array of imported wall hangings in Melbourne*'), photographic studios and fancy goods, newsagents and stationers, butchers and fruiterers, milliners and drapers, a wine and spirits merchant – and all with such an air of confident prosperity that their future seemed certain. And I grew familiar with the names as I walked these streets: Sweeney and Howard, the Misses Parry and Nott (dress and mantle manufacturers), Murphy the pawnbroker, Smith the watchmaker, and Roberts, an umbrella manufacturer. Also the grocer and corn dealer Nathaniel Beesley, with his cheerful greeting for everyone who passed.

A maze of small side streets, with livery stables and coal suppliers, artists and music teachers, a military embroiderer, and what on this earth was a pyrotechnist anyway? There were occupations I had never heard of. Bricklayer I could comprehend, but Brooks & Co., with their patent damp course composition factory, left me bewildered.

In the middle of it all, the Coffee Palace, where I read with relief, on the noticeboard above the desk where Mrs Murphy reigned supreme, the City of Richmond notice advertising the scale of charges.

Breakfast, dinner and tea	*1 shilling*
Board and residence	*from 21 shillings per week*
Tea, coffee or milk, with pastry	*6 pence*
Hot and cold baths	
Club and other rooms to let for Lodge or Meeting purposes	
Dinners or parties catered for	
Billiards – 2 tables	

I was reassured by the costs and unsurprised to find that my room, at the lowest rate, was toward the back of this rabbit warren of a building.

'You'll be wanting after a cup of tea, I'd think.' Mrs Murphy's accent suggested that she'd been in the immigrant role herself not too long ago, but she was a canny businesswoman, and wanted my money before her grim-faced husband battled my wooden chest up the narrow stairs to my room. Maybe some of her immigrant patrons hadn't been too trustworthy.

A small room, with a narrow iron-frame bed and linen that

had seen better days. But it was passably clean, unless one looked in the corners. It seemed better not to look under the bed, but just be grateful for the worn mat and the open hanging space for clothing, as well as a washstand with basin and jug. I sighed. In fact, the *Elberfeld* had provided more comforts. At street level was a café, where lodgers were confined to a back area while members of the public had the street-front tables. That first cup of tea, weak and lukewarm, was not a good sign and as I looked at the food on nearby tables I vowed to hunt the area for something better.

Davidson's Oriental Bakery looked promising, though what exactly an 'oriental' bakery would provide intrigued me. But there was nowhere to sit there, so I walked on to find something more appealing for this first day in a new land. More promising, number 59, where Caterer and Pastrycook gave hope of better fare. The sign above the entry was inclusive: Afternoon Tea, Light Luncheon, Banquets and Balls, Wedding and Birthday Cakes a Specialty. These were G. Ohlenrott's offerings, and the name at least was reassuring. It sounded of home.

If G. Ohlenrott was the baker at the back, he deserved thanks, for the glass display case had familiar cakes. *Streuselkuchen* and *Pflaumenkuchen* might have come out of my own kitchen in Lewin. For a brief moment a wave of homesickness swamped me, and the self-doubt I had been battling since arrival. What was I doing here, in Swan Street, Richmond, in the colony of Victoria, instead of comfortably home where I belonged?

It was a kindly face behind the counter and, above the spotless apron, a welcoming smile. 'What do you wish?'

I stood tongue-tied. He tried to put me at ease. 'Can you speak English, *gnädige Frau*? *Oder sprechen Sie Deutsch?*'

Did I look so clearly German?

'It is the cakes.' I answered in English. 'I have not seen such a splendid display since I left home.'

'And from where do you come?'

'A small place. Lewin, south of Glatz. In Schliesen ... Silesia,' I amended it quickly.

'I know the area. My wife and I are from Breslau.'

How comforting. Here was someone familiar, someone who knew my background, who might almost have been a neighbour. That coffee with Gerhard and Trudi Ohlenrott made me feel, for the first time, at home in this new country, and I shall always be grateful to them.

They shook their heads when they heard I was at the immigrant hostel.

'It is a useful place,' said the baker, 'for many of those who come. But most will be young men, here to find work and make better lives for themselves. And sometimes young women, who have a somewhat different idea of how to make their way in the world ...'

His wife shook her head in reproof. 'Gerhard, you must not say such things. You do not know what their lives are. And Mrs Murphy will not put up with bad behaviour under her roof. She has sent girls away if she feels they are too forward with the young men.'

'It is a big place, and even Mrs Murphy cannot be everywhere. But you are right, my dear. We cannot know. Frau Werner has paid for one week at the Coffee Palace; after that we will find better lodgings for her. And till then, she can perhaps come to us for dinner and some real food, not Mrs Murphy's Irish stew.'

By the end of the week we were good friends, and used the

familiar forms of address. So in this place I was Anna, and they were Gerhard and Trudi, and they knew the story of my search for Kurt.

'Just think,' Trudi marvelled. 'He may well have come into the bakery during his time in Melbourne. But I find it hard to understand – how he could leave you for so long without word. I can see how close you were.'

'You are right, of course.' I felt miserable at the admission. 'But there were circumstances. Probably not good reasons, but they help me to understand.'

They looked enquiringly at me.

'We had been close, that is true. I begin to wonder if we were too close, and perhaps his boarding the ship for Australia was a way of breaking this tie. Then, having done that, to admit that so much had gone wrong would have been a humiliation for him. And he is proud.'

'Even so,' Gerhard muttered.

'Then there was the accident. Well, no accident. The beating that he suffered after he deserted the ship. In fact, the captain could have had him arrested for desertion.'

'But from what you have told us, that might have led to more questions than the captain wanted about the way he was endangering the ship. He probably did not want authorities involved any more than your son.'

'Still,' put in Trudi, 'to have him beaten and left in the street was a shocking punishment.'

'It was so fortunate that people from the German Club found and helped him. That they have an organisation for care of the sick and needy. I want to find and thank these people. And, of course, to see if they can give me an idea where he is now.'

'We may be able to help here, Anna. Gerhard sings in the club choral society, the *Liedertafel*, and he has many contacts in the club members – though we do not involve ourselves in the social life of the *Turnverein*.'

'Is there a reason?' I asked.

They both laughed. 'Can you see us in the gymnastics groups? We like our own cakes and pastries too much – and we are getting on in years.'

I shook my head. 'You both look in fine health and condition.'

'But we do have another reason. Many of those in the *Deutsche Verein* are of the Catholic faith, whereas we are *Evangelische*.'

'Lutheran, she means,' Gerhard explained. 'They are fine people in the club, but most of our friends are in the German Lutheran Church, here since 1852 – it was one of the first churches built in that area in East Melbourne.'

'Ah, another bond between us. I too belong to the state church, the Lutheran church that the Prussian king demanded as the official religion.'

'And look at the divisions that led to,' Gerhard reminded me. 'So many of the old Lutherans refused to accept this, and emigrated to where they could practise their religion as they wished.'

'Here too,' his wife put in. 'We have many throughout this land who came here for that very reason. Some in our state, but many in South Australia, where there are whole colonies of these Lutherans.'

'But your church?'

'Ours does not believe in fostering divisions. We follow the official books and liturgies of the state church, and our main interest is in keeping our language alive and teaching our young. So our services are always in German, and there are many whose command of English is very limited.'

'But not yours,' I laughed.

'We could scarcely succeed in business if we did not speak English to our customers. And we have succeeded.'

I looked around the spotless shop. 'That's very clear.'

They were as good as their word, and in the weeks that followed I was truly glad that I had followed my instincts into that pastry cook's shop. Or was I led? I know that Gerhard and Trudi would have said that, for their faith was both simple and profound, and they saw God's guiding hand in all aspects of their lives. My own was a more fragile and uncertain matter, and I envied them the depth of their conviction.

'We have found you somewhere to live,' they announced a few days after our first meeting. 'We have a good friend – you will have seen her shop just down the road from here. We are number 59; she is number 175. She has a business sewing goods and small things – she calls them fancy goods.'

'I think I know it. There's a fruiterer next door, and on the other side a hatter. Just near Docker Street.'

'You really have learned the neighbourhood in a few days,' Gerhard said approvingly. 'Her name is Mrs Clark, and she lets out rooms to ladies in the upstairs section of her house. Her charges are low, about the same as the Coffee Palace, but they say she is an excellent cook.'

'She has a vacant room so we told her about you. At first she thought not, because you might only be there a short time. But when we told her your story and the search for your son, she changed her mind. Would you like us to take you to meet her?'

I listened with great relief. The Coffee Palace had been

adequate as a temporary measure, but the noise of clattering feet and coming and going at all hours had given me little sleep. Too many taverns in this street also, and drunken laughter and girls giggling in the passageways. Sharing bathrooms had not been pleasant.

I needed to put my efforts into the task I was here for. I needed to find my boy, and there had been little progress. Gerhard and Trudi were arranging for me to see people they knew in the *Liedertafel*, who might have a recollection of events of two years earlier.

The Lindners also asked questions of others in their circles in the German Club, and I was hopeful that someone might remember the German boy who had been so badly beaten. And I needed to meet workers in the Health and Relief Society. There was much to do, and I hoped that, if Mrs Clark accepted me, I would be free to start the search.

I had dressed carefully for our meeting, choosing a sober black skirt and jacket with a grey waistcoat for respectability, and my small black hat with ribbons that tied under my chin. I knew that she too was a widow, though I doubted that she would have shared my relief at the end of a marriage.

The rooms upstairs had a separate entry from the street, and she took me through this door and up the steep narrow stairs. The door through to her private quarters was shut, and I perceived she valued her privacy. That would not bother me.

Beyond was a passageway with four rooms for her residents. Small, yes, but spotlessly clean, and a bathroom that I would be able to use without fear of disease. I nodded gratefully.

'This would suit me well,' I told her, trying not to sound too eager. For after a week at the immigrant hostel these rooms looked like paradise.

'You know the costs?' she asked. 'And I provide a good breakfast – *Frühstuck* I think you people call it – and a substantial evening meal. But for the middle of the day you'll have to find your own food. I have my shop to care for.'

'I would be happy with that arrangement. I will often be out during the day. I think you know why I am here.'

Her sharp face softened. 'Yes, your friends have told me. I know what it is to lose a son ... but that was many years ago. I understand a little of how you feel.'

'It is the one thing in life that I want – to find my boy.'

'You deserve to have your wish. And if you are in the house during the day and need food, feel free to use my kitchen.'

A rare concession, I sensed. All I could do was thank her.

'What about your goods? Are they still at the hostel?'

'The Ohlenrotts have offered to help me move them.'

And so I became a resident at number 175, where once again my wooden chest was carried up the hazardous stairs by Gerhard. By now, I was beginning to view that chest with mingled gratitude and resentment. Sometimes, I had come to realise, what is most useful is also most onerous.

CHAPTER 19

Melbourne, Victoria 1889

These weeks have passed in a dream. The places I have been, the people I have met. Once, in the Countess's library, she showed me a small metal cylinder, a kaleidoscope – or something of the sort.

'Hold it up to your eye, Anna,' she instructed me. 'Then turn it slowly, and see what happens.'

'It is magic,' I breathed as I watched the swirling patterns shift and change, the small coloured pieces creating new worlds of beauty. The object fascinated Lydia, too, and we spent happy hours twisting and turning the toy to find new delights.

These last weeks are, too, a kaleidoscope. The many people who have become a part of this strange life I now lead. Who could have contemplated a year ago that I would be on the other side of a world? A part of this bustling city, filled with energy and activity and ways of life so new to me?

I wonder at the brash and confident Melbourne, smug in its prosperity in spite of those who foresee an end to such a surging tide, and say it must turn. I talk about this often with Margarethe for, true to her word, she has stayed in touch with me and we spend her free day each week together. It is a relief to her, as it is to me, to have a friend to speak to, someone else for whom this is all new and strange.

'They are very kind, the Bauers,' she told me. 'The parents are good people, and they do their best to make me feel included in the family life. But their girls are conceited little minxes; they think because their father has money it makes them superior to the rest of the world.'

'How do they treat you?'

'Oh, like a servant. I swear that what they are looking for is not a governess, but a maid to fetch and carry for them. I am not surprised I am the fourth governess their mother has employed in the last few years. Not too many would want to put up with their airs and graces, and their lack of interest in learning.'

I was surprised by the bitterness of her tone.

'What do the parents do about this?'

'I doubt they are aware. They are kind, yes, but Herr Bauer is occupied with his business and Frau Bauer is very sociable. She is always busy with friends in the daytime and in the evenings they entertain.'

I could not see my friend fitting into this household easily.

'Do they take an interest in the girls' education?'

'Only that they should appear well bred in the eyes of their friends. Theodora and Ernestine are expected to play the piano and sing as part of the evening's gatherings, and to be able to make polite conversation. But as for having any real learning ... no, that is not wanted.'

'So your role is not what you had expected?'

'I tell you, Anna, if I could find other work I would leave the Bauers. But they are good to me and the payment is fair. And what else could I do?'

'Do you have the chance to meet people?'

'Not many. A few through the German Club – Herr Bauer is important there, and he is happy for me to come to the social evenings one night a week.'

'Margarethe, what about the people you meet there? Are they congenial?'

'Not particularly. They seem overly concerned with fitness and sporting activity – this is, I gather, one of the purposes of the club. And they seem to think I am fortunate to be with the Bauers living in their grand house in Toorak.'

She took me there one day when she was free. The family had gone for an outing with friends in the nearby Dandenong mountains. There had been several carriages at the family home before departure, and packing of elaborate picnic boxes and lavish hampers for the coachmen to load.

'A free day,' Margarethe exulted, for the outing had included younger family members. 'They did ask me if I would like to join them, but I think were relieved when I said I had a friend to meet. So come. Let me show you the house and my room.'

I think sometimes of that splendid house; the lavish reception rooms with their heavily curtained windows and elaborately carved furniture – though I was intrigued by the draped legs on the tables and chairs ...

'Why?' I asked Margarethe, as we sat with Cook over morning tea in the spacious sunny kitchen. 'Even the piano legs are curtained with wrappings.'

The young housemaid sitting next to Cook giggled. 'They say it's not decent to show legs,' she explained. 'That'd be disappointing for my Harry.'

'Hush, Tilly. Enough of that,' Cook rebuked her. 'But that's the explanation. All the big houses drape the lower parts of furniture. Mind you, I can't see it m'self. I doubt that seeing a table leg is going to drive a young man mad!'

'Not like the real thing,' put in Tilly, with another giggle. Margarethe and I looked at each other; we knew what we were thinking. It was like being with Ida.

The WC fascinated me the most. Three of them in this house, each with its own flushing cistern and a long chain to pull. And new-fangled special paper to use. I thought of the long treks on cold nights to the little shed at the bottom of Mrs Clark's garden, and the pail of ashes to tip with the small enamel pannikin into the tin bucket way below the wooden seat.

'They do live well,' I commented to Margarethe.

'In some ways,' she said dryly, as we tied our bonnets and set off for the horse-drawn tram that would take us to the city and our planned walk in the Botanic Gardens. The Ohlenrotts had told me about these gardens with great pride.

'It was,' said Gerhard, 'one of our own church members, Baron von Mueller, who created these splendid gardens.'

'He is one of our most respected members,' put in Trudi. 'He paid for his own pew in the church – for life. Even though it cost him £10 – and he is not a wealthy man.'

I looked confused and she quickly explained. 'We pay a pew rent for our regular place to sit in the church; it costs us £1 a year, but he has bought his for life!'

'But we are telling Anna about his gardens, Trudi, not the church. Over twenty years von Mueller was in charge and even though another man took over the job fifteen years ago, the Baron is still the government botanist for our colony, and watches over his gardens like a father.'

'If you go there,' advised Trudi, 'you must see the giant waterlily. You will not see it flower, but oh, the sight when it does.'

'It is one of the most amazing spectacles of the world, but it flowers only at night. The first year it flowered, when they brought it from the Amazon – '

'Twenty years ago now,' she interjected.

' – crowds queued for hours to see it!'

Margarethe and I wandered the gardens for hours, stopping for lunch at the wooden kiosk, near the splendid classical Greek building completed only a few years earlier.

'I know this,' I told her. 'The Ohlenrotts said it is a rarity in the world. A Museum of Economic Botany. We must look inside. Not only is the interior magnificent, but also the displays. Especially – and of course they were proud of this – the model fruit display.'

Margarethe looked curious, so I went on.

'So many fruits, and all perfectly made. They are papier mâché models, made in Germany, and there to teach farmers about possible crops they might grow.'

'But of course.' Mararethe's smile was impish. 'If they were made in our homeland ...'

We grinned. It was good to have a friend with whom I could laugh at the fierce nationalism of our countrymen.

It was these same contacts and their pride in their background that was helping me in my search for Kurt. Little by little, person by person, I was uncovering the events of two years before.

The Lindners had taken me to the German Club and the welcome had been warm and genuine. Often in those weeks I visited the splendid clubrooms in the heart of the city, where

Skat was the most popular pursuit, just as it was back home. I found it comforting to see the players gathered regularly, intent upon their cards. The Melbourne German ladies whiled away many afternoons there.

I suspect they viewed me with suspicion – this woman who had travelled alone from the homeland. Not at all suitable for a lady! Yet as I sat at one of the small tables where the groups of three players earnestly peered at their cards before making a bid, they were friendly and sympathetic about my mission. My story intrigued them.

I had been introduced to Frau Ursula Polkinghorne, the matriarch of the Skat players, and I found myself one day playing with her and her daughter. A formidable pair, stout and commanding, and after I had won my round on a foolhardy bid, they looked at me with grudging respect.

'You play a skilful game, Frau Werner,' the older woman commented. 'You deserved that success. Have you had similar good fortune with your search?'

'It is difficult,' I admitted. 'No one seems to know of my son.'

'You must meet Dr Menge,' her daughter decreed. 'If anyone can help you, it will be him.'

They were right.

'You are his mother!' said Dr Menge, when the friends I had made led me to the *Deutscher Krankverein*, the German Sick and Relief Society founded in 1861. It was not the only organisation supporting needy and unemployed Germans, but someone recalled the story of a young lad cared for by that group.

Dr Menge remembered it well. It had been a brutal beating, and as he told me of the injuries my son had suffered I felt a sick anguish. If kindly people had not found him and taken him to the hospital, if there had not been German nurses in the hospital who discovered his background from whatever remained in his pockets, if there had not been an organisation like the *Krankverein* to undertake his care, my search might well have ended right at this moment.

Except that it would not have been ended *well*. I knew that if my only discovery had been his grave, my own life might also have stopped. There would have been nothing left to live for.

Recovery, Dr Menge explained, had been a long slow process. But, gradually, bones knitted together, and torn flesh healed. Other damage, they feared, might have been permanent.

'His ears will never be the same again. In one ear the hearing is almost gone – the blows to the head have left it beyond repair – but the other has recovered remarkably well.'

'*Gott sei dank*,' I breathed. 'Thank God.'

'For many months he seemed to remember nothing of his past. There was no sudden return of his memory. Little things came back to him piece-by-piece. Once he was physically stronger, we found him simple work. There was building at the German church, a new manse for the minister. We talked to Johann Koch, the architect, who is one of our members, and he persuaded the good Pastor Herlitz to take him on as a labourer.'

'But he knows nothing of building. He was an engineer, a steam man.'

Dr Menge's face showed sudden comprehension. 'That explains many things. For many months he seemed to have little memory of any sort of work he might have done. He showed no expertise. Until the exhibition.'

'But wasn't that many years ago? No, I remember. There was another one, just last year.'

'Yes. The second one; it has just finished. Pastor Herlitz took Kurt when he and his family visited the new exhibition not long after it opened. Last August it would have been. A little over a year ago. They were very kind to him, and treated him like one of their family. He is a good man, Pastor Herlitz, though he has some difficult members in his flock.'

'But the exhibition?' I prompted.

'It was the moment a curtain lifted in your son's mind. The exhibition included so many trades and activities. It was bewildering: so many countries throughout the world. Displays of goods in many fields – I think we were all astounded at the range of goods and products. I was amazed at the medical equipment on show.'

I listened with impatience. 'But Kurt? What has this to do with my son?'

'We thought for a few minutes that he was lost, but then there he was. Standing, totally absorbed, in front of models of steam boilers. It was a Melbourne display; in fact it had won a gold medal for the manufacturers. The rest of us had little interest in it but Kurt was fascinated, his memory switched on. He knew who and what he was.'

I was not surprised. If anything could have got through to Kurt's flickering memory, it would be steam.

'From there,' Dr Menge continued, 'his memory returned and he started to make plans for the future.'

'Plans. What sort of plans? Do you know?'

'I am truly sorry. I do not know what happened. My wife died at that time. I was occupied and lost sight of the young man. Not long after I heard he had gone.'

'I am sorry about your wife,' I said quietly.

He shook his head. 'She had been ailing for many years, and was in a hospital for months before her passing. It was a merciful release.'

Maddening and frustrating. To feel that I was so close and then to see the door close again.

'This is hard for you, Frau Werner. I wish I could help you further.'

'Who else might know more? Who would he have talked to? Did he have friends here?'

'I think you will need Pastor Herlitz. He is the one most likely to help you.'

'I need also to thank you, doctor, for all you have done. Without you Kurt might not have survived the beating he had – I do understand this, and I am grateful.'

He looked embarrassed. 'I would like the opportunity to be of further help. Perhaps I might call upon you next week, after you have seen the Pastor, to help you plan the next part of your search?'

For a moment the thought crossed my mind that Dr Menge might be motivated by more than simple helpfulness, then I took myself to task. Anna, I chided, do not delude yourself. Just because one man on a ship found you attractive does not mean that others will also think you have appeal. And he has been a widower only a year.

Yet the idea of further contact with that undeniably handsome man, with his piercing dark eyes and neatly shaped black beard was not unwelcome.

'We will take you to meet the Pastor after the Sunday service,' suggested the Ohlenrotts, when I told them of my conversation with Dr Menge. 'Do you mean that the young man we saw working on the new manse construction was your son? That is an amazing chance.'

'Not so amazing,' said Trudi. 'Our community is very close, and our members look after each other.'

Sadly, Pastor Herlitz could not give the help I was looking for. He had known and cared for Kurt, but had little sense of where he might be now.

There was a hint of disapproval in the minister's words as we sat in the office of the bluestone church. Until the new manse was complete, this was where his business was conducted. The morning service was over, and I commended him on both the church, less than twenty years old and replacing the first church they had outgrown, and the congregation with its full-throated singing of German hymns.

'Many of our members would like an English language service in the Sunday evening,' he replied. 'They say it would appeal to our younger people. Yet for most of us it is important to preserve our mother tongue.'

'The organ is particularly fine.'

'A donation from two sisters in our membership. The Lord has blessed them with worldly wealth, and they believe in returning some of it to the church.'

'About my son. Do you have no idea where he has gone?'

'I expected him to confide his plans to me. Unfortunately, he did not.'

The disapproval was obvious now. 'He talked about a wish to go northward. Someone had told him there were German settlements in Queensland, and he seemed interested in these.'

I thought of this vast continent with dismay.

'That is so far.' My voice trembled, and he looked at me with pity.

'He planned to find work along the way, and he looked forward to seeing more of the land.'

So like Kurt, I thought. Seeking adventure. Moving on. No concern for the rest of us!

'Did he not send a letter to you? He was concerned lest you should be worried, and he had planned to write. He truly did think of you.'

'Oh yes, there was one letter – and I can now see why there was nothing for so long. All that he could say was that he was travelling north – '

'That is what he told me he intended.'

' – working as he went. He talked of the border area between Victoria and the next colony … is it New South Wales? A possible destination.'

I touched my pocket, where Kurt's last letter, ever more crumpled and stained, sat in my pocket like a talisman.

Pastor Herlitz was adamant. 'It is thoughtless of him, and I am disappointed. However, he suffered greatly after the beating. Who knows? It may have affected his mind more than we know.'

'A friend on the ship suggested I should advertise in newspapers in areas where he might be. There's clearly no point in using the Melbourne papers. He is gone from here.'

'We will help you find the papers you need. I agree with your friend. An advertisement is your best hope. Many people go missing in a new land. The papers are full of Missing Friends advertisements.'

'You have been very helpful. And also, I understand, your wife and family. Would you please give them my thanks?'

'I hope you will meet them soon. Today is very busy. I have a large confirmation class this afternoon. You will be in Melbourne for some time yet?'

'I am filling in some of the gaps,' I replied. 'I don't know what comes next.'

I had written to Herr Eberhardt with my new address in Swan Street and I waited eagerly for his advice on newspapers to try. It came sooner than I dared expect, and with it a letter that was in no way improper, but made it clear he was hoping to see me again.

We placed the advertisement carefully, as he had advised, in a weekly newspaper that he told us had a wide readership in the area – the Riverina.

'Not just once,' he had cautioned. 'It can too easily be missed. You will be offered a package rate for six issues. Take it. If after six weeks there is no result, we may need to try further north.'

And meanwhile? I set myself a target. My money would last me six weeks. I was assured I would have no trouble getting employment. If no response came in that time, I would need to work and save money to travel.

I placed the advertisement as he had advised. Six issues, and it cost less than I had expected. A simple few lines.

Missing Friends

Kurt Werner of Schelesian, Germany,

please SEND ADDRESS to your mother,

175 Swan Street, Richmond, Victoria

The typesetter had misspelled Schlesien, but I thought this would scarcely matter. I wondered if, in this country, I should have used the English 'Silesia' instead. Too late.

I wrote to both Lydia and Hanna, but without mentioning my plan of employment. I did not want either of them rescuing me. I am an independent woman. I can take care of myself. Or so I like to think.

Yet it was comforting in those next weeks to have friends and companions. I could go to picture galleries and shops with Margarethe. One could live on very little money if one did not buy much, I discovered. So we wandered through the big stores in central Melbourne with their dazzling displays, and I studied the fashions with interest. Cook and Co. in Collins Street had moved premises, and sought to entice new customers with their large advertisement for French and English millinery, lace visettes and dust cloaks, silk and muslin blouses, embroidered French robes, black lace scarves, sunshades and umbrellas – how Lydia would have loved this world.

As she would have loved the fashion reports in the newspapers. Mrs Clark took daily papers, like the *Argus* and *Herald*, and together we shook our heads at the finery of the grand balls and evening soirees. Did the Governor attend? We always checked for the descriptions of the vice-regal costumes.

'You should read the accounts of the fine dressing at the Melbourne Cup,' she advised. 'It was the week you came, though I doubt you would have known about it.'

'I did get some sense of it,' I admitted. 'In the Coffee Palace all they could talk of was the horse racing, and what horses they would bet on.'

She insisted on finding the following day's papers, and we

pored over the accounts of the clothes. Oh Lydia, I thought, you should be here for this.

With the Lindners I went on excursions, like a trip on the brand-new electric tramway that ran from Box Hill to Doncaster – a wonder to behold. The tram had been on show at the exhibition, and now the local papers were full of this grand event, its inaugural journey. Is this the way of the future? And what will happen to all the horse-drawn trams in Melbourne?

I scrutinised the columns in the daily paper, while the weekly *Richmond Guardian* told me each Saturday was happening in the area. For the shilling entry fee I could attend concerts and plays, and even Wirth's Circus – such a display of gymnasts and acrobats as I had never imagined. Often, yes, with Dr Menge, who had come to see me in Mrs Clark's parlour one afternoon, and had passed her eagle-eyed inspection. The Ohlenrotts spoke highly of him and approved our outings.

'The doctor has had little enough enjoyment in his life, poor soul,' said Trudi.

'His wife was ill for many years,' added Gerhard.

'And not much happiness for him before that,' Trudi commented, despite Gerhard's rebuking look. 'You know that is true!'

'It need not be said.'

'Oh, you men. Women are more honest about things.'

It was rare to hear a note of discord. They had a marriage and a companionship that made me realise how barren my life had been. No wonder I had clung to Kurt as I had. Too much, yes, I could see it now. So was I wise to still pursue him here? I had come too far to give up the search.

I was not alone in wanting more. The advertisement columns

in the personal sections were filled with advertisements for palm-reading, Tarot cards, astrological predictions, and then – for those prepared to be more direct in their approach – the Matrimonial Notices, like the *thoroughly respectable lady, sensible, refined, no money, who desired correspondence with a gentleman of means and good principles, a bachelor, widower, town or country*. That was, I thought, casting a very wide net ...

Dr Menge's company was a pleasure, and again I blessed the education the Countess had given me. We listened to the Victorian orchestra's afternoon performances in the Town Hall, and discussed the Weber, Brahms and Mendelssohn on the program, or commented on the *Merchant of Venice* in the city theatre. Even the Temperance Society's productions, or *Little Lord Fauntleroy*, with Daisy Hopkins, the celebrated child actress in the title role, had their own perhaps unintended humorous moments.

We talked easily, in a way as stimulating as my conversations on board the *Elberfeld*. This man too was interested in the bigger issues of the day, and thanks to Mrs Clark's daily newspapers I knew about the debates over federating the colonies and the strong feelings that issue aroused. Dr Menge was interested in a world canvas, and we argued the merits of local organisations sending money to support the London Dockers strike – such questions were of no concern to others in my friendship group. With them I had other experiences.

Kaleidoscope it was. Yet always the matter of why I was there, and what the next step would be. After four weeks I was becoming discouraged and my spirits were falling. So the suppressed excitement on Mrs Clark's face did not alert me, when I returned from an afternoon visit to the Ohlenrotts.

'The post has come,' she said. Even then, I thought only of Herr Eberhardt. It was too soon for mail from Germany.

'On the hall table!' She almost pushed me toward it.

A hand I could barely recognise, but the postmark made me draw breath sharply. The letter was from Albury, the biggest town in the Riverina.

CHAPTER 20

Albury, New South Wales 1889

Trains. No longer the cause of trepidation they had been. Once the sight of long platforms, ticket sellers' windows and ladies' waiting rooms had been daunting. And the grimy firemen who shovelled coal into the voracious fiery mouths of engines that belched black smoke against the clear blue skies had seemed escapees from Hades.

No longer. I pondered the new worlds I entered. Worlds I had never contemplated. I could only shake my head in wonder at how my life had changed.

So the thought of yet another sortie into unfamiliar territory brought only slight anxiety. What was more fearsome was the thought of what would await me on arrival. I distracted myself for a time thinking about trains, fascinated just as Otto had been by the way these powerful beasts could eat the miles and subdue the distances.

Even more strikingly in this vast land, where the mania for building new rail tracks seemed to have reached unbelievable excesses. It worried Dr Menge, who shook his head with foreboding.

'This country has gone mad. You would not know, Frau

Werner, how the property prices have exploded during the last years.'

'But people say there is an economic boom.'

'We flood the land with investment money from England. We build railways as if there can be no limit on our expenditure. And everywhere people spend, spend, spend.'

I was intrigued. 'But this is Marvellous Melbourne. There is money enough.'

'A fool's paradise. It cannot be sustained. This bubble has to burst.'

He was, of course, right. But for now my focus was not on economic problems. Granted my financial worries were growing, yet there was enough for the next stage of my travels.

I thought about these things to push to one side the matter that had loomed over me since the letter arrived. Who am I deluding? The letter had become the focus of my life. This was what I had come for: to find this boy I loved so much. Boy? I had to think differently. Kurt was no longer a boy, rather a man of twenty-three years, an age by which his father and I had two children and many years of marriage behind us. But was he still the son who had left me so many years earlier?

I had tried to understand the letter that had arrived. He had made clear the shock he had felt when my he read the advertisement. Shock, yes, and guilt. It was there in every word, in the knowledge that he had been wrong in his long silence. Apology, but not an explanation. Perhaps there was none.

I had tried to discern the tone of the writing. I was to come to him – that was definite, and whole-hearted. He could scarcely have done otherwise, on discovering that I had made this remarkable journey to find him. I scrutinised his words, desperate to read his feelings. Had Hanna been right? That this new land was for him an escape?

My thoughts went in circles, and I found it hard to share the genuine rejoicing of my friends. It was even harder to find answers when they asked why there had been so long a silence. All I could say was that he would explain it when we met.

I was to come to him where he lived and worked, in a small German community some ten miles from Albury, the border city I had heard of.

The Ohlenrotts were, as always, ready to provide information, as was Pastor Herlitz when he heard the news.

'There is a large Lutheran settlement,' he mused. 'Mainly Old Lutherans – ' I was always amused at the way his lip curled under the heavy black moustache when he used this term, ' – who wanted to get away from the state church Prussia had introduced. They went first to South Australia, many to the Barossa Valley.'

'I know of that place. One of the young women on my ship was going there to marry.' I thought of Ida, and wondered if the wedding had taken place.

He brushed aside my comment. 'A stiff-necked people. And determined. Many set off with bullock wagons – perhaps thirty years ago – and made the long trip from South Australia to take up land just over the border.'

'In New South Wales?'

'They'd heard good reports, so they sent one of their own to investigate. He came back urging them to pack their wagons and go.'

'That must have been a major enterprise. Almost another exodus.'

Pastor Herlitz looked at me with approval. The Biblical reference had appealed to him. They were, I had noted, always a way to his heart.

'Their spirit was good, *ja*! They had their own ideas, that is true. Then, when there were disagreements, they divided into different synods. The foolishness. They would have been better to bury such controversies, and stick to the official church.'

I could see that he was congratulating his own church on having avoided dissension. He had made me wonder what sort of people I was going to find there.

Gerhard Ohlenrott was concerned for me.

'It is a long train journey. About eight hours, I think. At least these days the train crosses the river and goes from Wodonga, on our side of the border, to Albury, over the Murray.'

'There is a new bridge,' Trudi added. 'It was only opened four years ago. Before that train travellers had to leave the train at Wodonga and continue to Albury by coach.'

'That is, a new rail bridge,' her husband added. 'Now the trains can cross that mighty river and take travellers into New South Wales.'

'But there they all have to leave the train, even the ones who wish to travel on to Sydney. That is a different train.'

By now I was used to conversations with the Ohlenrotts. It was like the interweaving of pieces in a patchwork quilt.

'The stupidity of it,' Gerhard shook his head. 'It makes you see why there is so much feeling about the need for our colonies to join in federation.'

He saw that I did not comprehend.

'The rail tracks,' he elaborated. 'In Victoria the size of the track – the gauge – is different from that in New South Wales.

So no train can travel straight through. Everyone must change to a new conveyance.'

I smiled at the formality of his speech. Although his many years in Melbourne had made him fluent in English, he, like many of the new friends I had made, still showed their origins in their use of the new language. Elaborate and precise, it seemed pedantic. I sometimes wondered if my own sounded the same, though many years of practice with the Countess had given me ease speaking in this second tongue. I have read that if a child acquires a new language in the early years, it will remain. It seems so, and I often blessed the woman who had given me so much.

'Yes,' Trudi chimed in, as always adding her piece. 'You will find there are two platforms in the big new station in Albury. One side with one gauge for the train from Melbourne, then on the other side the gauge for the train from Sydney.'

'I wonder,' he speculated, 'if federation will mean that one day the whole land will be united in rail travel.'

She laughed. 'That will mean that someone must yield. No one will do that.'

I remembered this conversation the afternoon I finally stood on that platform, gazing down the impressive length of that showplace station, trying to quell the sick sense of anticipation that had been building throughout the journey.

But that was all ahead of me as I told my friends the news and prepared for departure.

'Kurt says that he will meet me at the Albury station,' I assured them. 'It will be late in the day when I arrive. His employer, Herr Bergmann, has allowed him to bring the wagon to take me to his farm. I am to stay there with him.'

Margarethe was concerned. 'You do not know where you are going!' She shook her head. 'This is too uncertain.'

'It seems this is where Kurt has been working for the past year. I find it hard to see what work he would be doing on a farm – it is not his type of work at all. Still, I suppose he could work as a labourer anywhere.'

'What sort of people are they, where you will be going? It is too unsure.'

'Margarethe, you did not know what sort of people you were coming to, when you set sail for Melbourne.'

She grimaced. 'That's what I mean. If I had known just how difficult those girls would be, I might never have taken this position as their governess.'

I had known that her life in the Bauer household was not happy, and I grieved for her. She had become a dear friend, someone I could confide in, and more than any of the others she understood something of the fear I felt about meeting my son. A thought had come to me of making her life more bearable.

'Can we,' I asked Dr Menge one day, 'take a friend of mine when we next go to the Gallery? I know she would enjoy the exhibition.'

Melbourne's National Art Gallery had just re-opened, after being closed for many months for renovations and repairs. He and I had spent happy hours there, impressed by the imposing State Library buildings to which it was attached. We stood on the green lawns surrounded by a wrought-iron fence and gazed at the bronze lions in the entry area, and admired the most recent acquisition, the statue of St George and the Dragon, which English sculptor Sir Joseph Boehm had just installed.

'Mmph,' grunted Dr Menge. 'At least his name is German, even if he is an English artist!'

I was constantly amused at the show of devotion to the Fatherland. A fierce nationalism, and the strength and numbers in the German Club seemed amazing in this new land.

This art gallery was, he had claimed, the oldest in the colonies. Started in 1861, and often extended. I knew Margarethe wished to see the new Buvelet Gallery, but I confess my wish to have her join us was not inspired only by a desire to show her paintings. I had hopes that my two friends might find each other pleasant company, for they seemed well suited ... Yes, I admit it; women are hopeless romantics. Or, in this case, hopeful.

The Lindners too were uneasy about my setting out on what seemed to them a perilous adventure. I smiled to myself. This seemed so slight a journey, compared to what I had already done. And yet, as my reunion with Kurt drew closer, this next stage seemed to me also more threatening.

They fussed about me, helping with preparations for the journey, checking train timetables and purchasing my ticket.

'We shall miss you at the German Club,' they assured me. 'You have become a part of our lives there. And Dr Menge will be sad to see you go.' Their smiles were arch.

'He has been pleasant company,' I replied. I did not add that I had done my best to ensure that he had company after my departure.

Mrs Clark was practical. We had an easy companionship; the loss of her son to typhoid fever during an epidemic had given her a warm interest in my search and sympathy for my feelings. Her joy at the way my advertisement had been answered was almost as great as mine.

'You do not want to take that big chest with you,' she insisted.

'It can stay here until you see what will happen. Take just a smaller valise. We can send the chest to you if you plan to stay there. If not, you will be most welcome to return.'

I hugged this option to myself like a security blanket. I knew, from talking to the other boarders in her house, employment would be easy to find. I could save money for a return trip to Germany. Or to stay here, where I had made friends. Or even to travel further, to Sydney, and see what life offered me there. I had come to see that my life was by no means over.

As I stood on the platform of Spencer Street Railway Station, I looked at my new friends with affection. The engine had been shunted into position at the front of the train, and porters were heaving the great sacks of mail into the carriages that awaited them. This was a mail train, providing communications throughout this huge country.

Goodbyes are always painful, and I hoped to make these swift. But the Ohlenrotts were determined to wait until the train left, and Dr Menge seemed forlorn. I touched his hand.

'I rely on you, my dear friend, to look after Margarethe for me. She is alone in that household, and I know she values your friendship.'

He was not a stupid man, and the look he gave me was shrewd and understanding. He nodded.

'I will miss you, Frau Werner, and the pleasure of our companionship.'

People were boarding the train, and whistles were sounding in warning of departure as carriage doors clanged shut.

We opened the door to my compartment, and stowed my luggage. A relief, I had to admit, to have abandoned the big wooden chest. Yet I felt almost disloyal, abandoning it after so much travel together.

'I'll come back for you,' I vowed silently, 'just as soon as I see what happens next.'

Part *Four*

CHAPTER 21

Jindera, New South Wales 1889

Though I have often tried to recall details of that journey, they remain stubbornly elusive. A haze of people. The young mother, with her baby clutched close to her breast while she tried to occupy the little boy who wanted only to escape the confines of the compartment and run into the side corridor that bordered these boxes. Had Kurt ever been as active, as hard to control as this imp? I thought not. The elderly ladies, who so carefully dusted the seats before settling themselves, and demanded the windows be closed lest smut and flying ash from the engine pollute our air. The young man who looked over his fellow passengers with boredom and retreated to the safety of the newspaper that obscured him from our view. Would Kurt behave like that? Round in circles, my thoughts. Always Kurt at the centre, and growing panic.

Jigsaw memories of the train making interminable stops at little country stations – for it was, after all, the mail train. Mailbags unloaded and received, before the long hoot of the whistle sounded and we rattled into life again.

Longer stops, I do recall, at bigger stations with their chances of food and drink. Seymour, Benalla, Wangaratta. At one of these, Benalla, I think, I held the baby in the station hall while her weary mother bought sandwiches for herself and her little boy.

'No, thank you,' I replied to her offer to purchase for me too. I could not have forced down food, though I recollect a cup of hot strong tea from a platform food bar. By then the little boy had fallen asleep, and the young man had escaped to the pleasures of solitude and a cigarette at the station. Why, I wondered, had he not chosen a smoking compartment? The fierce glances of the lady opposite him had made it clear that ours was not, when he first brought out his cigarette case.

Such bits and pieces come back to me. Of the countryside we passed I remember nothing, and little settlements with pretty names, like Violet Town, are only blurred memories. It was summer, that I knew. The foot warmers provided in each compartment remained unused and the view out the windows seemed an unending sea of golden wheatfields. Hours were lost in apprehension.

Even the last stretch of the journey, from Wodonga across the new railway bridge, has left me with no sense of the border crossing or of the mighty Murray River. My focus was ahead.

Albury station, and the longest platform, apart from Flinders Street Station, in the land. 'It had to be,' they'd told me. 'It had to take two full-length trains each side.'

Now I waited until the mother had managed herself and her children off the train, helped by the young man.

'Wait a moment,' he said to me, 'and I'll help you with your bags.' I silently apologised for thinking him surly. Would I have expected Kurt to chatter to a group of women on a train? I manoeuvred my two bags down the steps and gazed at the length of that enormous platform, wishing only to walk across it to the Sydney train on the other side. What had possessed me to do this? To come here?

No matter how I try, I cannot recall more than the first words we spoke. I can see him coming towards me, a dark head I recognised, his figure larger and clearer as he moved through the disembarking passengers toward me, my bags beside me. I might have been paralysed; my feet would not obey me.

He did not pause until he stood in front of me, then shook his head slightly and smiled. 'Oh, *Mutti*!' he said, and the years fell away at the sound of that childhood name.

We held each other close, and suddenly all my apprehension was gone. This was the son I loved, and the months, the years, I had lived through were forgotten. My search had ended.

It was only as we settled ourselves in the wagon, and the horses began the long trek home in the haze of this late-afternoon sunshine, that I looked back at the station. It gleamed in the full light. A building to rival any I had seen in my homeland. It was, I knew, Italianate in style, with the clock tower above the centre, though no clock face had yet been installed. The perfect symmetry of the two brick wings, the long verandahs with the double cast-iron columns, the detail of the pediments, the architraves, the arches, could have graced any European city.

'They said it was a splendid building,' I commented. We both sensed a need to keep talk light and casual.

'It is indeed. Not yet ten years old. There was a temporary station here, but this one was designed by Mr John Whitton, a name known to everyone in the area. It had a splendid opening, with the premiers of both the colonies attending. An unusual sight – to see New South Wales and Victoria together.'

'I understand there is great rivalry between the two. Back in Melbourne they are constantly telling everyone how superior it is to Sydney.'

'If federation does come about, there's going to be a problem with the choice of national capital. Both will expect it.'

'Perhaps they will need to find a new place and make it the capital.'

'Perhaps. Now we begin the trip home – more than ten miles we must travel, and these horses are strong but not fast, especially with this wagon.'

A pang went through me when I heard his easy use of the word 'home'. I looked around me at the city we were passing through.

'Tell me about it, about where we are going. And who will be there.'

'Right now we are leaving the city of Albury. I will bring you to see it properly some time soon. It's worth exploring – the way that you and I explored Breslau in the old days.'

That touched my heart, the recollection of our times together there. I knew that we would talk, talk properly, of what had happened. But not yet. We needed to feel our way back into our relationship, and it could not be forced. Yet so tempting to reproach him vehemently. *How could you do this to me? What did I do to be treated like this?* So tempting, but I bit back the words.

'So this is not really the city?'

'These are just the outskirts. We need to set off for Jindera, where you will be staying.'

'Staying where?'

'I had thought of finding you accommodation in one of the hotels in Jindera – there are four to choose from – but Carl would not hear of it.'

'Carl?'

'Carl Bergmann. I have worked for him on his farm for almost a year. "Your mother comes this distance to find you," he said, "and you think to put her into a hotel! She will stay here with us." '

I silently blessed this Carl Bergmann for his understanding.

'Who is in the household?'

The horses were keeping a steady pace, and already we were out of the settled areas and into countryside. I looked with interest at the cleared fields where flocks of sheep were grazing, quite different from the forest ranges outside Melbourne.

'Carl's wife died in childbirth just before I came to him. He was left with a baby son. I think that is why he took me on, to have someone to assist with the outside labour and to give him time with the children.'

'So he is quite a young man? Not much older than you?'

Kurt looked surprised. 'No, no. I have given you the wrong impression. I think he must have married late in life. He is actually quite old – even older than you, *Mutti*.'

I felt a flicker of annoyance. I had only just stopped thinking of myself as old, and I did not welcome being put back into that category. Still, to my son anyone of fifty would have seemed elderly.

'Who cares for the baby?'

'Carl's sister has come to help him. The older girls, Elsa and Adelina, assist with work inside and outside when they are not at school. It is a household where everyone works hard.'

'There are a number of children?'

'Six, if you include the baby – little Fritz, they call him. Also girls come from nearby farms to work when they are needed. It is the way things are done here. And there are other workers, but no one who understands machinery. Carl is a progressive man who wants to use the new inventions on his land.'

'I think I see why you would have found a place here. Always machinery. Any steam engines here?'

I laughed but Kurt took the question seriously.

'There are huge opportunities in this land for steam, *Mutti*. Landholdings are vast. One could develop all sorts of steam machines to help farmers.'

'Land instead of sea?' I asked.

'Perhaps. It could be done.'

'You would like to stay with him in this country? What about your homeland, and your work with ships?'

He paused and reflected. 'I think that last voyage on the *Hohenzollern* has cured me of a love of ships. I do not want to go to sea again. Can you understand?'

I did understand. The experience had been a nightmare for him. I was beginning to realise that he now saw his future in this land, not at home with me. And still I had not told him anything of home, not even his father's death, nothing of his sister. That was another life, one that he had put behind him. Or had the beating blotted out that life, I wondered.

'Then, you wish to stay with Herr Bergmann?'

'It's interesting that you ask. In fact, I felt my work with him was done, and that he needed me no longer. So I had decided to move on.'

'You haven't changed. Always the wish to move on!'

He shrugged. 'I know. There is always the feeling that better prospects are elsewhere.'

'It's an American proverb, Kurt. The grass is greener over the next hill.'

'Well, it's how I feel. American?'

'Yes, I recall the Countess telling me about it. She said it's a much older idea, and comes from a Latin poet. Ovid, I think.'

He ignored this diversion. 'I'd always planned to move on. I was making for Queensland, where a shipboard friend told me there were German colonies and good prospects.'

'I think you told me this plan.'

'Actually, more than a plan. I'd said my farewells to Carl and had set off up the road with my swag.'

'Swag?'

'It's what they call it here. Your bedding and equipment. The men who wander around the countryside looking for work are called swagmen.'

'And that's what you were going to do?'

'It's how I got here. If you're willing to work, there are always jobs available. Sometimes a day or two, sometimes longer. You get your keep and a little bit of pay if you're lucky.'

'You said you'd set off.'

'I can hardly believe it. I know you'll see it as God's hand – ' my son smiled indulgently, ' – and I almost agree. That day, just after I'd set out, Carl went to the post office where his copy of the paper, the *Albury Banner*, was waiting. He took it home to read with his morning coffee – and there saw your notice in Missing Friends, asking me to get in touch with you in Melbourne.'

It seemed incredible. Such an unlikely chance. He went on.

'Carl says he shouted out to his sister, "Magda, that's the young chap who's been working here. His mother's in Melbourne, and she's looking for him." '

I was listening in disbelief.

'So she said, "Go after him!" And he did. Got on his horse and chased me all the way to Walbundrie. Gave me a tongue lashing when he found me,' he said. 'Asked me what I thought I was doing, making you come hunting for me. Put me on his horse and brought me back. Sat me down and made me ride the four miles to the post office with the letter before sundown.'

There was nothing I could say. It was a remarkable story. If it hadn't been my son telling me I would not have believed it.

'I owe him a huge debt. Without him ...' I could not finish.

We travelled in silence.

The countryside had changed. The horses were labouring now, up hills that were no longer pastureland, but uncleared bush country. This was the 'bush' that they had told me of in Melbourne, and more like the ranges I had seen there. The road was rough and rutted, and I could imagine that in winter it could become impassable. Tall gum trees lined the route, and filled the valleys and patterned the hills with their green and grey. So different from home, and yet strangely beautiful. I could imagine winter bringing a carpet of green under the trees but now, in summer's heat, all was brown and yellow, with tall dead grasses drooping in the early evening warmth. Shadows were lengthening as sundown approached.

It was December, surely a time of snow and chill. I had trouble adjusting my thinking in this world of reversals. Soon it would be Christmas. How could one have a Christmas without snow? I pondered where my Christmas would be. My search for Kurt was at an end, what would follow? Strange that I had never looked beyond finding my son, never contemplated if this was to be the end of searching. A wave of affection swept over me, and I touched his arm.

'I am so happy to have found you,' I began.

He looked at me with the love I had come to depend on. 'And I, too, believe me. We have a lot of talking to do. Not today. Let us just enjoy the fact that we are together again.'

I nodded. Now we were through the hills. 'Is it much further?' I asked.

'That road was Jindera Gap. A gap in the mountains enabling the road makers to construct a route. This is the way the settlers came, bringing their covered wagons from South Australia. Whole families of them, opening up this land and making small villages like those at home.'

'Do the Bergmanns live in a village?'

'No. First we go through Jindera – we are getting used to the new name. When early explorers came, it was called Dight's Forest. Hamilton Hume named it after his friend John Dight, and for many years, even when our countrymen came, that was the name for the settlement. Then four years ago the name was changed to Jindera.'

'Where did that name come from?'

'No one is sure. Some say it was a native word from the tribes who lived here; others say it was just a made-up word. We don't know.'

'The Bergmanns have been here a long time?'

'Yes, Carl's father was one of the first, he tells me. For three years, groups of settlers came from South Australia. They had arrived in that colony hopefully, but the best land was settled, so they decided to try elsewhere.'

'Surely a brave decision, with families to care for.'

'His father brought them here in 1868 – it's odd to think that I was only a child of two back then.'

For a moment I was back in Lewin with a little girl of four

playing with her small brother, and Otto, young, strong and fit, coming home from Glatz at the end of a train-driving shift, to a wife who had never given him her heart. I would always blame myself for our lives together. I should not have married him. But if I had not, there would have been no Kurt beside me today, travelling through this southern land in the December sunshine. It was time to tell him.

Kurt did not seem surprised to hear of Otto's death.

'It is sad to say. I cannot feel grief. And I somehow knew it. You would not be here if he were still alive. You would not have deserted him, no matter what he did.'

It was true. None of it would wipe out the past, and we both knew it. Even my words about Otto's dying message to Kurt could make little difference. At least he could hold that thought and perhaps one day forgive his father.

'So is this Jindera?'

I was surprised as we entered the village. I might almost have been at home. Elm trees, twenty years old and flourishing in this southern climate, lined the main street, set out as it would have been in my own land, with houses that might well have been in Schlesien. Small places, some with just wattle and daub walls, others whitewashed and more prosperous looking. A mixture, and thriving. At least four hotels, one of them a square rugged two-storey building that looked long established.

Kurt's eyes followed my gaze. 'The Dight's Forest Hotel.' He commented, 'That one is very popular.'

I could see a substantial general store, with a familiar name over the verandah. Wagners. Also a butchery. Then a flour mill. A post office.

Kurt indicated. 'The Misses Spence. The postmistresses – and communications experts. They are the most efficient circulators of news in the village. They know everything that happens – and then so does everyone else.'

We smiled at each other. 'In a few years so much has been achieved.'

There was little time to gaze around for shadows were now falling, and we had four miles to go. Kurt turned the horses to a side road and the track became still rougher.

'There are a number of farms along the Four Mile Creek Road,' he said.

'Across the fields?'

'Here they are called paddocks,' he told me.

'Paddocks.' Another new word for me to try. 'And those are farm houses?'

'In this community we all know each other. And everyone knows everyone else's business. By tonight the whole area will be aware that Bergmann's man has a mother visiting from Germany. You will be famous.'

'That I can do without,' I said drily.

'Ah, but wait until you go to church on Sunday ...'

I was surprised. 'You go to church here?'

'Everyone goes to church. These people came to the colonies for the sake of their religion. They are not likely to abandon it now.'

'So they are Lutheran.'

'Oh yes. Not just one sort of Lutheran. They might have escaped the state church the King wanted to enforce in Prussia, but that stubborn-mindedness has led to further divisions. They take dogma seriously.'

I was puzzled. 'What do you mean?'

'They fled Prussia for freedom of religion, but here they cannot agree on exactly what they believe. In this tiny place we have two Lutheran churches, from the two main synods established in South Australia.'

'You are surely not serious. Two Lutheran churches in this Jindera.'

'And in all the other settlements in the area. Oh yes. At least both groups send their children to the one school. That was the first thing they did in 1868. Only a log cabin, but they built a school.'

'That has always been central in our faith. Church and school – they go together. Yet two churches! Such foolishness.'

'I can explain all this later. We are at the Bergmanns.'

By now the light had almost faded, but the animals knew where they were going, so we had not used the lanterns in the wagon. Ahead I could see the dim outlines of a house. No, of two houses. An older one, crouching white under massive overhanging trees. Then, beside it, separated by what looked like a garden, a newer house, a red brick square. From its windows, lamps cast a welcoming glow. As the wagon came to a stop, a door opened, and I saw a dark figure silhouetted against the rectangle of light, then come across the verandah toward us.

'There is Carl,' said Kurt unnecessarily. 'We are home.'

And, for an oddly comforting moment, I had a sense that he was right.

CHAPTER 22

Jindera, New South Wales 1889

How different my life has become, caught up these last weeks at Bergmann's farm. Or, *Lobethal*, the valley of praise, as I am learning to call it. It was the word the old man, the Bergmann father, used when he brought his wagons and his family to this untouched country twenty years ago.

They tell the story quite reverently, of how the man, strong and in his prime, gathered his children and his workmen and gave thanks to God for this land even before the wagons were unloaded and the first trees cut for the huts they would build. It will be, he told them, a place of praise to the good Lord who had brought them safely here.

Yes, brought here safely perhaps. He did not foresee that a mere two years later he would be carried on his wagon to the new graveyard they had established near the first church, a church he had built with his countrymen in the Dight's Forest settlement. Nor that his son Carl, still in his twenties, would inherit not just the land they were clearing and the house they were building, but also the mother he would now have to care for. The older sons were already gone, taking up land for themselves and the families they were creating, while Carl was left with his Valley of Praise to establish.

'My father's dream,' he said to me one night as we sat after supper in the big kitchen of the New House. 'I knew I had to make it what he had wanted.'

'You were such a young man,' I protested. 'It was a lot to undertake.'

'He died so young,' he meditated. 'There was so much he wanted to achieve here. Even when he lay dying under the tree that had felled him – '

'So it was an accident that killed him?'

'*Ja, genau.* Clearing the back paddocks. It's strange that he could have let this happen. He was a good woodsman. But even the best can make mistakes.'

We sat silent a moment, while he drew on his pipe.

'I was with him as he died. It was his last wish, with the little breath he could draw. "Make it a true Lobethal, my son." I have tried.'

'And so you have done. What you have achieved here is ... I do not know what word to use. Not just the Old House, now this new one too. And the land you have cleared and sown, the size of your flocks, all this. Did your brothers help?'

'When they could. They too were making their homes and had their families to care for. I think they were happy to know our mother would stay here with me.'

I must have looked my enquiry.

'She was not an easy woman to live with,' he admitted. 'None of their wives would have taken her in. I had none, so was willing to accept her for what she did for me. Without her those early years would have been more difficult.'

'And you? Then you married?'

'Against her wishes. She said she would never share her

household with another woman. Indeed it would have been a miserable existence, for Frieda also was a strong-willed woman. We built this new brick house to be our home.'

'Forgive me. I had thought your wife's name was Eda.'

I spoke tentatively, lest talking of the wife who had died in the last year might be painful for him. It did not seem so.

'No, Eda was my second wife. Frieda was the mother of my children – except of course for Friedemann, who came as Eda died. In childbirth. He was our first child.'

As if in answer to the sound of his name, there came the sound of crying from the next room, and Carl went to check. He returned with the child in his arms, where he settled and looked sleepily around the kitchen.

'It's a strange thing,' he sighed, bringing the infant to his chair in the firelight. 'I married Eda, God forgive me, to have a mother for my children. Now I have one more child and again no wife. If it were not for Magda, I would have even more problems to deal with.'

'You did not marry for love?'

'Eda was little more than a child herself. Only twenty years of age. She had worked here for Frieda, and I knew she would be a good housekeeper. There were reasons to marry, and the children seemed to like her. It seemed a solution to the problems when Frieda died.'

'Sometimes solutions do not work for the best,' I said. The picture of my wedding day with Otto was clear in my mind, and the picture of my wedding night.

Carl looked at me. 'You speak feelingly.'

'Some day I will tell you about myself. Not tonight. When you married Eda, you must have still been grieving, surely, for your first wife. It was so soon after her death, and I think that you had cared for her throughout her long illness.'

He shrugged. 'True. I think I was exhausted. And so fearful for the children. I should not have made such a mistake again.'

'A mistake?'

He patted the child, sleeping once more, and ran a ruminative hand down the trim dark beard with its streaks of grey. 'You said I was grieving. That is not so.'

I stayed silent. Questioning seemed intrusive. If he wanted to speak on, he would.

'I do not know why I am telling you this. I would like to be truthful. I was sad, yes. Frieda and I had been together for fourteen years. We had worked together. We had lived together. We had six living children, and the ones we had lost. She was a good woman, and I think she cared for me.'

He paused, and remembered, for a time.

'I should not have married her. It was her sister I loved. Her younger sister. It was Maria I loved, uselessly. Her heart was already taken. And Frieda and I were both getting older, and we wanted children. Perhaps she loved me. I know only that the affection I had for her was nothing like what I felt when I was with Maria. I should have listened to my heart. Instead, we married.'

'How did your mother feel about it?'

'She stayed in the old house, and would not move into this place with us. I think she knew she would be no match for Frieda. She died there. Perhaps it was her punishment for me.'

'Your marriage?' I asked tentatively. 'You were happy in it?'

'We were comfortable together, but she understood more than I realised. After she died I found that she had destroyed all pictures of Maria in the big Bible.'

The child stirred, and Carl carried him carefully back to the cot in the next room before returning. 'I should not have burdened you with all this. I do not usually talk about my life in this way.'

'Sometimes it is good to talk. Now I must go to bed. The children wake early.'

I took my candle and moved through the flickering shapes it cast on the hall walls until I reached the guestroom at the front of the house. The water in the blue-and-white-patterned jug at the washstand was still warm and I sent silent thanks to Elsa, whose nightly chore it was to take the water to the bedrooms. I paused as I washed my face, and ran a finger around the scalloped edge of the matching washbasin. How had I come to be having such a conversation with a man I had only known for three weeks?

Only three weeks. And they had made me so welcome. Kurt had realised, I think, that I had a different picture in mind. A burly farmer, rough of speech and limited in interests, absorbed in his horses and cows and sheep and pigs, looking only at weather patterns and the effect on his ripening crops. From the first night and Carl's quiet welcome on the front verandah I had had to readjust my picture of this household.

'Thank you,' I had said as we met. 'Without you this reunion would never have happened.' It was simple, heartfelt. I think he knew that.

'You must love your son very much to have come this distance. He is very fortunate.'

Kurt had gone to unyoke the horses and stable them, so my host picked up my bags and led me inside to the bedroom.

'There is an oil lamp; we will light it after supper. You must be very tired. I expect you will want to eat then retire early.'

He was right. I felt exhausted by the events of the day, and barely noticed the quiet chatter of children at the table. A good German *Abendessen* with a variety of cheeses and sausages, and familiar black bread. I was so tired I could hardly lift my knife. It was good to leave the table and unlace my clothes and fall into bed, pulling the light cover over me on this warm summer night.

Early nights are customary in this household, except at harvest time, when every moment of daylight is precious. Days begin early, and when the older girls and the housemaid returned from milking, Magda had breakfast ready.

'I would like to help,' I told her firmly, and she looked at me with appreciation.

'There is more than enough to do,' she said. I soon saw the truth of that, as we organised the older children for school, their lunches packed in their small bags.

'Elsa is almost fourteen,' Magda commented. She will be finishing at the school, though there is talk of her becoming a pupil teacher. Herr Wendt, the schoolmaster, speaks highly of her. Adelina and Hermann also are bright – like their father.' Magda smiled fondly, clearly attached to her brother and his family. She must have been. She had delayed her own wedding to help him with his baby.

'What about the others?'

'Willi is almost seven; next year he will begin at the school, and Helena soon after. Already they play at being at school during the day. They are good children, easy to look after.'

'It must have been difficult for them, losing two mothers in such a short time.'

'Their own mother was ill for so long that her passing seemed to happen gradually. The other one, Eda, was never really a mother for them.'

'She was very young.'

Magda sniffed. 'That marriage was a bad idea. If she had not been pregnant – '

She paused uneasily, and looked alarmed. 'I should not have said that. Carl would be very angry. Please forget it. My tongue gets out of control.'

I soon learned the routine of this hard-working place, and saw the many ways I could help. Much of the work of the household took place in the Old House, as it was always called. It fascinated me, I felt at home there. A house that could have been in Lewin, with its timber uprights and mud and clay infill for the walls.

'And straw and horsehair,' explained Kurt. Carl had sent him to take me on a tour of the farm. 'Horsehair keeps the earth sections solid. Then they whitewash the outside, which is why it looks so like home. The big verandahs are for this climate. You will be surprised how hot it becomes as the summer develops.'

The broad verandahs were indeed important, as the rooms all opened on to them, with few interconnecting doors. The house reminded me of a train carriage with its separate compartments, and deep steps led down to the coolness of the dairy and cellars below the rooms.

'That was Carl's mother's room.' Kurt opened the door to a square area with a wooden floor, unlike most of the rooms with their flattened earth underfoot. It too had one small window, and through the glass she would have been able to watch the development of the New House across the garden. I wondered how she had felt as she watched the growth of the new brick building where another woman would be mistress.

Beyond, I could see more buildings and outhouses. A black-smith's shop, with the forge already in full use as one of the workmen shod a draught horse, which neighed furiously as we walked past. Then another mud-brick building for winemaking.

'Yes,' said Kurt. 'The vineyards are now producing good crops each year. Vintage time is busy, and the wine good.'

The strong smell of wine from the big barrels along the wall backed up his words. Past the stables and other outbuildings, with their timber pole uprights and thatched roofs. Then the bails for milking and the clamorous activity of the poultry pens and roosting sheds. As we walked, I saw what had been achieved in these twenty years.

'All Carl's work,' said Kurt, in admiration. 'Now he wants to use steam power for some of his farming. That is why I was here.'

'Why move on then?' I asked. 'If you were happy here ...'

'A girl,' he said briefly.

'Can you tell me?'

'I will. Another time. It's a long story. Complicated.'

'When you want to.'

I had become aware of a familiar smell. 'Isn't this a pig yard?'

'Yes, see the sty? Well, actually there are three under that thatched roof – Carl is very proud of his pigs. And of the sausages they make at killing time. You would be familiar with that.'

'And the sausage making?'

'Of course. Made the old way. See there, behind the Old House.'

It was a smokehouse, a small grey building for the sausages

and sides of bacon that would hang there while the charred embers sent up the aromatic smoke to cure them. A familiar sight indeed.

'It is like a small village. I had no idea this was the sort of place you had come to.'

Kurt looked uneasy. He could see where this conversation would lead.

'You want to know, don't you, how all this happened. And why I did not contact you.'

It was not a question. We both knew that some explanation had to be made. And yet he seemed unable to begin.

'Let's sit down. We need to talk.'

We sat on the big log under the pine trees in the horse paddock. For a while nothing was said.

'Perhaps start with the ship?' I suggested. 'Up to then you had written, not often, but enough to keep me aware of your life. Then, suddenly, nothing. And after that just those few brief accounts.'

Kurt hesitated. 'I think it was, at first, that I could not bear to put it into words. The nightmare of the ship. It was overloaded, and we all knew it. The safety valves were screwed down so much that the boiler was unsafe. No matter what I said, no matter how much I pointed out the danger, he just ignored me.'

'Could you not have refused? Or gone to someone else in authority?'

'You do not understand the world of the ship. The captain is the ultimate authority – his word is law. If I refused he said he would have me in irons for mutiny. He would not accept there was danger – I was an ignorant idiot who knew nothing of ships.'

'So?'

'I believed that a disaster at sea was imminent. And I could do nothing. So I ... left.'

'That was when you deserted in Melbourne?'

'Yes, but having deserted I was a criminal. I had no rights to enter Victoria. No papers. And I could be picked up by the police as a criminal, as a deserter.'

'So why did he not report you?'

'Then the whole business would have been made public. And there would have been delays and police involvement. He could not afford a hold up; he had a schedule to meet. Those German marines he was transporting were due in Sydney, and the ship's owners would not have looked tolerantly on a delay.'

'Why not just ignore you?'

Kurt sighed. 'I had used intemperate language when we argued. I would not actually report to you the words I said. He was furious – he said I would pay for it.'

'The beating?'

'I recognised them. Two of the crew. I had never got on with them. They would have been delighted at the chance. They certainly earned whatever reward they got. I think even he would have felt me fully punished.'

I winced. 'Doctor Menge said it had been brutal.'

'If the people who found me had not taken me straight to the hospital, I doubt we would be talking about it today. And the real blessing was the *Krankverein*.'

'You were so fortunate to have found friends.'

'It was a long time before I could do anything. And even longer before I recovered my wits. My hearing, you will have noticed, will never fully repair; that apart, my mending has been better than anyone dared hope.'

'None of this really explains why you did not write to me.'

'For so long I was not capable. And then, after that – I find it hard to explain.'

We sat in silence while he tried to gather words.

'I do not really understand it myself. I fell into a sort of blackness. Nothing in life seemed worthwhile. I did not want people. I did not want affection. I was content just to work. Feeling for anyone seemed impossible. Even for you. Especially you.'

I swallowed. 'Especially me?'

'I do not know how to put this to you, or even to myself. Always you and I have been close. Even when I went away, you were always there. To Glatz, to Breslau. You came. And I was happy that you wanted to be with me. I needed to become a separate person, yet I didn't want to.'

He looked at my face.

'I do not want to hurt you. But it was as if we were too tied. I needed to separate.'

So Hanna had been right. And Kurt had had the sense to see it. I said nothing.

'How can I explain? I love you so dearly. I wanted to make up for all that you had suffered. At the same time I wanted to be free.'

'Free of me?' I whispered.

'Being here, in this country, I could not bring myself to do more than just tell you I was alive, that I was moving on and did not know where I would be.' He shook his head. 'I still cannot explain why I did not write to you from Lobethal. It was almost as if I were in hiding.'

It stabbed me like a knife.

'So now I have spoiled it – this escape of yours – by following you?'

He shook his head and his voice was vehement.

'No, do not say that. Do not even think it. The moment I saw you on the platform, it was as if the years had dropped away, and all I could feel was a flood of love for you and gladness that you had come.'

I sat silent on the trunk of the big tree in the horse paddock. What to say? My son turned to face me.

'Have I hurt you? I do not wish to hurt you, but I don't know how else to make you understand.'

'Would you like me to leave here?'

'*Gott in Himmel*, no! I am overjoyed you are here. Carl and Magda also, they are happy, not just that we have found each other, but to have you in the house. Please do not even think of leaving. Not for a long time.'

I got up slowly. 'Kurt, you have given me so much to think about. Let me be for a time, and then we'll talk again.'

'You are not angry, I hope.'

I shook my head and tried to sound reassuring. 'No, not angry. I am disturbed that I have been so blind. Give me time to absorb this.'

We walked in silence to the New House, where the midday dinner was already in preparation. I knew then that the next weeks would be a time of looking at myself and finding what I wanted from my life.

And so they have been.

CHAPTER 23

Jindera, New South Wales 1889

A curious time, as we slipped into a routine as comfortable as if I had been at Lobethal as long as Kurt. At ease with Magda as we shared the daily routines. Standing with her in the dairy as we skimmed the cream with slotted spoons from the huge pans of fresh milk, at times I would catch her sidelong look, almost appraising.

'You are enjoying your time with us, Anna?' she asked. By now we were on close and friendly terms. With the workmen and even with Carl, I still kept the traditional distance. We were still Herr Bergmann and Frau Werner, though to the children I had become Tante Anna; Elsa's request, and one that pleased me.

Elsa had taught me to drive the sulky, the cart pulled by one of the sturdy horses from the stables. At first the strange conveyance worried me, with its lightweight seat that seemed so fragile.

'It is quite safe,' the girl assured me. 'Even Adelina can manage it, and it is so convenient for going to Jindera for the post, or to the store.'

'I am sure you are right.' I could hear the lack of conviction in my voice as she urged me to take the reins. 'But we do not have these at home, and if you were not sitting beside me I would feel very nervous.'

She was right. It did not take me long to realise how easy this travel was, and although the Bergmann sulky had no sunshade top, it was a pleasant way to travel even in the hottest weather.

The whitewashed post office with its thatched roof made me feel at home, though the curiosity of the Misses Spence, the postmistresses, was at times intrusive. They were kindly in manner, though I have no doubt that Kurt had been right, and that every word I spoke as I gathered the mail was carefully reported. Their reputation for gossip was well known.

What a day for them when I received a letter from Germany, and exclaimed involuntarily, 'It's from my daughter!' I could not resist opening it as I stood there by the mail counter in the small room, nor could I have refrained from sharing the news.

'She has a new baby, a daughter, born eight weeks ago.' I had quickly calculated the time the letter would have taken, even on the fastest of the new mail steamers in the Norddeutscher shipping line.

'And all is well with them both?'

'So it seems. This is her third child.'

'It must be hard for you to be so far away at such a time,' Miss Alberta suggested, and her sister nodded. 'Will you return now?'

I gauged my answer carefully, knowing that by nightfall the whole community would know it.

'At present I am enjoying seeing my son before I think of returning.'

Non-committal, I could see no other response to give. It was true. Kurt and I had slipped into easy communication again, but it was subtly different. I no longer felt that all my happiness depended on him. I had come so far to find him; in the process I had also found myself. I was Anna, who had travelled across the world alone. I was Anna, who had made new friends in many places, friends I knew I would keep. I was Anna, who was still attractive enough for men to find interesting.

Going to Wagner's Store was a pleasure on these Jindera trips. No matter how self-sustaining our way of life at Lobethal, there were still small purchases to make, and it was rare to make the long trip by wagon into Albury. The store, with display cases running its full length and walls lined with packed shelves, was a delight. Along one side the groceries and foodstuffs, with tins and containers, and small compartments for spices and condiments, while underneath the big bins for staples were filled with the flours and sugars that we bought in bulk.

The other side pleased me even more, with ornaments and trinkets, soaps and decorations, and fancygoods – especially the array of small bone buttons and hatpins, as many as I had seen in the bigger stores in Melbourne. Plates and dishes, cooking pots, frying pans – whatever we needed could be found. Presiding over it all Herr Wagner, monarch of this empire, and his tiny bird-like wife, who was only in his absence allowed to use the sacred object, the cash register. This National Cash Register, their pride and joy, was a new invention, one of the very few in the district.

'Or in the land,' said a proud Hilde Wagner. 'My husband's brother brought it with him from America. In that country many stores are using them.'

She was a hospitable woman, and anxious to show off their new possessions. I suspect she felt that, coming from Germany,

I needed to be impressed by their modernity in country New South Wales. She took pleasure in inviting me to drink coffee with her in the new dwelling just added to the back of their shop, and I duly admired the sitting room with its green velvet chaise longue and ornate carving, and the elaborate arrangements of wax flowers under glass that sat on the small tables in all corners of the room.

'We are very up-to-date in Jindera, Frau Werner,' she assured me, her head cocked to one side and her voice more than ever like a twittering bird. 'I would not wish you to think us a backward society.'

'Indeed not,' I was emphatic. 'Your sitting room is equal to any I saw at home.'

She smiled, and took me through to the children's bedrooms beyond; then to the south wing with its kitchen and laundry. Here I was really impressed. A proper laundry room. Different from our Monday wash days at Lobethal, as we scrubbed sheets and clothing on the verandah of the Old House, and carted the hot water from the copper in its kitchen to the waiting tubs outside. Here too the flat irons waited for heating on the side of the oven, just as ours did in the Lobethal kitchen.

Outside, I unhitched the waiting horse and set off down the Four Mile Creek Road. It was, as always, with a sense that I was going home, and I pondered the question of how I would feel when the time came to leave. As I would have to.

The question. Where next? Herr Eberhardt was still pressing in his invitation to join his newspaper in Sydney, yet I knew there was more than just work involved in this invitation. There would be no return to Melbourne. A letter from Margarethe had made that clear. She had written, cautiously at first, of her growing friendship with Dr Menge, and I could sense the implicit question. Would this be a problem for me? Was he a special person in my life?

It gave me pleasure to assure her that he was a fine man and a good friend, and that I would be delighted if my two friends found more than just companionship with each other, a letter that brought an immediate response.

> *I am so happy, dear Anna, to hear this from you. Johan and I have found each other most compatible and I think – I hope – that he is beginning to care for me. I know that I feel for him more deeply than I would have expected. He is a fine man, indeed, and being with him stirs feelings in me that I did not know before. I hope it may be the same for him.*

In truth I was envious. Not because of Dr Menge – her news pleased me, and when I had brought them together it had been my hope. But to feel like that.

Still I did not know what Kurt had meant in his cryptic comment about a woman being the reason he wished to leave Lobethal. I had hesitated to intrude, wishing him to tell me when he was ready. Surely not Magda, many years older than him. Besides, she had her own lover, who came to visit whenever he could find the time.

'We have been engaged for a year now, Anna, and he becomes impatient. He has been reasonable about delaying our wedding until Carl's child is a little older but I cannot ask him to wait forever.'

'It is a real problem – I can see that.'

'Ideally, Carl should marry again. These children need a mother to care for them.'

I was surprised to find how little the idea appealed to me.

'He has told me he married Eda to have a mother here – and how he regrets it. It is not a good basis for marriage.'

'It was not the only reason. I think you have guessed that she was already with child when they married. He is an honourable man, and he felt he had to wed her. Have I shocked you?'

'Oh Magda,' I smiled. 'There is little in life that shocks me. He is a man, and an attractive man. If he was lonely after Frieda's death, it does not surprise me.'

'She was more than willing, and I doubt that Carl was her first.' She coughed, and raised an uneasy hand to her mouth. 'She is dead, and I talk too much.'

The rhythm of life at Lobethal was comfortable. On Mondays stoking of the fires under the big copper in the Old House for wash day; on Tuesdays the bank of flat irons heating on the kitchen stove for big ironing, while on Wednesday the smell of freshly baked bread and big trays of *Streuselkuchen* filled the house. Though the other workers cared for themselves, Kurt came often from their quarters to join us at the family dinner table.

Two days each week Rosa and Elfrieda would come from Mueller's farm to help with cleaning and I watched Kurt with them. His manner showed nothing but casual friendship, and I pondered his comment about a girl. Neither of these, I concluded. Perhaps at the church?

Sundays, the wagon was waiting in the yard with the two horses yoked and ready to transport us to the small weatherboard church that Carl's father had helped build. The horses paced sedately through the village, and out once more into countryside. I was surprised that first day when we did not pull in with other wagons at the grey stone church with its square tower and spire that looked so like those at home.

'Surely that is the Lutheran church?' I cast a puzzled glance at Magda, beside me cradling little Fritz, as we all called him.

She glanced up from adjusting his shirt. 'It's the other synod,' she answered briefly. I recalled Pastor Herlitz' explanation that in the new land doctrinal divisions still prevailed, and the Old Lutherans who had come for religious freedom had then split into groups. Often, in fact, bitterly hostile groups.

'You do not attend that one?'

She seemed shocked. 'We could not do that. Oh, we are still neighbours and friends. And our children go to the same Lutheran school. See, it is that building next door to this church. But we could never worship with them. And I could never have married someone from the other church.'

There was an absoluteness about it that startled me. Why should religious belief lead to such divisions? The horses plodded on and we turned into a yard already filling with sulkies and wagons, where bonneted women were walking toward the doorway of a small cream-painted timber building, its gable front topped with a wooden cross. No bell tower here, but a young boy hurried to ring the bell suspended in its tall iron frame near the entry porch.

'We go to the right,' indicated Magda, shepherding the children toward a back pew. Kurt, I noticed, was moving left to the men's side of the congregation, while Carl strode to the front pew, where two older men were already sitting.

'They are the elders,' whispered Magda, as the congregation settled.

A solitary fly buzzed lazily at the window, and already in the early morning a heat haze was hanging in the air. I gazed out the windows at the listless gums and yellowed grasses, wondering how one could celebrate Christmas in this climate.

Advent, and each Sunday a new candle was lit in the wreath at the front of the altar. As we stood outside after service there was talk in the women's circle of the Christmas Eve program the children would perform, and the making of new clothes for the event; in the men's circle – of course the two groups remained separate – of the coming harvest and the weather that might jeopardise it.

'You will be with us for Christmas, Frau Werner?' asked the pastor, as I left the church that morning.

'God willing,' I replied. It was the same response I gave to the enquirers in the women's circle, and Magda was quick to add her voice.

'We would all be disappointed if she was not part of our Christmas this year.'

I did not miss the significant glance that passed among the ladies, so I hastened to add that I must soon return to Germany to see my new grandchild. I did not want to start speculation.

I glanced across to Kurt standing with a group of the younger men, some casting surreptitious looks toward the gathering of unmarried girls. Soon there would be a few brave souls asking to escort a chosen girl for the walk to her home, if she lived close by. Or perhaps for permission to visit for one of the Sunday evening music entertainments that were so popular.

'Since Frieda has died, we no longer have these,' Magda had explained. I knew that the piano in the formal drawing room had not been opened in my time there, and the girls' music lessons had stopped during their mother's long illness.

'We used to go to a teacher in Jindera on Fridays,' Adelina had told me. 'He was a grumpy old man who came from Albury one day a week. Lots of my friends also learned from him. Do you play, Tante Anna?'

'I used to, but not well.' It was many years since I had touched the instrument.

'*Vati* plays the cornet,' volunteered Hermann. 'He played in the band until our mother got sick.'

The man was full of surprises. I had been intrigued by the bookshelves in his room, and the fact that our evenings were spent harmoniously with him reading in the lamplight while Magda and I sewed the never-diminishing pile of mending for the children.

'Where do your books come from?' I asked one evening.

'Many from the fatherland. When our people came, they brought not just seeds and farm equipment but also many books. And when we go to Albury, I visit the booksellers there and gain new stock for the coming months. You are welcome to read any that interest you.'

A mix of German and English, as I discovered when I took advantage of his absence one day to explore the shelves. Much theology ... old books that had come with his father on the ship. A complete set of Luther's *Table Talk* and many of the Church's confessional books. Books on agriculture, and on the new land they were coming to. Then newer books, a mix of history and philosophy, nothing more to my taste. No literature, no classics.

'Not a world I am familiar with,' he laughed, when I challenged this collection. 'I tell you, Frau Werner, we will go to Albury next week to buy gifts for the children for Christmas, and I will take you to my bookseller. You can choose books for me, the books you think I should know.'

'I'd like that. And I'd be interested to see something of the town. Before I return to my own country.'

'Yes.' A shadow crossed his face. 'I think you must find our life here very dull.'

'Not so,' I hastened to assure him. 'It's a life that I have not known, and I enjoy it greatly. I would like to see Albury. Will we all go?'

'I think not. Another time with the family. For this trip we will only take Kurt – he needs to buy equipment for a new device he is making.'

The children were easy to placate with the thought that we were planning to buy their Christmas gifts. And the house was filled with preparations for Christmas, with Magda and the girls in a flurry of baking and sewing for the day. I was pleased that Kurt was to come with us, otherwise I feared providing the gossip that would be sure to follow our excursion.

I look back on it now as an especially happy day. The children had all made their wishes clear to me before departure, and there was an easy companionship in choosing their presents. For Magda, a length of material, black with a finely figured pattern that shimmered as it shifted in light.

'It would make a fine wedding gown,' I murmured, then scolded myself as I saw his look. It was a problem he would have to face one day. Magda's husband-to-be would not wait forever.

'Now the bookseller.' He led the way out of the big department store crowded with pre-Christmas shoppers.

'This is Dean Street, where the newspaper in which you advertised began. We are very proud of the *Albury Banner* – they tell us it is the biggest country weekly in the land. Three years ago it was made larger, now it has forty pages.'

'I heard Kurt call it the *'Farmer's Bible'*,' I commented.

'That is true. We depend on it for many things – including the tracing of missing sons!'

I laughed. 'It's been very useful for me.'

'It is a very successful paper. The owner, George Adams, must be making money. In spite of the fire.'

'A fire?'

'The *Banner* offices were destroyed by a huge fire just before Christmas four years ago. It started in the draper's shop next door when a gas jet set alight a nearby display of laces. It was a huge loss – but now completely restored. Look!'

He led me to the side of the main street, and I smiled at his pride in the new buildings. They were, I had to admit, impressive: the new telegraph office and the Beehive Building, a splendid new post office. Even Mate's, the department store we had been in, had been rebuilt within the last few years.

'You would make a good agent!' I laughed.

He smiled sheepishly. 'Am I boring you?'

'No, of course not. You are right to be proud of your city. It seems so prosperous.'

'Wool prices in the last years have been at a peak; the entire country is profiting.'

In the bookshop Kurt soon disappeared to another section, fascinated by his new project and in search of books that would give him the information he needed. For me it was a matter of finding favourites I thought Carl might enjoy, and he shook his head at my eagerness to share them with him.

'You will need to stay here for a long time if we are to discuss all these books,' he laughed, as we carried the box of books to the waiting wagon. It was not an unpleasant thought. It would, after all, have been silly to come this distance and then to leave the country too swiftly. Besides, I had come to feel that I was earning my keep in the household, and I knew that Magda was grateful for the help.

'It is time that we eat something,' Carl paused in his stowing of our purchases in the wagon. 'Magda has packed a hamper for us to enjoy in the gardens. We will take the wagon there.'

'I shall leave you.' Kurt had other plans. 'I need to purchase equipment – parts for my project. Carl can tell you about it, *Mutti* – though I am not sure he believes it can be done.'

Carl tipped back his hat. 'I confess to doubts. I also have faith. If anyone can do this, it will be you. What about food though?'

'I will stop in at the Globe – it will be quicker. We can pick up my goods later when you leave.'

'He will get a good meal there,' Carl assured me as the wagon rumbled its way down Dean Street. He pointed to the hotel as we passed it; a two-storey building, impressive for this country town, with its balcony and verandahs. 'You see that balcony?' he gestured with the reins. 'The Governor has stayed in the hotel and spoke highly of it, and seven years ago the Premier of our colony stood on that very balcony and made a speech to Albury's people.'

I was embarrassed by my ignorance but as soon as he said the name I knew. 'Yes, Sir Henry Parkes. He is very involved in the federation matter; they told me of it in Melbourne.'

'It will be important if this country is to become a nation. We cannot have separate colonies all going their own way. We could do much better as a united land. But here we are.'

I could see how beautiful these gardens would be. Even in twelve years trees had grown impressively and lawns and flowerbeds made it an attractive spot. It was easy to relax and talk idly as we ate our way through Magda's provisions, and enjoy the bottle of their own wine she had included.

'I have been so impressed by all that you have created at Lobethal. And in such a short time. The way your vineyard is flourishing, and the orchards. You have fruits I have never seen at home. It is like a kingdom in its own right.'

'A kingdom I have to fight for. Have you not seen me shooting at the birds at dawn? They too want my fruit.' I had wondered at the gunshots.

'Kurt has an idea,' he continued, 'of creating a system of bells through the trees, that could be rung from the house. It may work. He is a man of many talents.'

'He seems very happy here with you, and I know this new idea is important to him. Can you explain? I don't know anything of it.'

The afternoon sun was warm, and we had eaten and drunk well, and Carl's explanation of a machine that would harvest the wheat more efficiently could not hold my attention.'

'A stripper, you say? A machine that would strip the wheat?' I murmured. I could feel my eyes glazing with weariness.

'Frau Werner, I am boring you.' His voice came from a long way away.

'I am sorry. I am just so tired; I cannot keep my eyes open.'

'You can lean against this tree – here, let me put this cushion in place. Or would you sleep on the rug?'

Tempting indeed. Yet how improper that would have been, in a public place. I had removed my bonnet, but to lie down seemed unladylike. Leaning against the tree – surely no one could object to that. And my eyes were closing.

When I woke, Carl had packed the remains in the hamper and was himself asleep on the rug. I looked at him. There was something so touching about his figure stretched out and defenceless. Strange to see this tall rugged man so vulnerable, no longer the master of his kingdom. He stirred in his sleep, and reached a hand toward me.

I swallowed. Caught by surprise, I realised I wanted to put my hand in his.

CHAPTER 24

Jindera, New South Wales 1889

With Christmas coming and no schooldays, there was little time for thinking in this hard-working household. Even the children were busy; all were expected to work in this way of life. My favourite time was the long light evening, when the household shared the after-dinner daily watering time. The summer had come, and I understood for the first time in my life the importance of water in the extended dry spells and intense heat of this land.

Each evening, as the sun sank toward the west beyond the curve of the hills, the horse was yoked to the furphy, a contrivance I had never seen before. Kurt explained it to me with enthusiasm.

'It is exactly the sort of thing this country excels at – people making what is needed for these conditions.'

I looked at the strange barrel-like water tank, where Carl was harnessing the horse. It stood patiently while the straps were attached to the long shafts of the cart.

Kurt continued. 'Each night we take it to the dam in the home paddock and bring it back with water for the garden.'

'I have never seen this done before.' I was intrigued.

'A new invention, that people all over the district are purchasing. It is the best way of getting water to where we need it each night. If we took too much from the house tanks or the underground wells we would run out.'

'Whose idea was it?'

'That's where the name comes from. A man from Shepparton – that's in Victoria – called John Furphy. So everyone calls them 'furphys' – see, on the front of the barrel.' He gestured to the round metal plate with its inscription *Furphy's Farm Water Cart.* 'A man with ideas can find real opportunities in this country. He will make his fortune with these.'

The heat of the day was yielding to the evening's long shadows, stretching horizontal fingers over the paddocks. We lined up at the furphy tap to fill tins and buckets, then adults and children tracked backwards and forwards from the cart to the rows of the extensive vegetable garden. There was no waste in this frugal household. Even Willi and Leni, only four and five, had their role and, equipped with discarded kitchen pots and leaking pans, ignored the drips and took water to the pot plants rowed along the front verandah.

By the time we finished darkness would be falling, and bedtime came early for most of the household. Kurt returned to the workmen's quarters in the Old House, and Magda, who rose early each morning to light the big stove in the kitchen, would soon carry her candle to her room. It was easy to sit on with Carl, reading under the gaslight we now used in the warm summer nights. I was concerned for Kurt, who had still said nothing more of the reasons he had left this place where he fitted so well. I did not wish to ask him directly, but I wondered if Carl knew.

'I have not asked Kurt, and I would not want you to betray confidences, Carl.' I still felt awkward using his name but it had become absurd in the intimacy of daily living and working to maintain this formality. I had been touched at his response to my suggestion that he call me Anna. His comment that it seemed more natural gave me pleasure.

He raised his eyes from the book. 'What is it, Anna?'

'Kurt has still said nothing to me of the reason he left. He said only that it involved a girl. And that one day he would tell me.'

'I know very little more. I think there is someone he came to know in Jindera – but who or just what happened I have not been told. All I know is that for a time he was asking me for use of a horse to go to the village.'

'You are fortunate your children have not yet reached that age. You wait, my friend, your time will come.'

'I can only hope that by then I will have someone to share the burden with. It would be hard to do it alone, and I cannot expect Magda to stay forever. She will go to her Lars, and you will return to your family. It will be lonely.'

A silence fell. I felt only an unaccountable pang that he was taking my departure for granted. It had to be broken.

'Who knows what the future brings?' I said as lightly as I could. 'You may find it easy to gain a companion.'

His dark eyes were troubled as he looked at me. 'With six children and two marriages behind me? I think not.'

Again the silence. 'You might be surprised,' I ventured finally. And I meant it. I had seen the way women looked at him outside the church. There would be many willing to provide friendship – and more – to this man. He was an attractive man with his height and bearing, easily commanding respect and attention.

Not just respect, I had come to feel. He was a man who could charm and stir, and if I had not known from Magda that his heart was still with his first love it would have been easy to allow myself to think of him more dearly than would be prudent. Perhaps I already felt more than was wise. I chose to not consider this too closely.

Magda had given me other insights into his marriage. She was, as she admitted, far too free with her talk. One could not blame her. Left here with little company, conscious always, as she had told me, of the passing years and a fiancé who was as eager as she for their marriage, she needed to share her feelings.

'I am getting older,' she worried. 'I am thirty-seven and Lars is forty. He wishes to have children. And so do I. I fear that if I do not set a wedding date soon, he might decide to look elsewhere.'

'Surely not,' I said with conviction. 'I have seen the way he looks at you.'

'Carl needs me here. If only he had married Maria when he wanted her so much ... she would be here now, and I would be free.'

'She is still alive?'

'Oh yes, and now widowed. I have said to him that it is not too late. He should try again.'

I found the idea distasteful, and was immediately repentant. 'What does he say?'

'He simply smiled at me, said that the past was past. I had the feeling that he might consider it, provide an answer to our problems. And I believe it is what he has wanted all these years.'

'Magda, he married and had children.'

'The marriage with Frieda was always a second-best and she, poor woman, knew her sister was the one he yearned for. And then Eda. That was such a mistake, but Maria's husband was still alive. Now he has gone ...'

That conversation burned into my mind. 'Do not delude yourself,' I spoke the words firmly in my mind. 'He has loved this woman all these years and is still in love with her.' It was not a happy thought.

It stilled my tongue when we sat together and talked of my return to my family. I would need to find the funds for a return ship; I knew that Kurt would be hard-pressed to provide money for me. I could return to Melbourne and look for employment. Or I could seek work in Albury. I knew from the weekly paper that it would not be a problem. That solution would keep me close to Kurt – and to Carl.

Foolish thinking. Matters of the heart so often are.

I turned my mind to the son I had come so far to find. It was his life that I should be concerned about. I needed to find out more about his feelings. Our time together had become easier since we had talked openly about our relationship, and I had schooled myself to look elsewhere for closeness. For too long I had relied on him.

He was surprisingly ready to tell me, when I finally asked him what he had meant about his reasons for wishing to leave.

'I have never felt deeply about anyone – except for you, dear mother. I had never imagined I could feel this way. There have been girls, of course. In Breslau, in Bremen. There are always girls available. I do not want to shock you, and this is not a talk one has with a mother. I can say that until now there has never been anyone I cared for like this.'

Once this thought would have distressed me. Once I would not have wished to share my son. Now I was only interested to know that his feelings had been at last engaged. Perhaps we were both breaking free.

'Tell me about her.'

It was a tangled tale that unfolded as he spoke. His exploration of the village and the discovery of the three graveyards. 'Not just our own, near our church. The other church also has its own, for their members – and there is a third for other faiths.'

'Well, there are four hotels. I suppose three cemeteries is not excessive.'

But he did not smile. This was to be a serious conversation.

'You know how I have always been interested in old gravestones?'

I nodded, recalling our times in Glatz and Breslau. He had come in search of the ones at Jindera. At one of these, he told me, he had seen a girl, a beautiful girl, weeping at a grave as she placed fresh flowers in the vase.

'They were lilies,' he said, recalling. 'And she was one of those girls who could cry without looking tear blotched and red faced.'

A lucky creature, I thought. He went on to describe how he had ventured to approach her, and offer help. It was refused. 'That time. But I went back at other times, and found she came regularly at that time of day. Always with fresh flowers.'

'Whose grave?'

'The headstone meant nothing to me, except to surprise. It was not one of the farmers' sons that she mourned for, but another man. A young man, our age, and titled. A minor member of the Prussian nobility.'

'Why was someone like that buried in a little country cemetery?' It seemed inconceivable.

'You are asking my question. Bit by bit, over weeks of our meeting there ... not every day. I could not have explained to Carl why I was visiting Jindera so often. Fortunately, he was accustomed to me finding my way around the area when not needed at Lobethal, so I met her often in the graveyard.'

'An odd place for a romance.'

'This was no romance, *Mutti*. Not mine, anyway. It was her romance with this man, the Graf zu Stolberg, who had followed her from a chance meeting in Albury. He had come to Jindera to find work near her, and they had been so much in love that her father had given way and agreed to the marriage. Her eyes filled with tears as she described their happiness.'

'Now he is dead?'

'Well clearly,' my son was impatient. 'He died of diphtheria three weeks before their wedding. He must have been popular. A large crowd came to the funeral. Even his friends from Albury.'

'That's terrible! It's not surprising she is still grieving.'

'The words on his tombstone were touching.' I looked up enquiringly.

> *As for man, his days are like grass;*
> *he flourishes like a flower of the field;*
> *for the wind passes over it, and it is gone,*
> *and its place knows it no more.*

Kurt recited it easily, and I saw that he must have dwelt upon the words.

'A verse we all know well,' I mused. 'He must have been very young.'

'Only twenty-five. He would have been five years older than I am. They were the same age. But here is the remarkable thing. His name too was Kurt.'

I suddenly felt there were too many Kurts in my life. Yet I had hardly given thought to the first one for many months, unlike my time at home when he had been a constant silent presence beside me. He had haunted me for too long, I now realised.

'What is her name?'

'Emma.' His voice softened, and the word came lovingly through his lips.

'And she has told you all this?'

'I had thought we were growing closer. I had asked her permission to call at her home. Her father has a blacksmithery in the village and their house is beside it. To my dismay she made it clear I would not be welcome. She feels that her betrothal has not been changed by her fiancé's death. And, as she pointed out, her family belongs to the other church. There would be no point in my becoming attached to her.'

'That was why you decided to move on.'

'There seemed little reason to stay. It would have only hurt more to see her and know she could never be mine. Now that you have come, things are different.'

'While I am here,' I sighed. 'Kurt, I must start thinking about departure.'

Kurt's surprise was obvious. 'I had thought you were happy here.'

'Yes, but that doesn't mean I can stay on. Magda will have to leave, and Carl will need to marry again. In fact, he may well have someone in mind.'

'I had thought ... I had hoped ...' Kurt's feelings were clear, so I spoke firmly.

'I need to go back to Hanna and the children. And I think Carl's affections are already with someone else. Someone he has loved for many years.'

Karl paused reflectively. 'I wonder if you are right.'

'Oh yes, Magda has told me about it. So I need to think about departure. Soon after Christmas. And you need to think about Emma. In spite of what you say, life moves on. Sometime I would like to meet her.'

'I think you would like her. She is a little older than I am, and strong-willed and determined. She reminds me of you. I think you would be friends.'

Now, as I sat with Carl, I pondered the subject of my leaving. Christmas, I thought. That gives a point of separation – and a way to introduce the topic.

'I am looking forward to Christmas at Lobethal,' I began. He stopped me.

'So are we all. This will be a very special Christmas for us, with you here.'

'For me, too. Then,' I steeled myself to continue, 'I must make plans for my return home.'

'Of course.' His voice was heavy. 'You have family awaiting your return.'

'And by the next Christmas you may well have a new mistress in the house.' It hurt to say the words, yet an impulse to kill pain with pain spurred me on.

He rose to his feet, and pulled the chain to stop the gaslight.

'It is getting late. Here is your candle. I hope you sleep well, Anna.'

As he reached the door to his room, I heard his parting remark. 'I had hoped that we had made you feel at home here.'

I felt quick tears come to my eyes. 'But I do, Carl. I do.'

It was too late. The door had closed.

CHAPTER 25

Jindera, New South Wales 1889

I had anticipated a bittersweet Christmas Eve. My last one at Lobethal, where I had been so at home. I recall there were moments of misery that almost blotted out the happiness. Moments when I wondered what I was doing here. Whether I should have left before my heart was involved. For now I had come to realise that it was so. Yet amid my doubts there were also truly happy moments as we prepared for the night.

I revelled in the wagon ride to the small weatherboard church on Christmas Eve. Here in this new land our old traditions were kept. Even Sir Ruprecht had come and gone at Lobethal, but with bells from the distant forests, forests now of eucalypts rather than pine. Here he came across the dead grass of summertime, not crunching over winter snow. He was not a figure of terror and punishment at Carl's. This Ruprecht wore a mask that did not frighten even Willi and Helena, and the older children joined in happy affirmation when asked if they had been good this year. As the bags of sweets were handed out and the wagon bells faded into the distance it was not a reprieve from terror, as it had been for Kurt. He looked at me, remembering his childhood.

When we settled in the wagon and made our way in the long light-filled evening to the church, Kurt and I were recalling a very different journey with a sullen Otto, forced for one night to be with us instead of at the inn. Here, for this night, church customs were relaxed, and Carl sat with us as we watched the children's Christmas performance, the nativity story told in recitation and play acting. The previous year Fritz had been the baby in the manger; Elsa the demure Mary who looked down at her baby brother. This year there was a new baby in the manger and Adelina was the blue-gowned figure watching over him. Elsa, in her first long dress, product of the Jindera dressmaker's skill, sat with us, now officially grown up, and Fritz bounced happily on his father's knee. I looked at these children, and realised how dear they had become to me – and how hard it would be to leave them.

Like the rest of the service, their performance was in German, and the sound of the familiar words in my own tongue was inexpressibly dear. From the front came the old, well-known words as they sang *Stille Nacht, Heilige Nacht* and with Kurt on one side and Carl on the other I felt as happy as I had ever been. Carl touched my arm gently. 'A happy Christmas, dear Anna.'

I looked around the congregation, wondering which of these women was Maria. He felt my stiffening, and withdrew his hand, sighing. Why did I allow this moment to be spoiled, I wondered, filled with regret.

Back at the house it was a joyous night. For once the drawing room was in use, and the locked door opened at last to the children who had waited impatiently all day for their first glimpse of the Christmas tree Magda and I had spent happy hours decorating.

Lars had joined us, and he and Magda sat, hand in hand, as Carl, our Saint Nicholas, called names from the labels and distributed gifts. We watched the opening with pleasure and listened to the squeals of delight. Carl and I looked at each other; we had done well with the present buying. My gift for him was small; there was no money for lavish buying, yet he seemed as pleased with the pocket watchcase I had embroidered as if it had come from an expensive store in Albury.

'I will give you your present later,' he whispered among the general melee of the presents. For the children, there was *Lebkuchen* and the special treat of Schweppes lemonade, which Carl had asked his friend, Gottfried Wagner, to get into the store for this night. For us, the traditional *Stollen* and eggnog, with schnapps for the men. The candles on the Christmas tree burned steadily while we watched carefully in case one of the brass candleholders slipped, and the nearby bucket of water became necessary.

I looked around as Magda played the piano and all joined in the familiar carols. The glow of happiness I felt had nothing to do with the eggnog, and impulsively I touched Carl's hand. 'Happy Christmas, dear Carl.' It was atonement for my earlier response, and he knew it.

The next day would be an early start for Christmas Day service, so we sent the children to bed, Elsa protesting vehemently that as she was now grown up she should not have to go. Sad that she was yawning widely as she objected – it rather spoiled her case. Magda and Lars had disappeared for a moonlight walk on this warm summer's night. Carl and I had looked at each other knowingly and had seen Magda blush. With Kurt's help we restored the room to order before he too made his way to the Old House where the workmen were having their own celebrations. Noisy ones, we could hear.

'A schnapps with me, Anna, to finish our work?'

It was not a drink I was used to, and the fiery liquid burned my throat. 'You drink this for pleasure?' I asked, coughing.

'It gives you courage,' he murmured. 'You are drinking it too slowly. It should be like this. He poured another one and tossed it back in a gulp. 'That is the way to drink schnapps.'

I shook my head.

'Perhaps I needed courage to give you my gift. I hope that what I have chosen will not offend you.'

As I opened the small jeweller's box, I recognised the name on the label. We had passed this shop in Dean Street and I had admired the display in the window.

'I gave you so little,' I protested, hesitating.

He had walked to the window rather than watch me open the box, and I was touched by his withdrawal. No matter what, it would give me time to plan a response. I could not prevent the small cry of delight when I saw the exquisite pendant on the velvet bed of the box. It was in the shape of a heart, enamelled and lovely.

He had turned back to me and suddenly I recognised the look on his face. A mixture of apprehension and longing.

'Anna. Have I offended you? Is it too personal a gift?'

I shook my head. 'It is so beautiful. How could I be offended?'

'Ach, do you see what it means? I am offering you my heart, Anna. You have had it for so long. How could I tell you? What could I give you?'

I found it impossible to speak, and his face fell.

'I was so afraid of this. That if I said anything, you would leave. And I cannot bear the thought of you going away.'

He turned back to the window. I knew I had to go to him. But I knew if I did, my life would change. Was this what I wanted?

There was no hesitation in my voice as I turned him towards me. I could say nothing except his name.

'Carl.'

It seemed to be enough.

I look back now on that moment with wonder. I had thought I had known one sort of passion with Kurt all those years back in the pine forests of Rauschwitz; I thought I had known another sort of passion in Otto's frenzied lovemaking; now I found I had never known passion at all.

When he came to my bed that night, I felt as if this was a first time for me.

'Be gentle,' I begged. 'It has been a long time.'

Then I found I did not want gentleness; my body craved his nearness. When he entered me I throbbed in every cell, or so it seemed. Surely this was not the Anna Werner I had known, had been, this creature who gasped in wonder as the tides of passion overcame her. This was like being born again. Renewed. New.

'You are wonderful,' he said. 'Your body is a treasure chest. What I am feeling is unlike anything I have known before. Your warmth. The way you take me into you. Anna ...'

'Yes, my love?'

'Nothing else. Just ... Anna. You are all I have ever wanted.'

He ran his hands wonderingly over my body and cupped my breasts.

'How can your body still be so young? Mine is old in comparison.'

'Yours? Old? No old body could do what yours has just done. I am sure of that.'

'And wants to do again. And again.'

His lips brushed my nipples and I felt them harden and grow.

'Oh yes,' he murmured. 'For me too.'

This time it was slower, gentler, but just as satisfying, and I cried out in pleasure in the ecstasy of the moment.

'It has never been like this before for me,' I said, almost shyly, as we lay together afterward. 'Never.'

'Truly never?'

I thought again of Kurt and the young Anna in the forest. What had that child known of passion? All that I had thought then seemed a distant dream, and I knew he was gone from my life forever. I looked at Carl's face close to mine, shining in the moonlight from the verandah window, and knew I could answer honestly.

'Never.'

CHAPTER 26

Jindera, New South Wales 1890

Kurt had been right. I did like Emma, when we met. That was still to come, and the months before seemed to disappear in a mist.

It had been strange facing Carl on Christmas morning. When I woke, very early, he was gone. It was a relief, for I needed time to think about what happened. It seemed strangely dream-like. Perhaps a schnapps-induced hallucination? No, not hallucination. I lay back and stretched lazily, reliving the moments that had been. What now?

At breakfast Magda looked from one of us to the other, and allowed herself a small smile before turning back to feeding Fritz in his highchair. I found it hard to meet her eyes, and busied myself serving the porridge that she had already made. I knew Carl and I would need to talk, but with the Christmas morning service to come, there would be no time. I had questions that needed answers. They would wait.

When the time came, and we sat together that night, I waited anxiously. There was so much I feared. Perhaps this had been a night when, carried away, we had risked too much, and there would be regrets. But no, the gift. Surely that had been planned.

'There is so much that I must tell you, Anna. I had thought to see you leave here without speaking, then I found I could not do it.'

I waited for him to continue.

'You know a little of my life before you came. You do not know how empty it has been. Always wanting something more.'

I feared what might be coming. Its potential to destroy my fragile happiness. I had to find out. 'I know how you felt about Maria, that she was the one you wanted. And it is possible for you to marry her, now she is at last on her own. Magda has told me. She is hoping you might bring a new mistress into your house. Then she can marry Lars.'

He gave a short bark of laughter. 'Maria! What on earth has Magda been saying? Yet Kurt hinted at the same thing when I spoke to him this morning.'

'What does Kurt have to do with this?'

'I would scarcely have this conversation with you if I had not consulted him.'

'So you do not plan to ask Maria to marry you?'

'Oh, Anna! What do you think! That is all so far in the past; only a romantic like Magda would even contemplate such a thing. Yes, there was a time I might have wanted it. But old affections can wither. Maria has become an overfed hausfrau. I would not be able to put my arms around her as I can with you.'

My face reddened at the memory of our night together, and the things we had said to each other.

'No, Anna. There is only one woman I want to marry, and it is not Maria. Before that, there are things I must tell you. I have made many mistakes in my life, and I do not want to make another one. I need to explain my marriage to Eda ...'

'There is no need, Carl. Magda has told me that there was a child coming.'

'I married Eda because I needed someone here, and I knew she was a good worker. Even though I could not be sure the child was mine – and yes, it well might be my child. I am not proud of what happened between us. All I can say is that I was very lonely, and I am a man. When she came to my bed after Frieda's funeral, I did not send her away. I should have done so.'

'This is all in the past. And you have Fritz who looks so like you.'

'I have not only Fritz, but five other children. How can I ask you to share my life? How can I make it clear that I am not looking for a housekeeper, for a mother to my children? You know I have married before for this reason.'

Any woman might well have wondered. I had contemplated the question. Would I ever be sure?

'Last night you did not seem to be looking for a housekeeper. Or a children's mother either.'

'It was why I did not speak earlier. I have wanted you since the night you arrived, so weary from travel, but so lovely. How could I ask you, you with your background, to come into a life like this?'

' Magda needs to leave, to marry Lars. She is desperate to get away. I was planning to seek employment in Albury. Would you like me to stay here instead as your housekeeper?'

He looked at me in blank surprise.

'*Mein Gott*, woman. Aren't you listening to me? I do not want you here as a housekeeper. I want you as my wife. I am asking you to marry me. First, I must know that you understand the life you will have. It will be so different from what you could have elsewhere.'

'I do not want that other life you are painting. I want only to be here with you. Does that sound too forward? '

He smiled lovingly. 'No, my dear one.'

After that it was easy. 'Yes, Carl, I will marry you.'

It was time, I knew, to write to Melbourne, and ask that my big chest be sent to me here. I knew that the friends I had made there would understand what this meant, and I wrote also to those in other places. To August Eberhardt, who would put aside the thoughts he entertained. The affection I had felt for him seemed trifling in the light of my new happiness, and I did not think he would be deeply grieved. To Hanna, who had been happy I had found Kurt, but had made it clear she was expecting my return soon. To Lydia, who would be amazed at the outcome of this journey she had helped me take.

'I owe you so much, dear Lydia. Without you I would not have this new chance of happiness.'

'Anna,' she replied. 'I am so glad for you. And yes, if I am truthful, envious. You understand what I am saying. We have never needed to put into words what our lives have been.'

To Margarethe, who I knew, in her new happiness, would recognise the value of what we both had found.

It was enough. There was much gossip, of course. There were those in Jindera who believed that I had come to Lobethal simply to take advantage of a lonely man's need. Those who knew us could recognise the truth, and those closest to us, like Kurt and Magda, rejoiced in our happiness.

'Dearest Anna,' she said. 'It is not only that I can now leave here, though I admit it was my first wish. I was not greatly concerned who would take my place. That it is you, and that my brother is now happier than I have ever seen him – that is such a joy.'

When she proposed the idea of a double wedding I did not demur. In fact, I was relieved. At least it would be different from what either of us had known before. I did not want to recall that marriage to Otto, and I had told Carl so much of my earlier life that he understood why I would wish this to be unlike my first marriage.

'Can we still call you Tante Anna?' asked Helena.

'For as long as you wish,' I told them. 'Some day, if you wish to change that, I will be happy.' It was not to be too many months before that happened.

'So *Mutti*,' said Kurt. 'I am to have a new father.'

'How do you feel about it?'

'When he asked my blessing – he said it did not seem necessary to ask my permission – I told him that nothing would make me happier. And I meant it.'

'One day your own time will come, I promise you.' I knew that no one would satisfy him but Emma. 'Give her time. She is still grieving.'

I came to like the young woman I met over the wedding festivities. On occasions like this, both churches joined in celebrating and theological divisions faded in the general rejoicing that weddings brought.

The night of the tin kettling, another custom from our homeland, brought scores of horses and traps to the home paddock of Lobethal, and food and drink to the great tables for the noisy merry-making. Magda and I kept well away, trying to occupy the children and knowing by the time the last revellers departed it would be well into the next morning. And our wedding day.

I had not expected Emma to come to the church, perhaps only to the village hall for the wedding feast. It had seemed to me that her plans, so sadly cut short, would cause too much pain. However, she came, dressed for the first time no longer in black, but in a soft dove grey with a matching bonnet. It was a lovely face, with its determined chin and firm and resolute mouth.

We talked a little, and she mentioned that Kurt had approached her blacksmith father to see if he could work in his forge. I was not surprised.

'It is his passion – steam.'

She nodded. 'I know. He has told me of the plans he has. He foresees a future in which steam engines will propel not just trains and ships, but many things in farm life.'

'His father was the same.' I could at last speak of Otto with respect. 'He was a gifted man, and Kurt has inherited his talents.'

'He wants more than just farming life, I think,' the girl continued. 'I like that. He is different from the young men here. Just as my fiancé was different.' Her face was sad, and I thought that Kurt would have a long battle to win this one.

It was another year before she yielded, and I suspect it was only her mother's urging that brought it about. Her younger sister was eager to marry, and convention said the older sister must be married first. Kurt was quick to take advantage of the argument, and if Emma had to marry at all, he was acceptable. My slightly built son was different from the big farmers of these parts. He was a man of different interests, a man who had travelled, read, had ambitions. A German, as her first love had been. And the same name. I could see why she agreed to marry him.

I wondered. I feared that her strong will and determination would not make for an easy life in the home they would now establish. I could sense that power and decision-making would lie with her, and I questioned what their future would be. Would she lie in Kurt's arms and murmur the familiar name, seeing not my son's face but that of the man she had loved so much? As I had done in Otto's bed.

Should I have counselled her? Told her that I had for too long cherished memories that made my marriage bed a place to endure? That it was not wise to hold too firmly to the past, that one must let it go? No, it was not my place to interfere, and I did not want to spoil Kurt's happiness.

He was happy and if at times I pondered on their marriage, his life seemed contented. When their first child came the joy on his face gave me peace. Emma too seemed happy in her own way, managing her household with a brisk efficiency I admired. But still making her pilgrimage to the graveyard each week with fresh flowers for the love she had lost.

'Does this disturb you?' I dared ask my son one day.

'I know she will always honour his memory.' He answered me carefully. 'Today she is my wife, and he is long gone. A few flowers will not change that.'

I wondered if he, like Otto, had to fight to blot out another figure in their marriage bed. Perhaps this was why so much of his life seemed bound up in his work, and why he allowed Emma to rule the household.

'She is a very strong woman,' Magda commented when

we discussed Kurt's coming marriage. 'She will always be in control.'

'Perhaps he needs this. Perhaps this is what he wants.'

Even their marriage had been her plan; in her own church, which Kurt now joined. There was no thought that she might have come to ours. That wedding in the grey stone building her forefathers had erected was perhaps a symbol of their future.

I could not help contrasting their lives with what I now had. The casual touch of Carl's hand on my arm as I worked in the kitchen, the way in which his eyes sought my face when he came into a room, the slight smile across a dinner table as we listened to the chatter of children.

So different, our marriage. As Magda and I had walked down the aisle of the small weatherboard church it was hard to say which waiting bridegroom looked more lovingly toward his bride. Magda, in the dress the two Spence sisters had made for her, the material Carl and I had bought on that shopping trip to Albury. Mine too a black dress, although I had considered a colour, a break from tradition which would have shocked the good ladies of the congregation. A thought to put aside, for I wished only to fit in with this new world. No veil, just a wreath of orange blossom in my hair, piled high.

Magda had shaken her head. 'No veil, Anna? Why not just a bonnet? Or one of the new small hats we have seen in Albury?'

I held firm. 'No, Magda. You must of course have it all. The veil, the flowers, everything. For me it is different. I will keep to tradition and wear a black gown, though much simpler than yours, but not the trappings.'

'You are so fortunate,' she lamented. 'You can wear the high neckline so well with your long neck. On me even a choker – the sort that the English princess wears – makes me look as if I am being strangled.'

'They say that Alexandra wears this jewellery to hide the scar on her neck.'

'Who knows? It has certainly become a fashion, as with everything she wears. As for the bustle,' she continued, 'if I have a properly fashionable dress, I will look like a circus figure. You, dear Anna, have the figure of a girl.'

'I still will not have a bustle!' I said firmly. 'A compromise perhaps. I will have the skirt draped to the back.'

'Not even a bustle petticoat?'

It was a little like being with Lydia, and I recalled our planning of Hanna's wedding dress. It all seemed so long ago. And so far away. While our letters told something of our lives, and my daughter kept me aware of the children and what they were doing, there was still no real closeness between us. It grieved me. Now I had a new family to think of and plan for. There was little time for regret.

It was a busy household, and with Magda gone, my life was full. When Kurt married and moved with his Emma to the house in the Jindera township, I had little time to notice his absence. I looked back with wonder on the time when he had been the centre of my life.

Yes, he was still dear to me, and I followed with interest the life he made in this young country. Emma's father had welcomed his new son into the blacksmith's shop, acknowledging the opportunities to expand his business into the new age of steam. It was a thriving business, and Carl spoke approvingly of the way Kurt was using the skills of his training in Glatz and Breslau, and exploring the rapidly changing world.

Kurt was becoming known through the area as the expert on matters of steam engines. He was frequently called away to distant parts, and often on the steamships that travelled the Murray. That river was still the lifeline for goods and transport in this land, like the barges criss-crossing the fatherland with their loads of people and produce.

'You are away from your family so much,' I chided him. 'You will miss your children's growing up. What does Emma say?'

'I think it matters little to her. She runs the household, and more and more she is helping her father in his work. She is an excellent businesswoman. Her attention to the accounts is more than his sons could give. Besides, they have all left. It was not the life for them.'

'Is this suitable for a woman? A woman who is also a mother?'

He laughed. 'Emma is like you in many ways. She is not too concerned with what is suitable. She likes to be in charge.'

'I worry for you. Are you happy together?'

'Happy enough. As happy as any married pair, I suspect. We have the children, and I have my work.' His eyes shone. 'I am working on something new. A different sort of steam engine. Some day come to the blacksmith's and I will show you.'

As happy as any married pair. I thought about his words. I felt almost guilty when I thought of Carl and me. Our lives were happier than I had believed possible.

In the busy routines of everyday life, in the companionship of quiet evenings as we read and talked, in the glow of the passion of our lovemaking, as he held me, murmuring only that he was besotted by me, in the quivering response of my body to his, our lives seemed complete.

'I could only wish that we were younger,' he said one night, running his hand down my arching body. 'I would have loved to have given you children. How I would have loved to feel life grow in you, to have seen you swell and have felt a child within you, my child within you, move.'

'No matter, my love. What we have is enough.'

Words that I had read came to life for me in ways I had never foreseen. *The lines are fallen unto me in pleasant places* – yes, the Psalmist had put it well.

Part *Five*

CHAPTER 27

Jindera, New South Wales 1894

So Emma was with child again. Kurt had come to me, his face joyful, to tell me the news. 'This little one will be a girl – I am sure of it. We will name her for you, dear *Mutti*. The boys have been named for Emma's forebears, and this one, she says, will have your name.'

'Surely you are jumping ahead of yourself,' I chided. 'You cannot be sure that this child will be a girl. And a little boy will not thank you for the name Anna!'

He laughed. 'No, I wouldn't do that to a son. This one, she says, is not the same as our two boys. She is carrying differently, and is sure it is a daughter.'

With these children I could at last feel myself a true grandmother. I thought guiltily of my lack of closeness with Hanna's three. For Liesel and Theo seemed like someone else's relatives; I found it hard to see myself in them. And I had never seen the new one, the baby, so when Hanna's mail came, with its photograph of the family, I studied it with a sense of wonder.

There they were. Hanna, stouter than when I last saw her, and standing behind her a Franz who seemed older and more fragile than when last I saw him. Hanna, at thirty, was still

Otto's daughter, with her heavy-set features and curly dark hair. On her knee she held the little one, Fredericka, no longer a baby but a sturdy three-year-old, while beside her stood Theo and Liesel. I studied their faces earnestly. No matter how closely I scrutinised them, I could see little trace of myself. Were these indeed my grandchildren? Where was my sense of grandmotherly devotion? They were strangers.

'Ah!' I could imagine Hanna's reproaches, the ones I had heard so many times. 'If they were Kurt's children ...'

I had to accept the truth. Kurt's children delighted me, and they were always welcome at Lobethal. For Dieter and Rolf it was a pleasure to come to Papa Carl, as they called him, and with infinite patience he whittled toys for them, and took them on rabbiting hunts and fishing in the dam. Or rode them on his knees, as they bounced up and down to the old familiar German rhymes.

'Hoppe!' they would beg on arrival, running to him. And 'Kuchen, bitte, Oma' to me. Carl would patiently listen to the squeals of excitement as they rode up and down on his leg joining in the familiar words – Hoppe, hoppe, Reiter, Wenn er fällt, dann schreit er – and waiting, in half-fearful excitement for the downward plunge when he reached the last line: Macht der Reiter plumps! He would then open his knees to let them swoop gently to the floor. Over and over, until an exhausted Carl shook his head and said firmly that the horse was tired and the ride was over.

'Off to Oma, boys!' and they would come to raid the cake and biscuit tins I kept filled for them.

With me it was drawing and writing at the big kitchen table, where I took delight in three-year-old Dieter's first attempts to write letters of the alphabet and his little brother's colourful scribbles. Somewhere, buried deep inside me, were the memories of Froebel and the kindergarten movement that had so fascinated me when Hanna and Kurt were young. I shook my head, amused, recalling that I had once thought I might even have liked to become a teacher in one of his 'children's gardens' – how long ago and how foolish such dreams now seemed. Now I found myself trying to put in practice some of his ideas.

I knew that when they got home Emma would shake her head and say to Kurt, 'Your mother spoils those boys!' I told myself that there was little spoiling in their home and it made coming to us a nice change for them.

Soon there would be a third baby in the family and they would need the new house they were building near the blacksmith's shop. It was fortunate that Kurt's work was prospering. Working with Emma's father had taught him many new skills, but his basic love was still the possibilities of steam, and I had seen his wife's tight-lipped face at the hours he spent reading in the small office at the side of his works. Understandably, it lightened when his new inventions, like the stripping machine for harvesting he had made for Carl, became well known, and orders flooded in from neighbours.

He was becoming known for his work with steam engines in a small way, and even the wealthiest landowners in the area called on his expertise. That too satisfied his wife, and made her involvement in the works more acceptable than the hours she saw him spending on other inventions.

'Do you think they are happy?' I raised the question yet again with Carl as we sat reading together. He sighed. It was a familiar discussion, and he marked his place before putting down *Jane Eyre*. He was reading the classic literature that I so loved, and we spent many hours debating the questions these books raised.

'In their own way, yes. She will never feel for him what she once felt for her first love, yet she is a good wife and mother. And Kurt has what he wanted, the woman he adored.'

'They say in every marriage there is one who loves, and one who is loved.'

'Do they indeed, beloved? And what do you say? Is it so with us?'

I smiled fondly at this man, so utterly dear to me. 'Whoever said that did not have what we have. I think – I believe – that we would be hard-pressed to say who loves more. We seem to be equal, balanced in our feelings.'

'Then let us just be thankful for that, and hope that Kurt and Emma may have even a measure of our happiness.'

It perturbed me, and I felt uneasy when I caught sight of my son watching his wife with an almost baffled yearning on his face.

There was no one I could talk to about it and, at times, I missed Lydia. To have a friend from childhood, a person to share memories with ... such a treasure. While I now had new friends in the village, for I had joined the ladies of the church, it was not the same as a friend who had known me all my life.

These women had thawed gradually, as they had come to realise that my way of life, as Carl's wife, was the same as theirs. Carl too had joined the Progress Association, and had returned to music with the village band. When the *Albury Banner* reported on life in local communities, his name would frequently be found in accounts of meetings, or plans for the new Institute. Kurt's name was there too, for he had realised that being part of the community was important.

'Important to Emma,' he remarked, when I commented on his new civic presence.

'Do not interfere!' Carl warned me. 'It is their life, and you cannot change it.'

I knew he was right; I should not meddle. This is not interfering, I convinced myself. Yet, when I took flowers to the cemetery for the grave of one of the women who had been quick to welcome me, I chose a time with care. A time when I thought I might well meet with my daughter-in-law on her regular pilgrimage. A time when I thought there might be a chance to talk to her alone, without children, husbands, friends around – and not easy to find.

'Mother Anna,' she said, with surprise.

'I've brought some flowers for Gerda Klinge's grave,' I said quickly. 'She was good to me when I first came. Many others saw me as an intruder in those days.'

'Now you are so much part of the community.'

'I feel very much at home. As does Kurt. Mainly because he is married to you.'

There was silence. A silence that became more pointed as I watched her continue her task, emptying the dead flowers from the urn on the Count's grave, and changing the stale water for fresh from the tank stand.

'You do this every week?' I asked.

'Always.' The air between us was heavy with unspoken thoughts. Finally she asked: 'Do you disapprove?'

'No, my dear. I can understand. How does Kurt feel about it?'

'He says that it does not concern him. That it is simply honouring the past and what we have now is the present.'

'But is it?'

I knew the question was intrusive, and I wonder now that I had the courage – no, the audacity – to ask it. I knew what Carl would have said.

The young woman eyed me steadily for a moment. She did not appear to resent the question, but to be considering her response.

'What do you think?'

'I think you are a very honest person. And an honourable one. I believe you would not have married Kurt if you had not thought you could be a good wife to him. And you are.'

'Thank you for that.'

'I too have lost someone dear to me, and clung to that memory for many years, so I can understand why you come here each week.'

Emma looked at me in some surprise. 'Forgive me, Mother Anna. I had understood from Kurt that your marriage was often difficult – unhappy, even. I am sorry if this is wrong, or if I am offending you.'

'No, child. You are right, and Kurt has told you the truth. In fact, he probably doesn't know how bad it was. I was not speaking of my husband.'

She looked up from her flower arrangement in surprise.

'I am not going to tell you a lot about my earlier life – that's no longer important. Before I was married, when I was very young, younger than you were, I was deeply in love with someone who loved me. Like you and Kurt zu Stolberg.'

For a moment she looked up in rejection of the idea that

anyone's love could have been like hers. She said nothing.
'He left me. No, he did not die. In some ways it is worse to be abandoned, I think. I'd loved him so much. He became the focus of my emotions. I couldn't forget what I'd had. Maybe I made it bigger than it actually was, I don't know. I didn't want to forget; to let it go.'

Emma nodded thoughtfully. 'It seems like a betrayal.'

'Not really. I let it mar my whole marriage because I could not forget him. And probably because I married the wrong man. I couldn't love my husband.'

'I do love your son, Mother Anna. Yet I feel I can't abandon what I had before. That it would be wrong.'

'You don't have to abandon it. That's what I've discovered. Finally, only here, with Carl. I know I can keep the place I had for my long-lost love, but still move on and love just as deeply, just as intensely, another man. And it doesn't seem wrong.'

'Do you really believe that? That you can love again, just as much as before?'

'What I've learned is that you don't measure love by quantity. As if it's – *this much for you, and this much for you, and – oh dear – I think we've run out!*

The younger woman laughed. 'I think I see what you mean.'

'You must have loved him very much.'

The girl's eyes filled with tears. 'I did. I still do. It was so romantic – we met in Albury, and we both knew, at once, how we felt. You have heard that he followed me here to be close to me?'

'Yes. I can understand what it must have been like.'

'He was so charming, so civilised. He knew the whole of Europe, and yet he wanted me.'

It was so reminiscent of my own experience that it was almost painful. 'He loved you enough to want to marry you.'

'And then I think he would have taken me away from all this.'

'Is that what you wanted?'

'Yes. No. Oh, I just don't know. Sometimes I wonder if that was what I loved. That he was so different from everyone here. He knew a bigger world, and I could have been part of it. It was more than that, though. I did love him too – I really did.'

'You can still love and honour your Count. But there's nothing wrong with also loving Kurt. It's not a betrayal. Just a recognition that love is an expanding emotion. There's more to go around than you've realised. He needs to feel this too.'

She had finished with the flowers. 'Do you think I should stop doing this?'

'No, not at all. Then you would feel you'd abandoned someone important to you. Just make sure that Kurt knows how much you love him too.'

She got to her feet. 'I think you are a wise woman. I'm glad you came here today. You have given me much to think about.'

When I confessed to Carl what I had done, he shook his head. 'You're a risk-taker, Anna. I love you for it. If you weren't you wouldn't be here now.'

There were more risks to take in the coming year. For when the new Anna was born, and my little namesake was put in my arms, I dared to ask my son about his marriage.

'She's a fine woman,' he said. 'A great manager, and an excellent mother. And look at all the good she does in the village. If there's anything to be organised, who do they ask to do it? Emma Werner! She's always the first one asked.'

He was rattling on, but not telling me what I wanted to know.

'Are you happy, Kurt?'

'What is "happy"? I have my children – look at this little one, our own little Anna – and I have my work. And I am married to a good woman who cares for me. Why would I not be happy?'

'Is this what most marriages are?' I asked Carl that night, as we lay entwined in the big bed. 'Is that what happens to most couples – *why would I not be happy*?'

He drew me closer. 'What we have is something special. How long is it now since you came into my life? Just five years, and I look back on all the time before as a desert.'

I nestled closer to him. 'Tell me more. I love it when you tell me.'

'Greedy! Well, if I lived in a desert, you, my dearest, have brought the water. And now I'm flourishing.'

So too was Lobethal. After the hard time of the early nineties, conditions were improving again, and Carl's face was serene as he went through his account books. Our lives moved to the rhythm of the seasons, and I looked with pride on the rows of jars in the cavernous cellar under the house. Rows of golden peaches and orange apricots, the deep red of cherries, and the big barrels of salted beans and cucumbers put away for the winter months.

In the Old House kitchen we sliced the sausages that came out of the smoke house, the reward for the labours of pig killing.

'Must do it before the warm weather sets in,' Carl would remind us as winter turned to spring and the orchard was a wonderland of blossom. 'I'll set a date with Magda and Lars.'

Pig killing was a family affair, just as, at home, it had brought together neighbours and friends. Here, as there, all had their appointed roles. Like the younger children I preferred to keep away until the animal was slaughtered. Once it had been tethered, stunned, and its throat cut, we could wait until the draining blood had been caught. Then all had their appointed tasks as the boiling water from the coppers was poured over the animal and the painstaking job of shaving the carcass began.

'Check the water,' Lars insisted. He was the acknowledged expert in the pig killing; it was usually his knife that dispatched the stunned beast. Now he tested the water, making sure it was not too hot. 'Add a dipper of cold,' he insisted. 'Otherwise it's going to lose its skin.'

With the butchering, it became Carl's empire, as the carcass was divided and the head removed. They cut along the backbone and began the dividing into hams and bacons, ready for smoking.

'Elsa, Adelina,' called their father. 'Time to come. Your jobs are waiting!'

Next the intestines were removed and turned inside out, before the scrupulous washing and soaking in salt water. Men butchered; women made sausages, carefully dividing the innards for the white puddings and the black puddings that would hang in the smokehouse, where the children's job was to get the fire going with damp sawdust and almond shells. As the long sausages were filled, the intestine skins were neatly tied at the ends, then handed to Lena for delivery to Willi in the smokehouse.

'Lena! Where is that girl?' rang out at intervals. Each year I cautioned her about her habit of finding a quiet corner for a quick read in slack moments. Each year she would look plaintively up at me with her big blue eyes.

'But Mama Anna, you understand. You love to read. You know what it's like when you are in the middle of a book.'

The trouble was that I did understand. 'Lena, there's a time for reading. And pig-killing day is not it! Off you go. And leave the book with me.'

'She will go far, Carl,' I said to my husband that night, as we lay exhausted after the work of the day.

'Too true,' he laughed. 'The little miss is getting plenty of practice. She is never where she's meant to be when you need her.'

'No. I am serious. We need to think about an education for her. More than she will get here.'

'What are you suggesting?'

'The Klein boy is going away to school. He wants to become a pastor, and the training for the church is in Adelaide. There are boarding schools there run by the church.'

'He is a boy.'

'Yes, but I have talked to Helga Klein about it, and she says the school accepts girls. We could ask Lena if she would like this. She would make a fine teacher.'

'Let her go all that distance from us? Anna, I am not sure that would be wise.'

I let the matter rest, knowing an idea had been planted. The next week I saw him in discussion with Joseph Klein, and smiled to myself. That evening, he called Lena to him.

Later, she came to me. '*Vati* has said I might be able to go away to school.'

'How do you feel about it?' I asked cautiously.

'I don't know. It sounds exciting, but I would be so far away. How I would miss you all.'

'There are holidays to come home. Would you like to go away to study?'

There was no need for her to answer the question. Her face told it all.

'*Vati* says there are two Lutheran schools in Adelaide. Immanuel, and the other is Con ... Con – something.'

'Concordia?'

'That's it. Each of our churches has its own school there.'

Typical, I thought. Such a little church, here in the colonies; still they divide and have their own schools.

'Well, we'll see what happens. It would be another year before you go. Meanwhile, work very hard at school so that you can be prepared. It will be a different world there.'

It was to be a different world here by the time she left for school. We did not know that yet.

CHAPTER 28

Jindera, New South Wales 1897

Who was to blame? In my rage, in the anguish of my grief, I needed someone to blame. Someone to be responsible. Someone I could rail at and accuse.

I think now, when I look back on that day, that I must have been mad. Surely it was enough to have driven any woman mad, and when I relive it the same blind inchoate fury swamps even grief.

Kurt had come with his children as so often before to stay with us for the slow hot Sunday afternoon.

'Not Emma,' he had explained cheerfully. 'This new baby is making her sick, and she is fearful of losing it. Like the last one.' A shadow crossed his face. 'Since Dieter and Rolf she has had trouble.'

'That's not uncommon. As women get older it becomes harder to bear a child. With Anna things went well, and there's no reason that this one should not be fine. After all, Emma is now four months on, I think. It should be safe.'

'Anyway, I have left her home to rest in peace with little Anna, just brought these little imps.'

They were active children, not so much naughty as eager and

adventurous, and Lobethal with all it offered was a favourite place to come. And to go yabbying in the dam with Carl was the best of all. They were quick to beg.

He shrugged resignedly. 'Come, Fritz, let us get the nets and buckets. Anna, can you find us meat for bait? And string for the lines?'

It did not take them long to set up the long sticks stored for yabby catching, or to check our nets for holes. The wire hoops with their discarded net curtains were getting worn. Still good enough, said Carl, for a few more uses. We did not know they would never be used again.

'Be good, boys, and mind what Papa Carl tells you.' I can still hear Kurt's voice as he bent to hug his sons. Dieter, now six, complained. 'Are you not coming with us, *Vati*? You always catch big ones.'

Kurt ruffled the boy's hair. 'No, I am going to stay to talk to your Oma. Look after your little brother, and bring back lots of yabbies. We will have a feast tonight.'

A feast meant work. I started to get out the big iron cauldron for the stove, and the piles of newspapers to cover the long table. A yabby feast was a messy affair, and it had taken me many years to get used to throwing the clawing wriggling creatures into the boiling water. The sight of the crowded family table and the sound of happy laughter could quickly blot out that memory.

'Who is home tonight?' asked Kurt, as Carl and Fritz shepherded the two little boys out the back door and toward the gate in the fence. I watched idly as Carl turned to wave goodbye before starting the trek across the long dry grass to the home-paddock dam.

'Almost everyone. Except Elsa – she will be in Albury with friends.'

'Is she still enjoying teaching so much?'

'Yes, but I think at twenty-three she is starting to have other things on her mind. I would hate to lose her. She is a great help to me here when she is home from school for holidays.'

'What about the boys?'

'Wonderful. Although Hermann is only twenty, Carl says he could not do without him. He could almost run the farm himself. And even Willi is a very capable sixteen-year-old. They work well with their father. I am more concerned about Lena. It is hard to get her to do anything except read or play the piano.'

'Well,' he said, smiling, 'she is fourteen. What do you expect?'

'More than I get. Although, when I think of myself at that age, and the way I read my way through the Chateau library, I can scarcely complain. Though I am sure my mother did.'

Kurt shook his head. 'She will enjoy going away to school.'

'Yes, Carl and I have come to feel this is the best future for her. These children are so dear to me.'

'Any news from Hanna?' As always, a pang when I realised how much less I was involved with her wellbeing.

'A letter this week, and I'm concerned. Franz has not been well. I think she is seriously worried about him. And she keeps asking if I intend to come home. She cannot seem to understand this is my life now.'

We smiled at each other. It was a pleasant feeling, to have this son I could talk to while knowing my life no longer revolved around him.

'Anyway, tell me what you are working on these days. You

are getting to be so well known. There was an article in the last *Banner* about a new engine you have installed.'

'I have almost more work than I can manage. We have put four new men on in the blacksmith's; it makes things easier there.'

I cannot believe, when I recall this casual chat, there was not some hint to me. Some shiver in my spine. A trembling of my body to warn me. Nothing.

Nothing until the door was flung open, and a dripping Fritz screamed at us both.

'*Mutti*. Kurt,' he was gasping. 'Come. Come quickly. *Vati* – '

'Where are my boys?' Kurt was ashen.

Fritz pointed. 'There. Outside.' Rolf was sobbing, his sodden clothes horrible to see. Dieter stood at the gate and wailed.

I swallowed and tasted bile rising. 'Where is your father?'

We were running toward the dam, and I cursed the long skirts that slowed me. I could see nothing, for the high ramp that circled the dam hid it from view. Before I reached the top and looked down, I knew what I would see.

Fritz had managed to pull him from the muddy water, and he lay at the edge, face down, his body sprawled defenceless near the kicked-over bucket. A last yabby crawled doggedly back to the safety of the dam.

'He was too heavy,' sobbed the boy. 'I could not get him out in time. I tried, *Mutti*. I tried.'

Kurt was busy at the body, leaning, pumping, cursing. It was no use.

'He could not swim.'

It had been a joke between us, every time he took the children yabbying. A regular farewell joke. 'Don't fall in the dam.'

Today I had not said it.

Later they told me about it. The deep waterhole at the side. Yes, I nodded. I know it. Rolf had wandered off and fallen in. Yes. That would be typical. And when Dieter yelled, Carl had rushed to get the little boy out.

It was hard to understand, from the distraught Fritz, what had happened next.

'I was on the other side of the dam,' he hiccupped. 'My lines were on the side, where I always fish.'

I waited.

'When I got round to them, he'd pushed Rolf out. But he was in the water, and he wasn't moving. His face was down. I couldn't see him. It was horrible.'

'What then?'

'I couldn't get to him. I got hold of a foot, but his shoe was still on. And it came off in my hand.'

I could see it too clearly. The panicked boy and the horror of the shoe.

'But you managed.'

'I tried and tried, and finally I got his trouser leg. And then I got him to the edge. He was so heavy. And the little boys were screaming. So I had to leave him there. I couldn't get him any further.'

I would not let anyone else touch his body when we had loaded him on the plank of wood for the older boys to bring back to the house. We put him on the bed, and I sent them away. This was my place, and no one else was going to clean away the mud and strip the sodden clothes from his dear dead body. He was mine, and I shut the door on all offers of help.

'See to your sons,' I told Kurt. 'And report this in Jindera. I don't know who must be told, or what happens next. But leave him to me.'

And the whole time that I prepared his body, touching it gently in places where I knew he had loved my touch, all I could think was that I had not said, 'Don't fall in the dam.'

CHAPTER 29

Jindera, New South Wales 1898

We were both widowed the same week, it seemed.

Hanna had been right to be concerned about her Franz, for the bleeding that had worried her had been only one of the signs that something was wrong. They had buried him in the churchyard at Mittelwalde, and she had settled to a life that would be much the same as what she had known for years.

Not for me. My life was very different. I look back now on those first weeks of raw anguish, and wonder how anyone survives it. In India, they tell me, the widow hurls herself upon the funeral pyre and dies with the man she loved. I could have done that too.

'Why?' I asked bitterly. 'So many years ahead of us to make up for the unhappiness of the past. Who is the God who has done this to us?'

The question could not be quelled. Why us? Why me?

Later, another thought. Instead of the accusing 'Why me?' perhaps it was a different question I should be asking: 'Why not me?' For I could see that I had been given so much. The years of happiness. They had been an unanticipated gift. Old teaching came back to me. *The Lord gives, and the Lord takes away.* I understood these words. I had learned them from childhood. I tried to cling to this acceptance, even in the times of total desolation.

'It will pass,' they told me. All those women who had loved and lost. There were many who came to comfort; in the years since we married I had made good friends in the village and among the church people. Yes, even from the two churches. They came from both, for deaths, like weddings, brought the community together. They offered me consolation. 'It will pass.'

I answered fiercely, 'I do not want it to pass. I do not want to forget him.'

'That is not forgetting,' they assured me. 'It is learning to live with the scar.'

'The scar?' My question was dull, and I did not care if anyone answered. Emma's mother spoke, for her husband had died the year before, leaving Kurt in charge of the blacksmith's shop. What did she know of how I felt? No one could know what I felt, or grieve as I was grieving.

'Frau Bergmann, we have all suffered this.' She laid her hand over mine. 'An old woman in the church explained it to me. Anna, we all feel like this at first. It is like a gaping wound, and it bleeds ...'

I knew what she meant. 'It feels like a limb gone. As if I have lost an arm. There is a hole ...'

'And it bleeds. I know. I remember.'

We sat in silence for a moment, then she went on.

'Like all wounds, it begins to heal. It forms a scab as the blood clots, and there is a surface over the wound.'

She did not rush me. She gave me time to think about her words. Then she continued. 'Like all scabs, it is fragile. Every now and then you will knock it, or be careless, and it will open a little and bleed again. And you will think: this will never heal.'

'True.'

'But it does. And one day you will find that the ache is still there, not so bad. It has lessened somewhat, and there is a sort of pleasure mixed with the pain. And there will be a scar where the wound was. That too will fade – but it will never go. Sometimes you will knock it by accident, and there will be a sharp misery. Other times, you will just see the scar. And you will remember. But it will not hurt the way it does right now.'

My eyes filled with tears. 'Thank you,' I whispered, as she got up to leave.

I thought of her words when Hanna's letter came.

I know things have not always been easy between us, Mama. I always knew that your feelings for Kurt were stronger than for me, and yes, I did resent that. Especially when you left us here to follow him across the world when I wanted you to stay to help me.

Yes, God forgive me, she was right. I could not deny the truth of her words.

Mama, I am asking you again. You went to Kurt when you felt he needed you. Now I need you. I so much want you to come home to me here. With Franz gone, my life is empty, and I find I want my mother with me. Will you come?

There was a great apathy on me. It hurt so much to be where every moment reminded me of Carl, where Hermann seemed a younger version of the man I had loved so much, and where I lay diagonally across the bed each night trying to fill the vast emptiness that was Carl's space. I could only cope by shutting down all feeling. Cope? No, exist. That I did not want.

Yet I was surrounded by warmth and care. I had not realised how much I had become part of this community, where the dour suspicion that had met me earlier, and the covert wary glances that had accompanied our marriage, had disappeared with the years and been replaced with acceptance and, yes, even friendship.

I went mechanically about my daily life. The routines of the years continued, and the rhythm of life at Lobethal resumed. It was good that Carl had worked so closely with his sons. They were able to keep going, and as we moved into harvest there were many who came to support them through that first year.

No one to blame. I knew it. My head told me that there was no fault to apportion, yet I found it hard to look at Rolf. If not for him, would we have buried the man I loved on a grey November morning? Kurt must have sensed this. He and Emma came less often to me, and when their new daughter was born there was little comfort when they named her Carla, for him. On her baptismal day I held the baby in my arms but looked at my namesake, the little Anna, and wondered what her future would be.

What would I have wished for her? Would I have wanted for her the life I had had?

Yes, and yes again. The pain of losing was vast, but the joy of loving, and of being loved, was even greater. The gift outweighed even the loss. I sought some understanding in reading, some sense that I was not alone. Others had felt it, I knew – the awful pain of emptiness, of a beloved gone. What little comfort they could give, I clutched desperately. There was Lord Tennyson, whose vast poem of lost love the Countess and I had read with tears. In those days in Rauschwitz before I had known of love. His lines came back to me – to mock or to console? *Tis better to have loved and lost / than never to have loved at all.* They offered me a mantra, and I clung to it. This I could believe, and it helped me through those moments when all I wanted was the feeling of Carl's hand in mine, and in the long nights his body cradling mine.

Rauschwitz, and my early life. So many years back, so far from all I now knew. Lewin, and my life with Otto. Motherhood and the daughter I had never given enough. Perhaps it was time to repair that damage, to offer now what I had denied her earlier, in those years when she had belonged to Otto as Kurt had belonged to me.

'Go,' he urged me. 'Hanna needs you, and perhaps you need her.'

'Go,' Magda advised. 'You need to leave here for a time. To get away. To forget.'

'Do you think I could forget?'

'That was foolish. Of course not. But it will help, I do believe that.'

'How can I walk away from here? This is my life. I am needed here.'

'They will manage. After all, Carl took over this place when he was little older than Hermann, and the boys and Adelina will manage well. And if you wish it, Lars and I will come to be with them while you are gone.'

'Fritz? He is only ten, and he still has nightmares of his father's death.'

He woke often in the night. I heard him cry out as he struggled with tangled bedclothes, reliving those awful moments as he tried to drag his father's body from the water. I held him close until the dream had passed.

Magda reassured me, 'I will care for him; after all, I have done that before.'

She was right; she had been the first mother he had known, and I do not think I had ever taken her place in his heart. Or his in hers. The children that she and Lars had so much wanted had never come. I knew she would slip back into her old role at Lobethal as if the years between had not occurred.

'You will come back, won't you?' they all persuaded. 'Take some time with your daughter, then come back to us. This is your home, it's where you should be.'

Their vehemence was comforting. And I knew they were right. 'Oh yes, I will be back. I'll not even take my chest. It can wait for me in my bedroom, where it has been all these years. It is part of my home.'

How Carl had laughed as we dragged the heavy wooden object to its position under the window. 'I find it hard to believe,' he commented, heaving it across the room, 'that you managed to get this from Lewin to here.'

'Ach, I had help. There was always someone who would assist me.'

When I looked back on that journey, it was true. Always there was someone who would come to my assistance, so the long desperate search had been manageable. And yet, when I recalled those weeks, those months, of my search, it seemed another life lived in my need to find my son.

I had found a son. But in finding him I had found so much more. A self I had never known. A new home. A new land to live the rest of my life. A new family. And now grandchildren as Kurt's life here became established. A little Anna to watch grow up. Carl's children, whose love for me I knew was real, and who would help to keep him close to me. As he always would be.

Yes, the chest could wait for me. I would return.

Epilogue

I have sought you, Anna, over all these years, and perhaps I have found you. Your voice has haunted me, and you have looked gravely at me from the one photograph that has come to us. You sit peacefully, your eyes calm and untroubled, your lips together, unsmiling but serene, looking out beyond the camera to someone behind the photographer.

Who is standing there? Is it Carl, whom you loved so much?

Your face is meditative, and you hold close the child on your knee. An infant, perhaps two years in age, his gown ruffled and a toy in his hands. Is it Fritz?

It is a small photograph, but you are lovely. Your hair is drawn back, and the ribbons of the small hat perched high on your upswept hair are tied loosely and hang over your breast. It is no surprise that men would be drawn to you. Above the high collar, your chin is firm, and there is a sweetness in your gravity.

You did not come back.

I found the news of your death in a brief report. A paragraph, non-committal, in the local news section of one of the regional papers. What else could they have said? It is the pedestrian prose of a local reporter.

Friday, 24 March 1899

Mr Kurt Werner's mother, who went home to Germany some time ago, had written her son, Mr Werner, blacksmith, that she was coming back again. The other day he received a letter to say that his mother was dead. This indeed was a shock, for the deceased lady lived here for some years and made many friends, who will regret to hear of her sudden death.

We know nothing more.

Is this what you have wanted to tell us? That you wanted to return here, where you belonged? Is this what keeps your spirit wandering restlessly in the shadowy realms where I have seen you?

I stand and search these photographs on my wall, the dour farmers and their submissive brides. Or so they seem. They too would have their stories; perhaps they wander the netherworld wanting to share their memories.

You are the one who came to me, Anna, asking me to search for you. Just as you yourself searched, and eventually found what you were seeking.

Your chest is still here, where you have left it, in hope of the return that did not happen. I touch it, running my hands over the surface of the battered wood. I turn back the lid; it is empty, filled only with the memories of the gowns it contained and, perhaps, an elusive whiff of the perfume you wore.

But you have returned; you live again in my words. Perhaps now your wandering spirit can rest.

ABOUT THIS BOOK

Fact or fiction?

It's sometimes impossible to draw a line between them. When you have a fascinating, almost unbelievable, story you begin to wonder how blurred that line might be.

Many of the events that form the basis of *In Search of Anna* really did occur in 1889, and much of the picture of those years is based on my research – details of daily life and historical events in nineteenth century Germany, shipping of the time, emigration experiences, and life both in the 'Marvellous Melbourne' of the period and in the small German enclaves in southern New South Wales.

Fact is also there in the old family story that is the focus of the book: that in 1889 my great-grandmother, an ordinary peasant woman in Silesia, now part of Poland, made her way north to the shipyards of Hamburg, and took ship for Australia, in search of the son who had gone missing two years earlier. A remarkable enterprise for a middle-aged woman, who knew only that her boy had deserted his work as ship's engineer, intending to set off from Melbourne and head north.

Fact: there are records of the actual ships that carried first him in 1887 and then her in 1889, and the problems of her journey, especially, are recorded in contemporary shipping accounts, as mechanical disasters on a much-publicised new steamship lengthened an already long journey.

Fact: on reaching Melbourne, she advertised in newspapers of the time in an effort to find where he might be. Reading those advertisements, week after week of them, is a poignant reminder of what a foolish enterprise this must have seemed.

Fact: the Melbourne address she gave in those advertisements is still there, today an excellent French restaurant in Richmond, and the owner allowed me to climb the narrow stairs to the upper rooms where she lodged during that time of waiting. Again, a moving moment.

Fact: her efforts were rewarded and, in a family legend that seems beyond credibility, her missing son was located in a small town outside Albury, in the Riverina, and they were re-united. Here she stayed for a number of years, then returned to Germany. But I don't want to pre-empt more of her story.

Bare bones of a remarkable tale, but only bones. This is where fiction takes over. Her character, her background, her family relationships, her connections with people during this saga – for all of these I have exercised the writer's prerogative and used my imagination. I now say a diffident apology to your ghost, Anna, and to all the others whose lives I have created – forgive me, and rest in peace.

Valerie Volk

ACKNOWLEDGEMENTS

I am deeply grateful to the many people and organisations who have contributed to the writing of this book.

Among the institutions who have provided valuable resource material are Burnley & Richmond Historical Society, City of Richmond Library, German Club of Melbourne: Deutscher Turnverein Tivoli, Lutheran Church Archives, Port Adelaide Maritime Museum, South Australian Migration Museum, State Library of South Australia, State Library of Victoria, Trinity Lutheran Church East Melbourne.

Certain individuals have provided special assistance, in some cases through the listed institutions, in other cases privately. They are included, with my thanks, in the alphabetical listing that follows: Claire Bell, Barbara Börste, David Briese, Pastor Christoff Dielmann, Jennifer Hand, Renata Jürgens, David Langton, Janette Lange, Hans Müller, Hans Roleff, Renate Shanahan, Greg Slattery, Siegfried Stehle, Roger Volk, Mark Worthing, Margaret Young, Lois Zweck.

I am grateful also to Michael Bollen and the wonderful staff at Wakefield Press for their support, especially to Julia Beaven for her meticulous and thoughtful editing, and her valuable personal encouragement.

Particular thanks are given to individuals who have been of special importance:

Elizabeth Newton and Keith Welzel, whose stories of my family background were the inspiration behind this book, and who provided information and resource materials;

my daughter, Felicity Volk, a brilliant writer whose editing skills and perceptive comments were invaluable;

two people whose enthusiasm and interest kept me writing, Anne Jantzen and Nicholas Volk – their frequent 'Please send me the next chapter!' was the stimulus that spurred me on;

finally, David Harris, who has accompanied me at every stage of my 'search for Anna' with love and support.

Valerie Volk